NEXT, AFTER LUCIFER

ALSO BY NEIL MCMAHON

Adversary

Cast Angels Down To Hell

Twice Dying

Blood Double

To The Bone

Revolution No. 9

Lone Creek

Dead Silver

Toys (with James Patterson)

L.A. Mental

"Creating a believable villain is the hardest work in the artistic world . . . which makes Neil McMahon's success . . . so stunning . . . In McMahon's assured hands, the duel between the rational, scientific doctor and the fascinating, frightening Freeboot . . . is an absolutely riveting read." (*Revolution No. 9*)
Chicago Tribune

"McMahon's stellar stand-alone offers a cunning technological twist worthy of the late Michael Crichton . . . (McMahon) easily makes a science fiction concept plausible in a pulse-pounding read that doesn't sacrifice intelligence for thrills." (*L.A. Mental*)
Publishers Weekly

"Reading *Dead Silver* is like discovering that the great Raymond Chandler wrote a mystery about Montana."
James Patterson

"Neil McMahon's thrillers have the precision of a surgeon's scalpel. *To The Bone* is a tautly written mystery embedded with characters as real as the surprises are many."
Michael Connelly

"McMahon is a writer and a half . . . his words carry for miles." (*Lone Creek*)
New York Times Book Review

"Reads like a cross between Raymond Chandler and Thomas Harris. More Monks please, Mr. McMahon." (*Twice Dying*)
Chicago Tribune

"A compelling novel by a first-rate writer. I urge you to read it." (*To The Bone*)
Robert B. Parker

"*L.A. Mental* is as much a mind game as it is a thriller, a scientific puzzle buried in a murder mystery, all set against the surreal world of Hollywood filmmaking. Blurring genres and expectations, this is a book that challenges and thrills in equal parts. I can't wait for the next book!"
James Rollins

"A mesmerizing thriller (with) a strong sense of menace . . . McMahon maintains the suspense to the bitter end." (*Twice Dying*)
Kirkus Reviews

"McMahon has now found his true voice with this splendid and suspenseful novel . . . It is the poignant and knowing prose that elevates this novel to literature." (*Lone Creek*)
Otto Penzler, New York Sun

NEXT, AFTER LUCIFER

Neil McMahon

Quinotaur Press

Missoula, Montana

Cover design by Jason Neal

Author photo by Kim Anderson

ISBN 978-0-9847750-0-2

AUTHOR'S NOTE
November, 2011

Almost thirty years ago, an aspiring author who'd had some minor literary success decided to try his hand at a horror novel. He'd never written a full-length book before, he only had a murky idea of how to go about it, and a lot of what he thought he knew turned out to be wrong. There was also another major wrinkle–the pesky need to make a living by some other means, which in his case took the form of swinging a hammer on construction jobs, trading that work for time to write.

As he got into the novel crafting process, he started comparing it to hiking in the mountains. You can stand on a peak and see a clearly marked trail leading down into the forested canyon below, then emerging on the other side and up to the next peak. At first, it looks like a straight shot from here to there. But what you can't see are the hazards hidden in those thick woods between the vista points–a bewildering network of false trails that branch off to nowhere, rockslides and brush-choked gullies, impassable deadfalls and rushing streams.

That labyrinthine trek through the prose wilderness ended up lasting several years and a couple of thousand discarded pages. Along the way, he adopted the pseudonym Daniel Rhodes, for reasons that seemed good at the time and seem better now.

Eventually, in 1987, the book was published as *Next, After Lucifer* (St. Martin's Press). A sequel, *Adversary*, followed in 1988, and a third horror novel, *Cast Angels Down To Hell* (originally titled *Kiss Of Death*) in 1990.

And then, quite suddenly, it was over. Daniel Rhodes was through with publishing (or more accurately, vice versa), those three books faded from print, and he faded with them.

Another decade passed before that writer re-surfaced as Neil McMahon (his/my real name) with a medical thriller titled *Twice Dying* (HarperCollins, 2000). My luck has been much better the second time around, with several more mainstream thrillers published to date. Writing them has kept me busy, and I haven't ventured into horror again (yet, anyway).

But those first three books, and the hope of getting them back in print, were never far from my mind.

The wait turned out to be a long one—roughly one-third of my life—but finally, thanks to a lot of help from terrific people, here they are.

"Look upon them again, I dare not," Sir Walter Scott said of his own earlier works—words that ring so true. As I've gone through mine this time, I've seen countless things I wish I'd done better. (It's a somewhat eerie experience, by the way—like meeting the ghost of who you were many years ago, and getting glimmers, or outright jolts, of how you thought and felt when you were that much younger.) I was sorely tempted to revise, but somehow, it just seemed right to leave them as they were. Except for very minor changes to improve formatting appearance, these are the original texts.

All in all, despite their flaws, I think they still hold up pretty well, and that there's more to them than might meet the eye—elements of religious thought, history, and perhaps most of all, a sense of how the supernatural is tied to human longing, promising the things we all desire but are unreachable to us by ordinary means.

In terms of what these books aim to do and how they go about it, I don't know of anything else quite like them.

I'll close by saying that I believe the story behind all this might be intriguing to readers interested in the writing process. So we've set up a website that's mainly devoted to discussing it in more detail—how the idea for the books first came, the thinking that underlies them (read: method to my madness), how they fared with reviews and the publishing world, my use of a pseudonym, and related issues such as this basic question about the horror genre: Why do so many millions of people love to be scared by stories like these?

Please visit us there at:

EvilAwakens.com

And also on Facebook at:

facebook.com/neilmcmahonbooks

PROLOGUE

*Millions of spiritual creatures walk the Earth
Unseen, both when we wake, and when we sleep.*

John Milton

Crouched in the darkness of a grove of ragged cypresses, Henri Taillou tugged uneasily at his beret and scanned his surroundings with narrowed eyes. He was not accustomed to the forest at night. It was strange how still it all was, how one could hear the tiny rustlings of animals creeping about their secret business, how the light of the moon seemed to magnify things and hide them at the same time. Shaggy clumps of leaves could have been the hair of weeping women, heads bent low. Ancient limbs twisted and gleamed like serpents' coils. Though not a breath of wind stirred the hot thick night, it was easy to imagine that they moved.

His gaze traveled up the mountainside. On its peak, the highest for miles around, the thick-walled fortress of Montsévrain had commanded the valley of the river Seyre for more than a thousand years. Now it was nothing but a bleak and crumbling ruin—to the people of the region, hardly more noticeable than the mountain itself.

But tonight the great fat egg of a moon hovered over it, throwing the walls into sharp shadowed relief so that he could almost feel their coldness, their grim ungiving strength. For the first time in decades, Henri Taillou remembered the stories used to frighten the young of his time, that the castle had once been home to a group of renegade Crusaders who worshipped the devil and drank human blood, that those silent dark stones had once witnessed the frenzy of nights filled with fires and cries.

He exhaled and shook his head. Such thoughts were for old women. He, Henri Taillou, was a man of practicalities. He had climbed to Montsévrain more than once in his youth, and while it was true that one could see the Côte d'Azur and out across the deep glittering turquoise of the Mediterranean almost, it seemed, to Africa, he had found nothing of use there—only rocks. And while the long-neglected grove of trees in which he crouched might have fascinated other men with its evidence of centuries-old cultivation, neither was he any historian. To him, the grove had suggested the presence of water.

He turned his attention to the clearing ahead, where his stupid son Philippe labored sullenly. An hour yet remained before midnight; the moon made unnecessary any light that might have given them away. So far, all was going as well as could be hoped. He took from his vest a flask of homemade Calvados, and let that and the steady thunk of metal against earth lull him. It was good to watch another man work.

The shoveling ceased. Henri Taillou's half-closed eyes watched like a cat's while his panting son took a drink from a jug of lukewarm barley tea. Philippe's undershirt was dark with sweat. The boy was too thin, he thought—the opposite of himself, a man of substance. Not for the first time, suspicions of paternity flicked through his mind. His Thérèse had been a bit of a gamine in her day. How could one be sure?

In a low voice, he said, "It is not my custom to pay a man for standing when there is work right in front of him."

"*Merde alors,*" Philippe said, in a tone that was half defiance, half whine. "This water has been in the ground a million years, but these Americans must have it out on the hottest night of the summer."

Henri Taillou fingered his mustache. "Don't forget that there are many young men in Saint-Bertrand who would give much for your job."

Philippe made a sound like spitting air, but picked up the shovel. "It would go twice as fast if you'd help instead of sitting on your fat ass."

"*Salaud!* Show respect for your father, who raised you. You know about my back."

"Your back, *oui.* How strange that it acts up when there is hard work to be done, but never makes you miss a game of *boules.*"

Sharp words hung on Henri Taillou's lips, but he let them pass and settled back against the tree. To argue with a fool was undignified. Perhaps it was true that his back bothered him less than he sometimes let on, but he believed firmly in the value of work for the young. It built

3

character. He unscrewed the cap of the flask and took a long drink, hearing the liquor begin to speak to him. His wife had done a poor enough job teaching the boy to behave. Philippe had become too big to chastise; but later, a slap or two would do Thérèse no harm, the brandy whispered—and never failed to ease his paternal doubts besides.

The summer had been the hottest in memory, with September the worst month yet. Water supplies had been evaporating with the speed of a plague. But to Henri Taillou, drought was good news. He owned the only backhoe and well-drilling rig this side of Grasse, and he had quickly begun to calibrate his prices to the desperation he read in faces. One of those faces belonged to a realtor, a Monsieur Colet, who listed the villa several hundred meters down the mountain from where Henri Taillou now crouched. The house was beautiful, expensive—and vacant for nearly two months, since the dwindling water supplies had forced the draining of the swimming pool. Now, it seemed, an American couple were interested, a couple for whom money was no problem. But who would rent a villa with an empty pool?

Although Colet's proposal was reasonable, Henri Taillou had at first shaken his head. There was no way to get this water but to steal it, and being a man of principle, he was not willing to do this cheap. But the bargaining power was on his side; after a *pastis* or two, they had settled on a figure half again as much. From there it had been a simple matter of walking the hills above the villa, pretending to hunt birds, until he spotted the grove of trees and confirmed his guess with the dowsing wand. He was still not sure to whom the land belonged. But he was convinced that the spring must supply dwellings farther down the valley, and that if he tapped the water at its source, one or possibly several households were going to try their faucets next morning and find only trickles. He turned his attention back to his son and considered offering him the brandy flask; but drinking on the job was to be discouraged.

"Patience," he said. "I tell you the spring is within a few meters of the surface, and I am never wrong."

"And I'm Marie Antoinette," Philippe muttered.

Again Henri Taillou checked angry words. Upon one or two occasions, perhaps even three or four, it was true that he had misjudged slightly, causing Philippe a trifle of extra digging. But what did the boy think he was getting paid for? At any rate, this time Henri Taillou was sure. The dowsing rod had plunged downward with a force that nearly tore it from his hands. Water there was, easy to get to and enough to fill the swimming pool for *les Américains*. And who knew? Perhaps the families down the mountain, dispossessed of their own water, would turn unwittingly to him for help. The idea appealed. Idly, he considered raising Philippe's pay, enough to allow him to buy the ancient Renault he coveted. But there would be time enough for all that. The boy had respect to learn first. Henri Taillou eased his rump forward, feeling the comfortable stretch of his waistband, and unscrewed the cap of the flask. Life was pleasant enough, he thought drowsily. The young were always in a hurry.

The shovel rang against something hard. Philippe threw it down, cursing and rubbing his elbow.

5

"Calm yourself," his father said irritably. "And keep your voice down." He drank again while Philippe probed the outline of the obstacle with shovel and bar.

"It's solid," the younger man said nervously. "The size of a wheelbarrow, but flat."

"Impossible." But Henri Taillou rose heavily, curious in spite of himself.

Philippe played the beam of a flashlight over the stone's surface. It was big, his father admitted—a seemingly regular rectangle, set partially upright like a door into the mountain. Further, the stone appeared to be granite, while the cliff's natural rock was limestone and crumbling shale. And around the edges—

"Impossible," he muttered again. It looked disturbingly like mortar. He reached forward with a crowbar and scraped red soil from the stone's surface. The bar's point lodged in a groove, then another. He scraped in the other direction.

And uncovered a carved letter.

"What does it say?" Philippe whispered.

"How should I know until you've cleaned it off?" snapped his father, who could barely read.

With a damp handkerchief and an old pocketknife, Philippe went to work. Henri Taillou stayed by his side, forgetting to drink. The creeping, rustling night moved behind him like a thing with life.

At last Philippe stepped aside. Henri Taillou leaned close. The top two lines read:

IN FLUCTIBUS AQUARUM
ACCLINAVIT ME

There followed three crosses in a horizontal line. Then:

QUIESCENTEM NE MOVETO

"Latin," Henri Taillou declared. "I have forgotten most of mine since they started that bloody new Mass."

"*Aqua* means water," Philippe said hesitantly.

"Any child knows that."

"We must get the priest. Monsieur Boudrie will–"

"*Crétin!*" Henri Taillou wheeled on his son. "Don't you understand what we're doing? Do you want to go to jail? That's all we need, the priest butting his thick head in here."

He turned back to the stone, glaring as if it were an enemy. Again his gaze rose as if pulled to the looming moonlit fortress; again he remembered the old tales of the castle's human vampires; and he was suddenly touched by the haunting memory of a thousand lonely childhood nights, lying on his attic cot in the old family home while the icy *mistral* winds howled against his window.

But an equally sudden anger surged. This buried chunk of rock had destroyed the peace of his night, tried to cheat him of his reward.

"*Eh bien,* my friend," he told it grimly. "I, too, can play rough." He turned and strode toward the truck.

"Wait," Philippe said, sounding troubled. "We need to find out what it says."

"It says *water*. Now shut up and set the grappling hook."

Henri Taillou hauled himself into the driver's seat of the old flatbed truck. The noise was a risk they would have to take. Mouthing the mixture of wheedling and threat that passed with him for prayer, he pushed the starter. The engine cranked reluctantly and loudly into life. By the time he had maneuvered into position, the hook was set behind the top lip of the stone. Henri Taillou engaged the power takeoff for the front-end winch and slowly began to reel in cable The line went taut. As if he were playing a giant fish, the truck began to jerk, then cough. Cursing, he put the accelerator to the floor. The engine leaped with a roar that must have been audible all the way to Grasse. For seconds, machine and stone fought each other, until he was certain the cable must snap. Philippe stood gripping the crowbar, gaping, useless.

Rage lent youth to Henri Taillou as he leaped to the ground. He tore the bar from Philippe's hands and shouldered him aside. Again and again he drove the bar into the mortar that held the stone, hissing like a madman crushing the life from an enemy.

"Give it some gas, you clod!" he shouted, and as Philippe ran to the truck, he planted the bar with a last vicious lunge. The engine's rumble rose again to a roar. Henri Taillou threw his weight against the bar.

The stone burst from the ground, spraying earth and shattered rocks, and a wall of cold black water slammed into him, carrying him backward into darkness.

He was moving through a corridor cut into the earth, black but for a faint phosphorescent glow that seemed to rise from the stone walls themselves. The only sound was the distant dripping of water. How long he had been walking, he had no idea, but he was suddenly aware that he had never in his life wanted anything so much as he wanted to turn back from whatever he was approaching.

But something was behind him: something he felt more than saw, a creeping dark blur. From it emanated a sense of anticipation, of lust, that brought a hot wave of dread crawling across his skin. His strained breathing rose in his ears to join the hammering of his heart. He took step after agonized step, fingers trailing the cool damp stone of the wall.

The dripping grew louder. The corridor was opening into a vault. In the center of the floor was a depression, filled with water that was absolutely black; and he understood that what he dared not approach lay in that pool. Now there was a rustling sound behind him. Moaning softly, helpless to resist, he took a final step and leaned forward.

On the floor of the pool lay a skeleton, bones still glistening from the draining water. He stared at the ferocious grinning rictus of the skull, the blank dark sockets of the eyes—

Blank and dark until the right one opened.

It stared back at him with a calm, knowing evil. The grin widened.

The skeleton began to rise.

He stumbled back, arms flailing for the support of a wall. But what his fingers touched was not rough *stone. It was soft and wet. He hung, paralyzed, while his mind registered what it was:*

A mouth, with teeth in it.

The distant sound in Henri Taillou's ears began to separate itself into syllables—"*Papa! Papa!*"—sharp and staccato, like the blows that stung his cheeks. His eyelids fluttered, but closed instantly at the bright light that shone into them. "Papa, wake up!" the voice chanted. Henri Taillou found his right hand and made it move clumsily to push the light aside.

"Papa! You're alive!"

He opened his eyes and inhaled in a gasp. A white orb of a face hung before him, suspended against the blackness of night. But then his clearing vision assured him it was all right. This face had flesh on it. It resolved itself into someone familiar, and at last he understood that he was staring at his son.

"I thought you were dead," Philippe whispered.

When Henri Taillou opened his mouth, the sound came out a snarl of fury and fear. He heaved himself upright and found he was soaking wet, sitting in a stream of water that flowed from a dark cavelike opening in the mountainside ahead.

"You must stay here. I'll go for help," Philippe was saying. "Your face is the color of wine—"

Words finally exploded from Henri Taillou's mouth. "Stay here? Are you mad? Help me!" Hesitantly, Philippe gripped his outstretched hand and pulled him to his feet.

"Home, for God's sake," Henri Taillou groaned, and moved with a heavy half-run to the truck.

"But the water—"

"Leave it! Just get me out of here!"

Philippe moved quickly, rewinding the winch and throwing the other tools on the truck. As he drove, he glanced in wonder at his shaking father, whom he had never known to be anything but blustery in the face of fear. There was nothing in the clearing—only the moonlit grove of trees, the shadowed brush, the gleaming trickle of water.

But there had been a moment, when he had first knelt beside his fallen father, of a strange, sinister tingle. Almost as if something, or someone, most unpleasant were suddenly there at his shoulder. It was not unlike stepping over a log and feeling something rubbery twist beneath your foot.

And had he imagined a whisper of laughter in his ear?

He cut the engine and let the truck coast down the slope in darkness.

"Put on the lights," his father growled. Philippe shrugged and obeyed. Henri Taillou shifted restlessly, staring out one window, then swiveling to another. "You must come back tomorrow and connect the pipe. You'll just have to take your chances on being seen."

"But—what happened?"

"My lifetime of hard work has caught up with me, thanks to your useless help."

Philippe shrugged again. It would be almost a pleasure to work without the old man breathing down his neck.

But as he listened to his father's uneasy movements and ragged breath, that moment of sinister tingling came creeping back. *Quiescentem ne moveto*–had he heard the phrase before, or was he just imagining that it had something to do with not disturbing what rested? That it was in the nature of a warning. He decided to copy the inscription next day. He might run across someone who would translate it without inquiring too closely into its origins.

Henri Taillou remembered his flask, took several long drinks, and then grudgingly handed it to his son. In the familiar safety of the bouncing, rattling truck, he remembered to hope that no one would happen along to discover what they had done.

But as he stared down at the hand that had gone into that loathsome cold mouth, he knew beyond doubt that he would face trouble, fines, even prison, before he would ever set foot on that mountainside again.

PART ONE

Philosophy is odious and obscure,
Both law and physic are for petty wits,
Divinity is basest of the three,
Unpleasant, harsh, contemptible, and vile;
'Tis magic, magic that hath ravish'd me.

Christopher Marlowe

ONE

On the patio of his newly rented villa, John McTell washed down a last tart bite of blue cheese with a swallow of chilled Vouvray, pushed his chair farther into the shade, and settled back to survey the domain that would be his for the next months. Around him as far as he could see rose the steep craggy hills of the Alpes Maritimes, soil baked to the deep rust color of a ceramic glaze, forming a bright mosaic with the thick green vegetation. The sky was like a polished slate of sapphire. No other dwellings could be seen, nor, the realtor had declared, could any others see this one. Though the heat was intense, the villa's tiled oval swimming pool was filled with cool clear water, procured mysteriously during this season of drought.

McTell's gaze moved to the woman who stood beside the pool. My wife, he thought. In the eleven months of their marriage, he had yet to get used to the term. Her name was Linden, and she, too, was taking stock of their new home; her eyes were hidden by sunglasses, her arms folded critically, her mouth compressed.

He turned back to the postcard-perfect ruin that topped the highest peak, dominating the countryside like an ancient, failing, but still grand lord—built against the Saracen invasions of the seventh and eighth centuries, he supposed, when the faith of the Prophet had swept like a tidal wave of fire and blood across the known world. The great stone walls, sparkling with mica, were the color of old bones. He wondered again if the ruin and the for-ever-lost times it symbolized, times of romance and mystery and faith, were the real reason he had held out for renting this house over several others, closer to the social life of the coast, that Linden had preferred. But she had given in with good grace, and all was well, with the place, with the marriage, with his career—with his life.

Why, then, the touch of melancholy?

The telephone rang inside the house, a harsh buzzing that fell off at the end as if it could not quite sustain itself. Linden hurried inside, sunlight catching auburn streaks in her pulled-back hair, outlining her shape through a loose white linen blouse. McTcll glanced at the remains of lunch before him, bought that morning at an *épicerie* in Saint-Paul de Vence—*patés*, cold chicken, fruit and cheese—and braced himself to clean up. The inside of the house was a clutter of boxes and clothes delivered earlier in the week; the car was still full of traveling gear. Once he began the process of organizing, of shelving his books and arranging his desk, he would enjoy it; but beginning was hard and the wine and heat were no help.

The brisk slap of Linden's sandals brought his head around. She was a striking rather than pretty woman, her face a little too severe, body a little too spare, except for the generous breasts nature had almost cruelly given her; a malformation of mysterious organs would keep her forever childless.

"That was Monsieur Colet," she said. "He's found us a cook and gardener." Colet, the realtor, was a sad-eyed little man with a drooping mustache, who had reminded McTell of Charlie Chaplin.

"And filled the pool."

"Yes," she said—with a trace of displeasure?

"You need to take some time for yourself. Lin," he said. "Lie around a little. Get bored. You never stop."

Perhaps a second too long passed before she smiled.

"Of course you're right. Well. Ready to tackle the chaos inside?"

He stretched. Colet had mentioned that the fortress—Montsévrain, he had called it—had once been a stronghold of the Knights Templar. That was all it had taken to fan McTell's professional curiosity into flames. He squinted at the ruin, gauging its distance.

"Actually, I was thinking about some exercise."

"Yes?" She leaned a hip into him. "It *has* been a while."

He let his hand drop to caress her ankle.

"I meant the vertical kind. How about it—up for a hike?"

She shaded her eyes and followed his gaze. Her mouth settled into a line.

"It looks like hard hot work."

"So does unpacking."

"That's productive hard hot work."

McTell sighed. "Always the pragmatist."

"It got you through your last book, didn't it?"

Though her tone was teasing, her words annoyed him.

"You're a one-woman Salvation Army, Lin," he said.

For a moment neither spoke—sensing, he knew, that the dance had gone as far in that direction as it comfortably could.

Then, too casually, she said. "Let's cut for it."

He glanced up, about to argue. Her luck at games of chance was a standing joke between them, and she kept a pack of playing cards in her purse to settle good-humored disputes. It amused him and exasperated him about equally. But, he reminded himself, it was she who had made the real concession in agreeing to rent this house.

"The stakes, specifically?"

"If you win, you do what you want. You know, climb around that hot old mountain with the bugs and poison oak. I unpack."

"And if you win, I unpack. What do you do?"

"I might be persuaded to help," she said, smiling, "if the offer was sweetened. Want to shuffle?"

"It never makes any difference."

He watched her fingers hover over the spread cards as if they could read the hidden faces; then drop and draw one out.

"Read it and weep," she said, and turned over the Queen of Diamonds. She folded her hands, looking demure.

He stood to conceal his annoyance, and paced. Abruptly, on a whim, he crouched beside the pool, dipped his cupped hands, and splashed water on his face.

"Baptized," he said. "Now I'm ready." He slid a fingernail under the first card he touched–

And as he began to lift, he suddenly understood that he was going to win.

It was the King of Spades.

He stared down at it. His premonition had not been a hunch but a certainty: something that was suddenly there in his mind, unasked for but unquestionable. About to tell her, he saw that her disappointment was plain; and he hovered on the edge of relenting, of spending the afternoon with her and their baggage.

But his desire was urgent–less to see the fortress, he realized, than to have a few hours alone. He had been a solitary man for most of his adult life, but was increasingly aware that he had married a woman who required little privacy herself The constant companionship of travel had tightened the strain.

"You'll find that I'm magnanimous in victory," he said with mock formality, "unlike certain people I could name. You're free to do as you please while I'm gone."

"You're a prince," she murmured.

He leaned forward and quickly kissed her unmoving cheek.

"I'd better find my walking shoes." As be turned, his glance caught the cards. For an instant he imagined he saw complicity in the king's handsome unblinking face.

He hurried through the villa, gaze averted from the havoc of clothes and luggage on the floor; rummaged through the BMW until he found his rucksack and camera; changed quickly, slipped a bottle of chilled white wine into the pack, and went back out to the pool.

There he stopped in surprise.

Linden was prone on a lounge chair, wearing only sunglasses. Her clothes lay on the deck in a tangled pile. She was smoking a cigarette and reading a copy of Paris Match while a glass of Vouvray sweated in the shade beneath her. It was nearly the first time he had seen her abandon herself to indolence.

"Are you magnanimous enough to oil my back?" she said, and he heard with relief that humor had returned to her voice.

He knelt beside her and began to work in the scented lotion, feeling her muscles relax under his fingers. She was travel-weary too; they both needed rest. Her skin was pale, hot now with the sun that rarely touched it, slick with oil; her flesh just beginning to acquire the delicate softness of a woman leaving youth. He slid his fingertips lightly up the insides of her thighs to their joining. She made a deep contented sound.

"I'll be back in two hours." he said.

"What if the mailman or somebody comes while you're gone?"

"That will give us both something to think about."

"What if you run into bears or rattlesnakes?"

"They'll just have to take their chances."

"I'm doing this for you, you know—cultivating laziness. That's what men really want, isn't it? Naked, oiled, always-available women? Who don't threaten them?"

20

McTell's gaze scanned the mountainside until he saw what looked like an overgrown switchback. He patted her rump and stood.

"I want you to be happy, Lin," he said.

A graveled path led to the edge of the grounds.

From the villa the ancient stones had seemed a mark of permanence, but as McTell approached, they brought to mind the boast that Shelley had reported, with such cruel irony, carved into the time-ravaged remains of a monument to a long-dead king: *Look on my works, ye Mighty, and despair!* The mountain itself had been hewed off flush with the fortress's walls on three sides, while a steep brush-choked ravine guarded the entrance. The archway had undoubtedly once held a portcullis, and McTell remained unable to shake the inner voice that whispered of being herded in at spearpoint, prisoner of some savage feudal lord bent on revenge. It was a relief to step into the open courtyard. He crouched with his back against a shaded wall, opened the wine, and took several long swallows. It was tart and fragrant, and his head lightened suddenly.

The building's outline was an approximate rectangle, perhaps forty yards wide by sixty long. The walls were many feet thick, largely crumbled away; in only a few places did vestiges of battlements remain. He paced the rough lichen-covered paving stones, footsteps loud in the silence. Stubs of what had probably been interior foundation walls were choked by squat, ugly nettles. He remembered that the Templars had built their great churches round; but this was a minor outpost, no doubt acquired either as a spoil of war or as a gift of a noble who had joined the Order. That the place had not been maintained was obvious, although an iron grate, badly rusted, was set over an opening in the ground–most likely a dungeon. But the south wall, and the vista it promised, called to him first. He climbed carefully to the top, testing for loose stones. There he crouched, safely back from the vertigo of the sheer drop down the mountainside, and raised his eyes.

Perhaps twenty miles south, thousands of feet down, shone the vast azure expanse of the ancient world's sea of seas, horizon barely distinguishable from the lighter blue of the sky, as if it went on forever. The Mediterranean, he thought: the middle of the earth.

In Provence more than anyplace else, he felt the almost boyish swell of wonder that had sparked his love affair with the remote past. Perhaps it had to do with the Roman remains that lay everywhere: the arenas, amphitheaters, aqueducts, built centuries before the great cathedrals, themselves ancient beyond his comprehension, had even been conceived. Before the Romans, the Greeks had colonized the southern coast of Gaul, and before the Greeks, peoples whose histories were shrouded in mystery and myth; and McTell recalled that when Schliemann had exhumed Homer's Troy, dead and buried for three thousand years, he had found beneath it the ruins of six previous settlements.

It put a certain perspective on the self-preoccupation of the modern world.

He turned, taking in the mountainsides that sloped sharply into vast draws sweeping to the sea, rusty soil interwoven with emerald vegetation. To the northeast lay the handful of buildings that made up the village of Saint-Bertrand-sur-Seyre. The slender jade band of the river flowed through it, winding around the bases of the mountains, so nearly dried up that it had pooled in places. Back toward the sea were red tile roofs scattered in thickening clusters, black ribbons of roads with insect cars moving imperceptibly along, and the thicker traffic-clogged artery of the coastal highway. The gleaming mass of a city would be Cannes, with its harbor of swan-like yachts; and offshore, hazy spots of land could only be the Îles de Lérins, where the Man in the Iron Mask had spent the last years of his wretched life. McTell reopened the wine, and, warmed by sunshine, slipped into the introspection he had been craving.

At the age of twenty-two, John McTell had turned from the study of law—against the stern wishes of his family and of the professors who had overseen his honors-laden undergraduate career—to that of medieval history. The reasons he had been able to give at the time were unsatisfactory even to himself, and years passed before he understood the simple truth: that in his last year of college he had fallen in love, for the first and only time; had lost; and had gone into a lifelong retreat.

For a few months the world had been transformed, as if by a magic lens, into a place of wonder and beauty. But she had left him for another man; and when, over the unending year that followed, he found himself plunged back into a lonely, passionless world, it had been almost more than he could bear. His heart had turned away from practicality, from the mainstream of contemporary life,

23

and sought comfort in the romance of the past. Its mystique provided an almost-adequate substitute for what he had lost.

He remained a brilliant student, and he channeled that brilliance into the study of history, mastering languages, cultures, eras. The honors continued: two well-received books by the age of thirty-five; a full professorship at one of the nation's prestigious universities at thirty-eight; and last year, at forty-eight, the publication of the book that had raised his reputation from modest fame in academic circles to worldwide eminence. *The Death of the Lance*, a study exploring the end of the chivalric age and the seeds of the Reformation, had won the recognition of even the bitterest pedants. Through the territory was well traveled by previous historians, McTell's book was profound, academically impeccable, lucid, and provided that rarest of commodities in scholarly research: a genuine insight into vastly overworked material, a fresh and important perspective.

But the real story lay in the ten empty years between receiving his professorship, at thirty-eight, and the publication of *The Death of the Lance*.

Once McTell had achieved the things he had considered so important—status, reputation, career—his world had not grown brighter still, as he had always assumed it would. On the contrary, it had begun to crumble—not from any cataclysm, but a little at a time—into apathy, boredom, and the suspicion that what he was doing was not after all very worthwhile. A series of romantic involvements interested him progressively less. His popularity with students was undermined by his increasing sense that, at heart, all of them were toadying for grades. And the material he taught came to seem dull and unimportant in the context of the lightning-quick technologizing of the modern world. How was he supposed to impart weight to the teachings of Abelard or Aquinas when his students went home to computers?

McTell was not the sort of man to fall into bitterness, but he was easy prey to ennui. He liked to think of himself as a soldier who had fought too many battles, and who had at last come to understand that winning or losing meant little–the result could only be more war. His publications ceased; he lectured from the same notes year after year; and he began to detect in the manner of his colleague the sort of knowing condescension reserved for those who, once tenured, never exerted themselves again. But even pride could not rescue him. He lapsed instead into cynical passivity, and began to drink during the day.

Until one April afternoon, when a graduate student in journalism named Linden Sumner appeared in his office, asking to interview him for the school newspaper. When McTell declined–wearily amused, and slightly drunk–the request became a demand. He had sat up then and taken a closer look at the woman confronting him: attractive in a severe sort of way; brisk and determined; in her early thirties, but seemingly undismayed at her late start on a career. He soon learned that she was recently divorced, and something of an heiress.

He consented to the interview. It took the form of several long conversations over a period of weeks, moving from coffee to drinks to dinner—and away from European history toward his personal one. Soon she decided that he needed a part-time assistant. With that same brisk determination, she took charge of his office and then of his life, and when she finally led him to bed, she demonstrated that she was just as efficient there as behind a desk. By then it was clear that his existence was infinitely simpler with her than without, and they were married. Linden finished neither the interview nor the school year. But under her firm influence he began to work again, and while she typed and researched and organized relentlessly, he found that the brilliance he had thought dead was only dormant; and he emerged from his ten-year decline stronger than he had ever been.

So here he was, at the peak of his life and career: healthy and vital, with the sort of rugged good looks that aged attractively; well enough off so that money need never be a problem; on the verge of producing another great work; and blessed, at last, with a wife.

Yet he could not escape the growing sense that while in his days of drinking and cynicism he seemed to have given up, he was really waiting—waiting for the person or event that would arrive suddenly and change his life; that would, if only briefly, ignite his world once more with the priceless flame of passion.

And the contrary: that while in the eyes of the world he had recovered his dignity and become an object of admiration, he had truly quit this time. The unspecified adventure he dreamed of had been unlikely enough anyway; but now that he was married and settled, he felt he had forfeited even that slim chance. He finally understood that he had never really healed after those months of youthful heartbreak. Rather, the magic lens of passion had scarred over. It had grown dimmer still through the years, overlaid with a laminate of disappointments, missed chances, and his own failures, until it was almost forgotten. Now it was only left to him to wonder, during moments like this, at what precise point he had accepted its never coming clear again. He supposed there had been many such points, like stepping-stones across a brook of time, bringing him to a far shore of endless if not unpleasant grays. The last of those stones had been the exchanging of vows with a woman for whom he cared deeply, with an affection that was mature, companionable, fitting for his age and place in life—but whom he did not love.

He glanced at his watch and realized with a start that he had been gone almost the promised two hours. The sun was deceptive, motionless in the sky, and the passage of time difficult to gauge. He pictured Linden wandering around the empty villa, unable to lie still beside the pool for long; starting dinner; perhaps beginning, a little forlornly, the chore of unpacking. He quickly corked the wine, and paused for a last look at the vista below.

What scenes had the Templars gazed out upon from this spot? Crusaders and bands of pilgrims on their way to the Holy Land? Enemy hordes sweeping across the countryside, with the smoke and cries of pillage rising on the wind? A little reluctantly, he shouldered his pack and made his way back down the wall.

As he crossed the courtyard, the iron grate set into the ground caught his eye—a grim reminder of the darker side of medieval life. A few yards from it, a stone slab the size of a tabletop protruded from the pavement. Its purpose puzzled him. Late though he was, he could not resist a closer look. The dungeon was doubtless long since filled with earth and debris.

But when he looked over the opening's stone lip, he was startled to see that it was filled with water. Blinking, he leaned closer. Not black and stagnant water, but clear and steaming, as if it were a bath.

A young woman was rising out of it.

For perhaps one second, McTell's astounded eyes locked onto the details of her profiled face and form: rich chestnut hair pinned atop her head, with loose strands trickling down her neck; tiny beads of sweat on the bumps of her spine; the flex of muscle in her thighs; the delicate puckered rose of her breasts–

Suddenly she turned to face him, stepping forward as if into his arms. With a strangled cry of shock, be threw himself backward, catching what might have been a fleeting look of alarm in her own eyes.

An instant later, he found himself gripping a rusty iron grate, staring into a passage cut at a steep angle some fifteen feet into the earth. Remnants of a flight of stone stairs led to what might once have been chambers where the sun never shone, but was now only a heap of parched soil and rocks.

TWO

Mélusine Devarre found her gaze moving again and again to the girl who worked silently beside her in the kitchen. Alysse was always quiet, her temperament naturally gentle and subdued; but this evening there was a quality to her withdrawnness—a sense of disturbance or worry—that Mélusine could clearly feel. It disturbed her in turn.

She glanced at the clock. It was six-forty, twenty minutes before Alysse usually went home to her spinster aunt and supper. Mélusine considered; then she sighed aloud and stepped back from the counter, patting at her forehead with her apron.

"What heat!" she exclaimed. When Alysse looked up. Mélusine winked and said, "Time for a little drink for the galley slaves."

Alysse gestured doubtfully at the cobbler she had been layering with fruit.

"I'm not done—"

"Pah, we've worked enough. *Un petit Campari?*"

The girl nodded timidly, her eyes large and grave, then gave a quick smile. She was an orphan, the aunt she lived with poor as a mouse; and ever since the Devarres had moved to the village the year before, Mélusine had wished she could have known Alysse much earlier, adopted her to raise as one of her own. A bond had sprung up between them instantly, mysteriously powerful–almost more so than that of blood. But Alysse was seventeen now, nearly of age. The best Mélusine could do was to give her light work helping around the house, and contrive excuses to overpay.

"Put the fruit away, then," she said. "I'll make the drinks."

She moved around the kitchen, a handsome, strongly built woman in her mid-forties, limping slightly on her polio-shortened leg. Her dark skin, almond eyes, and slightly harsh features spoke of Eastern blood; her hair, black as a raven and carefully hennaed, was just beginning to show strands of gray. These she made no attempt to hide; on the contrary, they pleased her. Accept it with grace, she thought, and with a shrug added another splash of the sweet, mild apéritif to the ice and soda in her glass.

In the parlor they sank into chairs. "Will it never rain?" Mélusine said.

"It's bad this year," the girl agreed.

"But you," Mélusine said accusingly. "I think the *lys* in your name must stand for water lily. You always look so cool and lovely."

Alysse blushed, lowering her eyes. Mélusine watched the girl's slender tanned fingers turn the glass, and thought, Heavens, child, with proper clothes and a touch of gold, you could be on the covers of magazines. But not quite. There was the thing that kept her features from perfection: her nose, strangely flat across the bridge–a peasant nose pressed onto the face of a princess. And yet even this added an inexplicable charm, the mar that true beauty must have. Mélusine found herself toying with the idea of an unobtrusively expensive necklace for Christmas.

But, she reminded herself, there was a reason for this drink, this little breach of routine. She knew that the girl had no real communication with her aunt, who still wore corsets and, while kind enough, disapproved of the very air she breathed.

Firmly, Mélusine said, "Come now, tell me what's on your mind. A young man, perhaps?"

Alysse's forehead creased, but she did not look up.

"I've raised two daughters myself, remember," Mélusine said, "and even an *ancienne* like me has had her day with men. You'll feel better if you talk."

"I don't have any boyfriends," Alysse finally said. "It's just that it seems silly. This afternoon when I was bathing, I looked up and thought I saw a man in the window, watching me."

Mélusine's face tightened, but she made herself relax. There was no point in adding to the upset–yet.

"You're sure?"

"I thought so. Only–it's impossible. The window is much higher than anyone's head; there are no trees or rooftops. But the face was right there, not two meters away, as if it were hovering in the air. I must have imagined it, but it was terribly real."

"Terribly?" Mélusine said sharply.

Alysse nodded. "It was very ugly, and grim, with a big nose and cruel mouth–and only one eye. The other–there was no patch. It was just empty."

Mélusine's fingers tapped the chair arm. She sipped her drink, watching the girl's face closely for a sign of guilt or, Christ forbid, madness. But Alysse was telling the truth, or at least believed she was. Mélusine was sure, and about such things she was never wrong. Hallucination, then? Something to do with the tensions of approaching adulthood, or as simple as a chemical imbalance in the diet? Could the girl have been experimenting with drugs? It was impossible to imagine.

"You've never seen this man elsewhere?"

Alysse shook her head. "It happened so quickly. But a face like that . . ."

Mélusine nodded. There was no one in the village who remotely answered to that description. A wandering *clochard?* But how would he have reached the window?

"Well, perhaps it's a new form of satellite TV, coming directly to you in your bath. Let's just hope they're not broadcasting your charms to the world." Alysse giggled, hiding her face behind her drink. "Keep your door locked at night," Mélusine went on, "and if you see this man anywhere–if anything at all strange happens again–you must tell me at once."

The front door opened and closed; a cheerful greeting came to them from the hall. Roger Devarre was the town's only physician: semi-retired, he saw perhaps a dozen patients a week, and spent most of his time happily, if badly, painting. A moment later the high-pitched whine of the bathroom faucets came on. He was forever pushing up his glasses or scratching his head as he paused to survey his work, managing to spread nearly as much pigment on his skin as on the canvas. Luckily, he used mostly watercolors.

She rose and saw Alysse out, took from the refrigerator the pitcher of dry martinis she had made earlier, poured one into a chilled glass for Roger, and left it beside the parlor table where he would spend the next half-hour with his newspaper. Then she turned to the business of dinner. As she sliced and chopped the assortment of vegetables on the counter before her, she thought again of what Alysse had told her, and felt a sudden fierce surge of protective anger that anyone would dare to interfere with the girl in such a way. If it were true, if it were somehow a vagabond or voyeur, she would see to it that he regretted the day he had set foot in Saint-Bertrand-sur-Seyre–

Abruptly, she was staring in amazement at the thin line of blood welling up from the web between thumb and forefinger of her left hand. With a gasp, she hurled the paring knife clattering across the counter.

It lay beside the sink, inert, innocent, only a knife, with nothing to suggest what it had been–seemed, she corrected herself–an instant before:

A snake, flat evil head reared back, eyes locked malevolently with hers–then twisting and striking with a blur of speed at her free hand.

Snakes, the creatures she loathed most in the universe.

She leaned against the counter and waited for her breathing to even, the hammering of her heart to slow. But another glance at the knife brought the sudden feel of the cold deadly writhing in her hand. She gagged and hurried, limping, into the parlor. Roger Devarre glanced up from his paper. His good-natured face sharpened instantly with concern, and in two steps he was examining her hand.

"Vapors," she said, managing a smile. It was an old joke between them, from the early days of marriage.

"Well, it's not serious," he said. "I'll just put something on it that stings enough so you'll be more careful."

"Slicing vegetables. You'd think I'd never done it before."

"Vapors," he agreed; then, as if to a patient, "Wait here, please." She watched him stride off to get the necessary supplies, a lean craggy man with clear eyes and springy step; and while his concern was sometimes stifling, just now she was very glad of it.

He was right, the stuff he painted onto the cut stung harshly. In the process, she noted with amusement, he unobtrusively took her pulse. Then she was bandaged and safe, the pain subsiding to a dull throb.

"Now I prescribe a good stiff drink," he said, "to be taken in the company of, say, an admirer." He returned from the kitchen with another chilled martini. She sipped, coughed a little. The pressure in her hand and heart lessened again.

"So you're getting clumsy in your old age?" he said.

"Actually, I had something like a waking nightmare."

His eyebrows rose. Too casually, he said, "Ah?"

Psychiatrist too, she thought. "A clear-cut anxiety dream," she said, teasing. "I was attacked."

"By what?"

"A snake. Of course you know what that means."

He snorted and she laughed, but a pang of worry remained. Many years before, visions and premonitions of a gentler kind had not been uncommon in her life. The parents of her great-aunt Mathilde had themselves been caravan gypsies. It was this aunt who had insisted on the infant girl's being named after the Mélusine of legend, a mythical creature half woman and half fairy; this aunt who had whispered to the child of the gift she possessed and must learn to use, but who had died before that education was more than barely begun. The birth of Mélusine's own children had put an end to any such doings—or so, for the past two decades, she had assumed.

Now this. There was no knowing what it might portend. She only hoped that if visions were to begin again, they would not be in the same vein. Snakes. *And I will put enmity between thee and the woman, and between thy seed and her seed.* She shivered, finished her drink, and got out the pitcher again.

"Another?" Roger said, surprised. She drank little, and rarely.

She shrugged, resisting the urge to tell him the truth; it would worry him to madness. Though she had borne him three healthy children, two now with babies of their own, and had hardly been sick a day in her life except for the polio, her withered leg made her an invalid in his eyes, to be cherished and protected obsessively.

Well, she would have to face the kitchen sooner or later. She walked in firmly. The knife was just that, a knife, and she gripped it without hesitation; but a faint sickness touched her. She was not sure she would ever trust the thing again. She rinsed it, put it in a drawer, and began to sauté the vegetables.

But it was not just the knife, or what Alysse had told her, or the fear that there might be more to come. Something else was nagging.

Then she had it. It was the sense that something had been *let out* which should not have been. As if you knew that a viper was loose in the house, and that any time you opened a closet or reached into a drawer or slid your feet into bed . . .

"So what is it?" Linden murmured. "Sea air? Exercise? Or am I finally irresistible?"

They lay uncovered on the bed, sweat beginning to dry on their bodies. McTell felt her fingers twisting lazily through the hair on his groin, occasionally moving with a fascination of their own to touch his still-wet penis and measure the progress of its shrinking.

"I've been that bad?" he said.

"Let's say you seem to have had other things on your mind."

"Travel," he said vaguely. "Takes a lot out of an old man like me."

"Hah. You were forty-nine going on eighteen tonight."

"You bring out the animal in me, darling."

"I wish I could do it more often."

"We will," he said. "I promise." He began to stroke her back, pressing the heel of his hand into the muscles along her spine, feeling her relax with a sound like a purr. And he thought of what he could not or would not tell her: that with her so physically near those previous weeks, joining their bodies had been almost too intimate, as if he feared that in becoming so close they might merge, and that she, the stronger in some mysterious primal way, would absorb him until he ceased to exist. The time when he would have welcomed such a union of souls was long gone. There was even relief in having a mate who lived with him and cared for him in the world they shared, but who never crossed the threshold of the world where he walked alone.

But there was more he could not say. She had been a little cool when he returned from the ruin an hour late; and a dozen times, as he stood with cocktail in hand and watched her set out the dinner things, he had been on the edge of sharing with her his strange vision of the afternoon. Their stay in the house had begun inauspiciously enough; it would have been a simple way to overcome tension, reestablish intimacy.

But each time, something had intervened—something almost in the nature of a warning voice. It was not that he wanted to hide anything from her, he had finally decided, but that in some way he could not quite pin down, the vision of the girl had been too private, too much a part of his own inner world. And, the voice of common sense added wryly, few wives would be pleased to hear that their husbands had been imagining beautiful young nymphs bathing.

Linden's breathing had evened. He kissed the top of her head and disengaged himself, turning onto his side. She made a small sound of complaint but did not wake.

McTell, too, sought the deep sleep he needed after weeks on the road. But the face of the girl rose and floated before him—not a face of common abstract beauty such as he might have imagined, but sharp and clear, right down to the strange detail of an incongruously broad flat nose. He remembered that last flash of alarm in her eyes, as if she had seen him too, as if she had actually been there, as if, through some impossible warp of time or distance, it had not been his imagination at all.

For a long time he lay with his wife's breath warm against his shoulder, until he seemed to be drifting, as though in a boat on a gentle river, through the interface between sleep and dreams. A hand was beckoning. He floated obediently after it, and saw that it was gloved in a heavy metal gauntlet. It led him through a land of gorgeous fluid dreamscapes, vivid, seductive, tantalizingly familiar. At last the hand descended into an opening in the earth and began to scrape at the red crusted soil. It dug steadily deeper, until McTell was looking into a compartment blacker than anything he had ever imagined. Something was in there, he understood—something terrible and powerful and wonderful; but as he hovered, in the manner of dreams, wanting and fearing to reach in and find out what it was, a sudden hard pressure pulled him away.

He opened his eyes to see his wife's tense face. Her hand was gripping his arm. Seconds passed in the room's dark stillness, and then Linden smiled timorously.

"Sorry," she whispered. "Bad dream."

With murmurs and caresses they settled back down, and at last he dropped into a sleep that was sweet and profound.

THREE

The exterior of the cathedral of Saint-Bertrand was pleasing but unremarkable, McTell decided after a few minutes. The design was standard Gothic: transepts extending out to both sides like wings, a semihexagonal apse in the rear, a row of high-arched clerestory windows whose stained glass depicted an assortment of saints and biblical figures. He was sure even at a distance that these were not original, but replacements from the eighteenth or nineteenth century. The good glass had probably been made away with for the private chapel of some noble, destroyed in the frenzy of the Revolution, or looted by Napoleon's agents and sent to Paris. Carved in stone on the west-facing façade above the great main doors was a tympanum of the wise and foolish virgins; the cornices of the spire sported gargoyles weathered featureless by the centuries. But while the little church offered nothing of magnificence like the great cathedrals of Chartres, Amiens, and Notre Dame de Paris, McTell was, if anything, more moved to awe by the incalculable labor of peasants and tradesmen, perhaps lasting generations and hundreds of years, in erecting such an edifice to a God who so often seemed dedicated to making their lives a misery.

He squinted up into the merciless sun. He had left the villa only a quarter of an hour before, but his shirt was already plastered to his back. Linden had remained, declaring that she had seen enough churches in the past six weeks to last her a lifetime. He was secretly, if a little guiltily, pleased.

It had occurred to him that the girl of his vision the previous afternoon might be a known phenomenon–an apparition that haunted that particular place and appeared under certain conditions. McTell had never had any sort of psychic experience, and was inclined to skepticism; probably she had only been an image of his fatigued mind. But there was no denying he had seen *something*, and there was a possibility, however faint, that a few discreet questions might shed some light. He started for the entrance, hoping he might encounter a talkative priest or caretaker.

Inside, the coolness was refreshing. McTell walked through the nave, conscious of his echoing footfalls in the deserted building. Apparently, the village was far enough off the beaten track so the *curé* feared neither theft nor vandalism, at least in daytime. The ceiling was high and groined, supported by fluted stone pillars; the aisles narrow, the altar simple, the walls hung with the Stations of the Cross. Not until he reached the farthest corner of the south transept did he come upon anything of real interest.

At first glance, there was only a dusty triptych screen presenting some sort of pageantry. He quickly dismissed it, like the windows, as an imitation from a later century. But perhaps because it seemed so oddly out of place, he was impelled to peer behind it. Hardly visible in the darkness of the corner, about waist-high, was some sort of carving on the stone wall. He glanced around; the church was still empty. He edged behind the screen.

Immediately his excitement jumped—instinct and judgment both assured him that the work was early and genuine—and rose again when he bent to examine it. The carving was small and crude—done hurriedly, he had the sense, on a single block of stone—and time had taken its toll. But the scene had been rendered with obvious ability and care.

He was able to make out two figures for certain, and what might have been a third. The first, at the far right, was clearly of a man fleeing, with arms outstretched and mouth open wide in exaggerated horror. The second was of his pursuer, and this portrayal caused McTell to study the block intently for some time. The figure was very short and squat, muffled entirely in a hooded garment. A single limb was extended in pursuit; McTell would not have called it an arm because he was not at all sure the creature was intended to be human.

The third figure was only a vague outline in the background. It might have been that of a tall man, standing on a hillock, watching. Behind him rose a mountain with a building on it. Beneath the scene were letters that McTell had to squint at to make out:

S. BERTRANDE
QUI DEMONIA EFFUGAS
ORA PRO NOBIS

In smaller letters still was added the legend:

ann. Incarnationis veri Dom. mcccvii
D. f. descripsit

"Saint Bertrand, who makest demons to flee, pray for us," McTell said quietly. "Incarnation of the true Lord, 1307. D. f. hath drawn this."

He straightened up and looked around. The church was very still. Though illustrations portraying the miracles of a saint were not unusual, he had never seen anything like this. Then he noticed that the small window in front of him had side panes of clear glass. Although the glass had become viscous over the years, his recognition of the scene outside was instantaneous. He was facing south, as had the sculptor, who had etched the landscape into the stone precisely as he saw it. The mountain in the background was Montsévrain, visible in the distance; the building atop it, the fortress as it must have appeared seven centuries ago, before decay had set in.

That much of the scene, then, was from life. And the figures?

The pursuit was probably allegorical, he decided–the common enough theme of Death hunting down the human soul, here in a somewhat offbeat representation. In any case, it was certainly worth a photograph. He took several with varying exposures, and was putting the

43

Nikon away when he heard the echo of footsteps. Feeling like an intruder, he stepped quickly from behind the screen and walked to the nave to advertise his presence.

The newcomer was a tiny wizened man in a beret and blue workman's smock. He gave McTell only a glance and a "*Bonjour,* monsieur," as he hurried back to the apse. A minute later he reappeared, carrying a pile of vestments.

"Excuse me," McTell said in French. "Are you by chance the sacristan?"

It had been McTell's experience that while the French would condescend almost graciously to strugglers with their tongue, they tended to be outraged at foreigners who dared to speak it well. Or perhaps it was a thyroid condition that made the little man's eyes bulge.

"Yes, monsieur," he said. "I have kept this church these twenty-three years, and my father before me."

"Can you tell me anything about that carving?

The old man's gaze followed McTell's pointing finger, then returned to his face, this time seeming reproachful, as if McTell had betrayed a trust.

"Carving, monsieur?"

"The one behind the screen."

"Ah," the sacristan murmured. "Monsieur has examined our church closely. I fear I know little about such things."

Amused and irritated, McTell said, "Surely there must be a story to it."

The little man glanced at the screen, then shrugged.

"Long ago there was a bad business with some wicked knights."

"The Templars who held Montsévrain?" McTell said sharply.

"I know very little," the sacristan repeated. His eyes seemed in danger of popping from his head. "Now, if monsieur will excuse me—" He held up the pile of clothes and edged toward the door.

McTell's hand had already gone to his pocket. "For your trouble."

The sacristan stared at the fifty-franc note, glanced quickly around the church, and set the vestments down on a pew. The bill vanished into his smock.

"It was their leader, the giant—" McTell did not quite catch the name; it sounded something like *suloy*. The little man had stepped close and was speaking in a low voice, looking furtively around. A bit melodramatic, McTell thought; amusement was gaining.

"He was the most evil man who ever lived, monsieur. Even now it is not good to speak his name. It is said that he made a bargain with the devil himself, that the devil granted him the power to command spirits. There was *celui*"—the French word meant simply *the one,* but the sacristan gestured nervously at the carving—"always with him. He had a magic book bound in human skin, and he killed people and drank their blood to appease the devil." His voice dropped to a whisper. "It is said that he could raise the dead."

McTell looked into the old man's eyes, and realized suddenly that he was genuinely frightened—that this was not a show for a tourist. The church was very quiet.

Gently, he said, "And what happened to this man?"

"Burned, monsieur, by the Inquisition," the sacristan declared. "But even death could not stop him. A group of priests had to"–here came a phrase McTell understood as *bury the restless ghost*–"and the doors of the cathedral were closed because evil had penetrated them."

Questions flared in his mind. What did it mean, "Even death could not stop him"? How could you bury a ghost? Who or what was this *celui?* And what was the origin of the carving?

But the old man had evidently decided he had given his fifty francs' worth of information.

"Many thanks, monsieur," he said, backing away and picking up the vestments. His look of reproach was back, as if McTell's money had induced him to tell something he should not have.

"But I'm very curious," McTell said, reaching for his wallet.

"Many thanks," the old man repeated, this time shaking his head firmly. Then he paused, and finally said, "But if monsieur would care to meet the *curé*, perhaps he can satisfy you. Monsieur Boudrie knows a great deal more about such things than I."

McTell had considered calling on the priest anyway, torn between the hope of learning some interesting history of the region and the fear that he would be bored by a thickheaded provincial mired in dogma and peasant life. If the second proved to be the case, at least the encounter would be brief.

"*S'il vous plaît,*" he said.

"Then if monsieur will come with me."

The sunlight was blinding, the heat like a blow, but both were welcome after the almost sinister darkness of the church. He followed the hurrying sacristan around the apse, skirting the ancient graveyard, to the rectory next door.

"Monsieur Boudrie, a visitor, a foreign gentleman," the little man called crisply as they rounded the corner.

McTell found himself looking at a man bent over a car's open hood, feet braced wide apart, head far into the interior. He was wearing overalls and heavy black brogans, and as he backed out from under the hood, McTell saw that he was broad as an ox. His worst fears surged.

But only for an instant. The *curé's* face was heavy and purpled with the broken veins of a drinker, and his graying hair flowed almost madly back from his forehead; but there was quiet determination in the set of his jaw and a deep, watchful intelligence far back in his eyes. For a moment neither spoke, and McTell had the sense that his entire being was measured by those eyes and filed away irrevocably in that massive head.

Then the priest held out his right hand as if it were something he had recently found on the end of his arm and did not quite know what to do with. It was enormous, with cordlike veins crawling under the skin and short stubby fingers black with grease around the nails. A stream of bright sticky blood was drying across the badly skinned knuckles.

"It would be my pleasure to shake your hand, monsieur," Boudrie said, "but as you see . . ."

47

McTell smiled and held out his own hand. The priest wiped his palm on his overalls, then seemed to realize the gesture's futility. As they touched, McTell was conscious of his own slender white fingers.

"If you will excuse me, messieurs," the sacristan said, bowing and retreating.

They watched him go. "Little René, always in a hurry for dinner, or lunch, or an *apéritif*," Boudrie said. "One would think he would be as fat as me."

"Perhaps he worries his weight off."

Boudrie turned to him with interest. In English, he said, "You are American, monsieur–?"

"McTell. I didn't realize my accent gave me away so quickly."

"On the contrary. It is only that I knew several Americans well"–Boudrie paused, then finished vaguely–"long ago. But I fear my English is–how do you say?–rustee." He waved deprecatingly at McTell's protest, and continued; "You are passing through?"

"Actually, my wife and I are renting a house here, the de Renusson villa."

"Ah yes, I know that house. It once belonged to a family of that name, de Renusson. But it was sold, and now it is only used for vacations. There has been some trouble renting it, this summer has been so dry." The priest's pause was almost imperceptible, just long enough to make McTell wonder if Boudrie had heard about the use of precious water for something as frivolous as a swimming pool. "The farmers are throwing up their hands–and not forgetting a convenient excuse to drink away their afternoons."

48

"A pity," McTell murmured uncomfortably.

Boudrie shrugged. "This year drought, next year it will rain too much. Mysteriously, though, it all continues. Like this—this beast." He swept his hand at the car. It was a tiny two-seat 2CV with a gearshift protruding from the dash; almost comically old and battered, rusted, upholstery in tatters. McTell found it difficult to imagine how the priest wedged his big body behind the wheel. Then he noticed that one of the hood hinges was torn loose, leaving fresh sheared edges of metal.

"Odd," he said, pointing. The car did not appear to have hit anything. "How did that happen?"

Boudrie's face clouded. "It is old like me, Monsieur McTell," he rumbled, the hard syllables of the name almost crackling from his lips, "and brittle. Things give way unexpectedly." He clasped his hands behind his back; his gaze turned inquiring.

Here was a man with things to do, McTell thought, glancing with wry sympathy at the preposterous little car. Sparring was over. He chose his words carefully.

"I've heard several bits of information about a rather lurid history of the fortress up there. I'm a historian myself, and I confess I'm intrigued."

The priest looked sternly in the direction of the sacristan.

"I trust this information did not cost you too much?"

McTell grinned. "Not too much."

"My good little René, filling people's ears with fancy. Worse even than his father."

"In all fairness, I should tell you that I pressed him. I noticed that strange carving on the transept wall."

49

"Ah," Boudrie murmured. He turned to gaze at the ruin of Montsévrain, looking, McTell thought, a little weary, like a man regarding the stronghold of an ancient and unroutable enemy.

"Perhaps I shouldn't have been prying."

A moment passed before Boudrie turned back.

"History refuses to stay buried, Monsieur McTell, as you surely know. But sometimes it emerges in a distorted form, and perhaps this particular distortion is not one for either this region or the Church of Rome to be very fond of. You translated the inscription?"

"Yes."

"*Eh bien,*" Boudrie said. "About that carving, I can tell you who did it, and when, and something of why. Saint Bertrand du Cians was a famous exorcist of demons, and during credulous times such things were always on people's minds. I know a little, too, about Montsévrain and its occupants. You are correct, there is some quite unpleasant history connected with that place. But as you see, I am not exactly in a position to chat. Perhaps you could come by tomorrow and join me for coffee."

McTell pictured himself stiffly sipping coffee in a room lined with sanctimonious books and pictures of dewy-eyed Christs exposing their hearts—hardly the ideal setting to get the priest talking. He decided that the sensible thing would be to describe his vision to Boudrie right then and there, to find out if anything like it had been known to happen before. But again, that strange reluctance to share it overcame him; and a better idea came instead. Unless he was very much mistaken, the

50

priest was fond of drink. A good meal with plenty of it would surely loosen his tongue.

"Why don't you join us for dinner?" McTell said. Boudrie looked uncertain.

"I have to warn you, we're heretics," McTell continued quickly. "Perhaps it isn't proper for priests to break bread . . ."

"These days, monsieur," Boudrie said gravely, "what is proper is of no account—only what is convenient. The honor would be mine. It is only that I am reluctant to impose."

"Not at all. We've hired a cook from town, so it's no trouble. And you won't have to suffer American cuisine."

Boudrie smiled. "Anyone's cooking is preferable to one's own, *non?*"

For the first time, it occurred to McTell that the priest was a bachelor—and if poor enough to fix his own car, then probably poor enough to keep his own house as well.

"Tomorrow night?" he said.

"Surprisingly, my calendar happens to be free."

"About six, for an *apéritif.*"

Boudrie bowed and again offered his hand. Their eyes met briefly, and McTell realized that the subtle game of wits already developing promised to be as entertaining as the story the priest had to tell. This much was sure: Inside that clumsy body hid a man to be reckoned with. Above all, there was that watchfulness, that measuring, far back in his eyes.

The heat continued, relentless; McTell had been thirsty for some time. He pulled away from the curb, heading for the red and white awning of a bistro on the village's main street.

Étien Boudrie wiped his sleeve across his forehead and watched the American's car pull away. A BMW sedan, new and expensive; clearly, the rumors of money were true. A pleasant man, too: intelligent, decent, possessing the sort of quiet confidence that suggested he was used to getting his way without having to fight for it.

Only—there was something. An unhappiness that had come once or twice into his eyes, that suggested a disappointment, an unsatisfied longing. Boudrie had been a priest too many years not to recognize it. There was no one who did not long for something he could not have. Though Boudrie was known as something of an expert in the history of the area, the truth was that he knew a great deal more about the mean and petty vices of its inhabitants. He had long ago given up the fiction of the confessional's anonymity. It was impossible not to identify the voices coming through the screen, and all too often, he understood what was on a sinner's conscience before the stammering words began.

He had, of course, known McTell's name, that he and his wife had rented the villa, and that old Amalie Perrin had been hired to cook for them—the last probably before they themselves did. These were among the dozens of bits of gossip reaching his ears every day, in a place so dull that the tiniest event was seized upon, examined, embellished, with connotations attached and stances taken until the utmost drama had been wrung from it.

He had known, too, that water had been mysteriously procured for their luxury, and though its source
had not yet been revealed to him—which made it a very
well-kept secret indeed—he had little doubt that it involved an illicit undertaking by Henri Taillou.

Well, *la Perrin* laid a good table, even if she did have
a voice that could cut glass, and a decent meal would do
him no harm. By informal arrangement, she usually
cooked something extra and dropped it by the rectory
two or three times a week, but now that she was working
full-time, that practice, and his stomach, would probably
suffer.

He turned back to the automobile that had been his
companion for more than a decade. Already old when he
had received it secondhand from a wealthier parish, it
seemed at times more of a nemesis than a helpmate.
Although he had of necessity become proficient at keeping it alive, today it had struggled with him like a wild
thing with a will of its own. The last spark plug was always tricky to reach. This time it had simply refused to
budge until Boudrie—knowing better—applied too much
pressure with the wrench and snapped the plug in half,
stripping the skin off his knuckles in the process.

Whereupon, enraged, he had seized the hood and
ripped it halfway off the car.

This had happened only a few minutes before the
American's arrival. Luckily, he had had time to cool
down; his appearance had been embarrassment enough.
He leaned under the hood and surveyed the damage. The
plug would have to be drilled and tapped, the hood hinge
replaced or welded. Glumly, he wondered if American

priests worked on their cars. He wiped his forehead again and longed for a glass of beer.

Was it his imagination, or was there some subtle strangeness touching his little world? One could not spend thirty years in such a place, with a finger on its spiritual pulse, and not be sensitive to such things. This business with the car–it was as if some imp of perversity had goaded him on, blinding him to common sense. Yesterday evening he had seen young Philippe Taillou hurrying off to the bistro to spend the little bit of wages his father did not deduct for room and board. At the best of times, the boy had the profile of a rodent and a furtive look–too long under his father's heavy hand–but last night he had resembled a hunted man. And earlier that same afternoon, Boudrie had passed Mélusine Devarre, the wife of the new *médecin,* doing her marketing. Though he did not know her well–they were not church-goers–she was the most pleasant of women, never failing to pause and exchange a few words. But she had clearly been preoccupied, her brow furrowed, her mind else-where, and had passed without seeing him–considering his bulk, not an easy thing to do.

Now there was this Monsieur McTell asking about the carving–the first stranger in years to have even noticed it, let alone be interested in its significance. The little church did not get many tourists; there was nothing of particular interest. Boudrie liked it that way, and had deliberately placed the triptych screen to hide the carving from the idly curious. What instinct had led McTell directly to it?

But it was a *fait accompli,* and he began to segregate in his mind certain information there would be no profit in repeating—for instance, that the carving's inscription, chiseled by a peasant stonecutter who could not even read, was a laborious copy of the last entry that a four-teenth-century canon named Larmedieu had made in his journal, only hours before meeting his fate at the altar— and at the hands, so legend had it, of beings that were neither human nor, strictly speaking, alive. He had always found it interesting that the name Larmedieu meant "God's tears."

Nor did he plan to mention that the Americans from whom he had learned his first English were members of an OSS unit in World War Two.

Well, it was coming into the season for odd events. Though the sun continued to say summer, October was not far off and it would bring the *mistral.* Many a windy autumn night he had stood by his study window with a nameless sense of unease, the restlessness of the ele-ments seeming to find a deep, secret response in his soul. At such times it was almost possible to believe, like some of the older peasants, that the wind truly did carry the spirits of those who did not lie easy in their graves. Or had never lain in graves. It was no accident that *mistral* was the old *langue d'oc* word for master, and there was no doubt in the mind of Étien Boudrie that the gloomy autumn storms affected the living if not the dead.

But here he was, thinking dark thoughts in the middle of a scorching afternoon. He turned reluctantly back to the car, then brightened. There was no point in continuing; he had none of the proper tools. He would simply have to get old Gauthier the mechanic to perform the work for the good of his soul. Not for the first time, Boudrie admitted that the suppressed Church system of selling indulgences had had its points; it would be far easier to persuade Gauthier to fix the car free if Boudrie could guarantee a century or two eliminated from the time the mechanic most assuredly had coming in purgatory.

Trying not to be pleased, he hurried toward the rectory, where several frosty bottles of excellent Kronenbourg beer waited in the refrigerator. He could picture exactly where they were.

He was rounding the corner of the building when he saw Alysse walking along the street across the square. His heart jumped, as it always did, at the sight of her—as it had from the moment she had arrived in Saint-Bertrand, a bewildered five-year-old orphan, and along with an overwhelming crush of grief and guilt, he had recognized the terrible, wonderful possibility.

He stood a moment in the shadows, watching her lovely springy walk, the glorious mane of chestnut hair bouncing down her back, the flash of tanned arms and legs against her white frock. When he stepped forward, she saw him and waved.

Étien Boudrie waved back, eyes misting at the memories she brought him of her mother, who had been his lover eighteen years before.

The town was like a thousand others in France, McTell thought: the small square, the main street of shops and taverns, rows of houses enclosed by high masonry walls and iron gates painted bright green. A hundred yards to the east he could see the lazy glimmer of the Seyre, emptying its last late-summer reserves from the Alpes Maritimes into the Mediterranean. He parked the BMW in front of a dusty building with bolted wooden doors, which looked like a warehouse that had not been opened since the Revolution. Beneath the striped awning of the bistro, a parted curtain revealed several men standing at the bar.

Like most French taverns, it was too brightly lit. A large sign read SERVICE N'EST PAS COMPRIS, the Gallic way of letting customers know they were expected to tip. Silence fell as McTell entered; he felt the indirect stares of the sharp-eyed faces, topped with berets, decorated with identical mustaches. The bartender was young and deeply tanned, sporting a gold chain around his neck and a carefully groomed haircut. His face was vulpine, his deference exaggerated.

"La Meuse," McTell said, naming the first beer that came to mind. There were no women present, no sign of anything feminine. He almost smiled, remembering his first timid ventures into bars as a young man, the feeling of being measured by veterans. Conversations began again—muted, rapid, in a *patois* of which he caught only bits. He suspected he was their subject. The bartender opened a sweating brown bottle. McTell paid and obediently tipped, then carried the beer and glass to a table by the window. He sat with his back three-quarters turned to the gazes that had followed him, imagining with amusement the low-voiced comments: *It must be nice to be a rich American, to hire a cook and do nothing all day but sit in a bistro and drink.*

The beer was not cold, but it was rich and malty, soothing his throat, relaxing him. Idly, his gaze roamed the storefronts across the street—a grocery, a butcher's a cleaner's—while he planned his interrogation of the priest tomorrow night.

The door of the bakery opened and a young woman stepped out, calling something back over her shoulder. She wore a white summer dress and sandals; rich brown hair fell nearly to her waist. A long baguette was tucked under her arm. She shut the bakery door, glanced across the street toward where McTell sat, and turned in the direction of the square.

He remained stunned in his seat for seconds. Not until he was rising, fast, did he remember where he was. He gripped the chair-back tightly, straining to see her, ignoring the stares that again swiveled toward him. She was walking rapidly away, calves slender and bronze under the hem of the dress, willowy body moving with a trace of adolescent awkwardness.

He waved, without turning, at the bartender's obsequious "*Au 'voir, monsieur,*" and strode into the street. The girl had disappeared around a corner. He stopped, gradually realizing his position. He could hardly go running after her; he was behaving strangely enough as it was. *Those Americans, they cannot hold their liquor. The monsieur from the villa came in here only this afternoon and hardly touched his beer, then rushed outside, no doubt to be sick.* He started walking, trying to appear casual, and turned down the street she had taken. She was gone.

You must have been mistaken, he told himself. You got only a glimpse. She was a hundred feet away. The sun was in your eyes.

Slowly, he turned and started back to the car.

Behind the seat, he put both hands on the wheel and stared unseeingly at the distant hills. There was not a shred of doubt. She was the young woman he had seen stepping from her bath in the empty dungeon at Mont-sévrain.

As Linden strode through the living room, her eye was caught by a painting that was slightly askew. She straightened it automatically and stepped back, surveying the room sternly for any more departures from perfect order. Then, realizing what she was doing, she sighed. She made herself walk more slowly to the dining room, lit a cigarette, and stood before the sliding glass door that opened onto the patio. The vista of brightly colored mountains went on endlessly, set off by the magnificent ruined fortress and capped by the flawless Mediterranean sky. Flowers grew in profusion on the grounds; the pale purple of wild lavender sprinkled the hills; four massive, ancient *cyprès d'acceuil*—the traditional Provencal cypress of welcome—graced the entrance to the drive. The house was lovely too, built of thick-walled stucco, with a gorgeous curving staircase and second-story balcony, ten-foot ceilings, handsome Louis XV furniture—and modern plumbing.

But on their second day of residence, she was already bored.

Although she cooked, sewed, kept a comfortable and even elegant house, and did it well, she did so out of duty; and though she had dabbled in more than one career, her inheritance had given her the luxury of doing just that, dabbling. In truth, she had been waiting for something, and when it came in the form of a somewhat cynical and too-often-drunk college professor, she knew it immediately. McTell had needed someone to take over the reins of a career that had started brilliantly and languished; she had needed a worthy object for her organizational abilities, her drive, her skill in dealing with people. She had moved him out of his shabby old apartment and into a house, away from his reclusive habits and back into the society of his peers—and most important, had weaned him away from the bottle and back to finishing *The Death of the Lance,* which had lain half-completed for five years. In the process, she had developed a reputation as a hostess, and took her greatest pleasure in parties where she could let shine her wit, intelligence, and grace, qualities which in her own mind were so infinitely more important than domestic concerns.

The thought of several more months here brought her back sharply from festive memories. Her shoulders sagged a little, and she walked aimlessly through the room, stubbing out the half-smoked cigarette. Well, his work came first, and a few months of seclusion were not much of a sacrifice. Once he began to write she would again be needed, to type, organize, research, and suggest; and the days would pass quickly. Meantime, there would be company; her half-sister, Mona, had called from Paris and would be down within the week, along with her husband and whatever entourage the two of them had collected during their endless ramblings among the wealthy of two continents. Linden's mouth twisted. Seeing Mona was not always relaxing, but it was nearly always interesting.

Though the baggage was mostly unpacked, a thousand odd jobs waited, and she began to order them mentally. But a glance at the clock told her that only an hour remained before the new cook arrived. Almost with resignation, Linden realized that it was time to sunbathe.

She had decided to do this when she realized how much trouble John had taken over the pool. She knew it was intended mainly to pacify her. It was just like a man to try to buy you off, she thought with irritation, and with such a foolishly misguided gesture; she was not the kind of woman who enjoyed lounging in the sun while the hours slid vacantly by. But it soon seemed clear that the whole thing meant more to him than met the eye. Wasn't that what they said when your stodgy husband, out of the blue, suddenly presented you with a sexy negligee? It might amaze you, amuse you, even anger you—but you wore it. She had not been entirely joking the previous day in her remark about men wanting their women oiled and nude; she had been probing for a response.

When the whole thing had started, when John had began negotiating with the realtor, Linden had stepped into a hotel bathroom one afternoon and examined the skin on her arms. It looked pale—even, suddenly, unhealthy. Quickly, she had unbuttoned her blouse. The cutoff line from faintly tanned neck to white breasts and belly was clear. A feeling almost like panic touched her: She had been ignoring a hint literally as broad as a swimming pool. It was not the suntan itself–that was only a symptom, an almost laughable cosmetic. It was what might lie much deeper. Who could guess what fantasies of lissome brown-skinned girls lurked in even such a distinguished mind as her husband's? And so, a little ruefully, she had bowed to a part of her psyche beyond rationality, and set out to reshape herself in order to please the man she loved.

Upstairs, she undressed, slipped on a white terry-cloth wrapper, and pulled her hair into a ponytail. Then she gathered up the necessary equipment for her ordeal of indolence–oil, sunglasses, cigarettes, magazines, and a glass of chilled wine. Stepping onto the patio, she hesitated; even though it was protected by a chest-high wall and there was no one around, she still never felt comfortable being naked out of doors. She dropped the wrapper and quickly lay down.

But the heat was pleasant, relaxing; her skin warmed quickly, beading with sweat. She took a sip of wine, then began to cover herself with Bain de Soleil. Automatically she assessed her features as her hand rubbed in the fine film of oil: legs good, belly and buttocks flat, if perhaps a little too spare. Can't be too thin or too rich, she reminded herself. Her hand moved to her heavy breasts, and she smiled faintly, imagining her husband's penis between them.

Through half-closed eyes she watched the water shimmer in the pool, hypnotic, inviting. Her sunglasses slipped partway down her nose, and she saw that a strange indefinable haze had entered the air, though the sun was still bright and fierce. Puzzled, she briefly squeezed her eyes shut. The haze remained, an almost imaginary overcast that was somehow troubling. She sat up, swaying with the sudden rush of blood from her head; a little alarmed, she decided to go back to the cool of the house.

But as she stood, she found herself thinking, You haven't yet been in the water. The water will make everything all right. Think of all the trouble he went to, all those years of waiting. He'll be very disappointed if you don't go in.

The shimmering filled her vision as she moved closer, stumbling a little, and then stepped over the edge into the deep end. The cool water gently caressed her skin—soothing, wonderful, almost sexual. She drifted near the bottom, turning slowly, luxuriating. Somewhere far away, a pressure was building. It did not concern her; nothing was important but the mounting delicious sensations that surrounded her. There was no reason to go back. She opened her mouth to fill herself with the loveliness that urged to be inside her as well as out, to make itself hers—forever.

But as the first bit of water hit her throat, a tiny red light of panic flared.

All those years of waiting. What did *that* mean?

Suddenly she was struggling for the surface, fighting to keep her lungs from yielding to the need to open and suck in. She turned and turned, wild-eyed, but she had lost up and down, everything was the same pale blue. Her

63

vision grew dimmer, and the soothing sense of a moment before was now an iron hand in a velvet glove, holding her under, forcing her to give in. At last she understood dimly that one of her thrashing feet had broken the surface. She clawed her way to it and burst free. For long seconds she hung on the side, coughing, and finally managed to pull herself out.

Slowly, trembling, she gathered her things. On the doorstep she turned to stare at the pool. The water sparkled blue and innocent.

Then came the familiar sound of the BMW pulling into the drive. Glad for it, she stepped into the house, eager to tell her husband what had happened, to be held. But he stalked straight across the living room to the bar, without so much as a glance in her direction.

"John," she said.

He swiveled and stared, then smiled.

"Hello, darling," he said, and came forward to kiss her.

But in that instant, he had looked at her as if she were a stranger.

FOUR

McTell capped the bottle of Rémy Martin and carried snifters across the room to Linden and Étien Boudrie. The priest was sitting upright on the couch, holding what looked like a doll-house coffee cup between his thick thumb and forefinger, regarding it as if he feared it would snap in two at any second. His black clerical suit was shiny at the knees and elbows, and while the meal *had* been extraordinary–McTell sensed that the cook, a dried-up little woman who could have been fifty or seventy, had outdone herself for the priest–he had eaten like a man half-starved. He had also arrived on foot, to McTell's acute embarrassment–only then had he remembered the damaged car–and that embarrassment had increased when Boudrie's eyes had lingered on the swimming pool. But the priest had said nothing, and during the meal his conversation had been polite, general, and wedged in between bites of *coq au vin*.

So now, my friend, thought McTell, it's time for you to earn your keep. He noted the interest in Boudrie's eyes as they followed the cognac's progress across the room.

"Monsieur *le curé*," he said formally, "if it would please you to tell us a little of this region and its history, we'd be honored."

Boudrie accepted the Rémy with a rumble of contentment.

"Monsieur McTell," he replied with equal gravity, "I spend a great part of each day listening to my own voice, speaking to what I believe you call in English an 'audience captive.' I say Mass, I preach sermons, I console the sick, I give penance and absolution. And yet, I rarely tire of listening to myself. Strange, is it not?"

Linden smiled, a quick flash of teeth, and McTell saw that she was beginning to relax. She had seemed withdrawn during the day, tense at dinner, and he wondered if his own unrest could be communicating itself. She settled back, crossing her legs, peach-colored gown fanning out against the deep burgundy of the couch, and Boudrie seemed to ease his own stiffness a little.

"I take it from our conversation of yesterday that you have a particular interest in Montsévrain."

The game was beginning, and McTell moved carefully.

"The Templars have always fascinated me."

"To be sure, a most interesting group of men—and a most grim episode in history. Yes, they did once inhabit Montsévrain; I myself have seen documents to that effect. Of course, the fortress has changed hands many times since those days, and was finally abandoned in the nineteenth century. I believe that land reverted to a family from Anjou, or perhaps Champagne, but it hardly matters. They never come here."

66

"So it's just sat there untouched for a hundred years or more," Linden, said, "Hard to imagine."

Boudrie looked puzzled. "You have no such unused land in America? Have I not heard of the 'wide open spaces'?"

"Not this close to a place like the Côte d'Azur. Somebody would string signs along the highways for five hundred miles, set up concession stands, and charge admission."

Boudrie nodded judiciously. "But what one must understand is that thirty kilomètres back from the Côte, one may as well be in another country—and almost, another century. The wealth you see in Cannes never reaches these little places like Saint-Bertrand. Much of the land has been farmed too long; it is easier to go to a city, Marseille or Lyon, and find a better living in an office or factory. The young especially have no love for a life of struggle and poverty. They want automobiles, television, glamour. And who can blame them?" Boudrie's gaze, moving back and forth between their faces, came to rest on Linden. "So you see, madame, these people have no use for a desolate mountaintop and a pile of rocks. As for tourists, there are many ruins in France better preserved and far more accessible. A few times a summer someone takes the trouble to climb up there. But it is hardly an attraction."

Since seeing the girl in the flesh, McTell had abandoned his apparition theory. Still, it was possible that something about the place was known to cause psychic phenomena.

"There's no history of unusual occurrences there?" he said casually.

The priest's gaze moved to him and held steady.

"What makes you ask, monsieur?"

Wrong move, McTell thought. Anger at his mistake brought a creep of blood to his face. He raised his glass and half-turned away, shrugging.

"With all these mysterious rumors, it just seemed like the sort of place that might be haunted."

"You have climbed up there yourself?"

"Yes."

"And did anything unusual happen to you?"

McTell hesitated. Then he said, "I started daydreaming and got home an hour late for dinner."

"Nothing unusual about that," Linden said under her breath.

Boudrie joined in their laughter, chuckling in a deep growl, and McTell glanced gratefully at his wife.

"A great many unusual things are said to have happened there, Monsieur McTell, but not for some centuries."

As if on cue, Linden declared, "I'm dying to hear this story. A wizard with a magic book, commanding demons and raising the dead?" One shoe dangled, tapping against her foot.

Boudrie looked reproachfully at McTell, who smiled and said, "Just repeating what I heard."

"*Mon petit René,*" Boudrie said, shaking his head. "Half a bottle of *vin rouge,* and he would have thrown in the Second Coming of Christ."

"Then perhaps you'd better set the record straight."

Boudrie took a sip of coffee, a longer one of the Rémy, sighed appreciatively, and rearranged his big body on the couch. McTell settled back in anticipation.

"You are right, it is better you should have facts than fancies," the priest began, "although you may find that the fancies are more entertaining. But you, Monsieur McTell, undoubtedly know a great deal more about *les Templiers* than I."

"I'm familiar with most of the standard accounts, and a few not-so-standard ones."

"Well, I'm not," Linden said. "just because we're married doesn't mean John talks to me."

Boudrie coughed into his hand. "Of course I know little of marriage," he murmured. "Perhaps, monsieur, you could take a moment to speak to your charming wife of these knights?"

They laughed again, and McTell thought, Good: easy, casual, not too interested.

"What I mainly know," he said, "is that most of the information we have about them is highly questionable. But you're the one onstage."

"Very well. Please correct me if I am mistaken. The 'Poor Knights of the Order of the Temple of Solomon'—a name that turns out to be tragically ironic, as you will see, madame—were a holy order of men who were a combination of soldiers and monks. This order was created after the First Crusade, sometime in the early years of the twelfth century. These knights took vows of poverty, chastity, and obedience, just like other clerics; but their avowed mission was to protect the Holy Land and its pilgrims, by force. For many years they were the idols of

Christendom-the bravest of warriors, the most fervent of the religious, almost more gods than men—and their ranks swelled with the greatest nobles in Europe.

"Their riches and holdings swelled too, and perhaps it was inevitable that, over time, they achieved a new and less desirable fame—for their wealth and arrogance. Perhaps if they had stayed as poor as their title boasted, they would yet exist. But instead they were destroyed by the king of France, Philippe le Bel, who had them seized by the thousands in a single night—a Friday the thirteenth, interestingly enough, in the year 1307—and handed over to the Inquisition."

McTell's fingers tightened around his glass. He had not made the connection until now: 1307 was the date carved into the stone of the cathedral's wall.

"It is generally agreed that the charges against them were for the most part fraudulent," the priest went on. "How do you say? Trumped up. Philippe le Bel was a king with much luxury and many wars to support. He hated and feared this powerful order, who by their charter owed no allegiance to any secular authority. But he was able to install a pope in Avignon who was his creature—a sad chapter in the history of the Roman Church—and then he dared to bring down the Temple. In doing so he accomplished the double aim of ending their threat and seizing their wealth.

"To justify his actions, Philippe seized upon rumors that were already in circulation. The Holy Land had fallen again into the hands of the infidel some years before; it was widely thought that the Templars had allied themselves with Saracen princes and fought against their brother Christians, that they had become little better than an army of mercenaries, and even that at the last they had sold the Holy Land outright into Muslim hands. There is good evidence of at least some truth to these accusations—*n'est-ce pas,* monsieur? Do I speak satisfactorily?"

McTell bowed, impressed. The priest's account was accurate and succinct.

"Whether or not these charges were valid, no secular power alone, even one as mighty as the throne of France, could destroy that great order. It was necessary for Philippe le Bel to enlist the aid of the Church and its terrible hammer, the Inquisition. Thus the accusations made against these knights had to be transferred to the realm of religion; and thus when they came to trial, it was not for treason or other crimes against their fellow man, but for crimes against God: in the main, heresy and blasphemy. In those times they were easy labels to apply to an enemy one wanted to destroy, and with the aid of torture, the Inquisition rarely failed to find sufficient evidence for convictions. Many of the Templars were burned or left to rot in prison, including a number of their important leaders.

"That these knights used strange rituals which were unorthodox, if not deliberately heretical, there can be no doubt, although it seems that these were harmless enough. What is finally certain is that many innocent and even pious men came to cruel ends because of a rapacious king and a weakling pope. Though some few escaped in France, and remnants of the Order survived in

71

other countries, the Temple was broken, and never rose again."

From the dining room came the brisk clattering sounds of Mlle. Perrin, the cook, clearing the table. They jarred oddly with Boudrie's words. He picked up his brandy glass distractedly, but it was empty, and he hastily put it down again, looking embarrassed. McTell was already on his feet. He filled the glass over the priest's weak protests, and unobtrusively left the bottle by his side.

"For heaven's sake, don't stop now," he said. "What about our neighbors up the hill?"

Linden nodded, eyes exaggeratedly round. "This is better than summer camp."

"And true up to this point, madame. But now, I fear, is when the story enters the realm of the fantastic. As you are surely aware, monsieur, the line between heresy and sorcery was, to the Inquisition, very thin. We read in accounts of the Templars' trials that they were said to have variously worshipped a black cat, a talking head, an idol named Baphomet—even the demon-god Belial, a practice thought to have originated in very ancient Eastern worship. But of these charges of sorcery and diabolical worship, no real evidence was ever found. There was evil done, to be sure, but mainly by the Inquisition.

"At least, this is as much as we can glean from official accounts. But according to the legend of this region, at least one man among the Templars *was* an avowed sorcerer and worshipper of Satan. This man was the Master of Montsévrain"—McTell nodded; the giant *suloy*

72

of whom the sacristan had spoken—"and absurd though such rumors might sound, he was with reason greatly feared by the peasants. Leaving aside any question of magical powers, he was undeniably a savage and evil man.

"When the king's agents arrived to seize the Templars of Montsévrain, they of course moved with all secrecy. The Templars were, after all, great warriors, and the fortress was a stronghold; the king's men wanted to avoid either a battle or a siege. So they took certain of the villagers into their confidence. How exactly it was brought about is not clear after so many centuries, but the peasants contrived to open the fortress gates to the king's men at a time when they knew the knights within were weak and unprepared—perhaps in the aftermath of one of the blood orgies they were said to have conducted. The peasants were necessarily familiar with the Templars' habits, since they provided them with supplies and menial services—and, it would seem, victims.

"In any case, the unsuspecting knights were seized and hurried off to trial at Nîmes—all except for the Master. It is a measure of the terror in which he was held that trying to transport him so far—a journey that would have required several days and, more to the point, nights—was considered too great a risk. The king's agents were hardened soldiers, but they were swayed enough by the peasants' fear to agree to put that man to the stake immediately, before the fortress gates. According to the legend, he never uttered a sound, even to cry out in pain, from the moment he was taken. An exaggeration, no doubt."

McTell rose and stalked to the sliding doors. Just enough evening light remained to silhouette the brooding outline of the fortress. There, before the entrance, where he himself had stood, a man had once been burned alive. He remembered his uneasiness in passing through the archway.

"Oui, monsieur," Boudrie said. "On that very spot." McTell turned back to find the priest's gaze resting on him, steady, unreadable.

"As for the rest of that group." Boudrie continued, "they were tried, tortured, and burned in due time. It is from these trial records that I have a little evidence to bolster this story. Besides the accusations of unholy worship there were others that have a more credible ring, including the disappearance of a number of people. But who knows? When the Templars fell, they became a great scapegoat, and everyone will leap upon a scapegoat in a time of trouble."

Abruptly, Mlle. Perrin thrust her sharp face into the room. Her springy gray curls were tightly bound by a kerchief; an ancient pair of glasses pinched her thin nose. She rode a bicycle to and from the village, and McTell realized with amusement that the image of her as the Wicked Witch of Oz had become firmly fixed in his mind.

"*À demain,*" she said brusquely. Boudrie hastily swiveled around in the couch and delivered a series of compliments about the meal; although McTell could not follow all of the rapid *patois,* it was so heartfelt that it brought color to the old lady's cheeks. For the first time, he saw her smile. He supposed it would sour any woman to spend decades being stigmatized as a spinster–with

74

"Mademoiselle" every time someone addressed her, especially in an old-world place like this.

"Well," Linden said. "This Master must have made quite a reputation for himself."

"To be sure, madame. You must understand first that those were times not only of great superstition but of barbarity as well. No doubt the two are companions. It is perhaps impossible for us to imagine the day-to-day cruelty. Not uncommonly, those on their way to market would pass heads impaled upon stakes, men hanging in chains, dogs tearing at quartered bodies in the streets. Floggings and brandings were meted out like parking violations. Men were blinded and mutilated for the tiniest of crimes, or for no crime at all. The nobility thought of the peasants quite literally as animals; and for all the faults for which the Church of Rome must rightly be charged, we must remember that it was the Church that first spread wide the concept of mercy. Still, the record of abominations is endless and chilling, and for one man to stand out as a monster is no small thing. But if even a little of what is said about this Master of Montsevrain is true, his wickedness would be bard to equal.

"He joined the Templars as a youth, it is told; one would like to believe that he hoped to curb a nature whose ferocity he recognized already, but more probably he sought an outlet for his violence. His place of birth was near the Norman coast, wild and desolate even today, and for centuries the favorite route of invading Norsemen and British. The people of that region knew well the meaning of savagery and terror.

"He grew to great size and strength, and in the Holy Land won acclaim as a fearless and merciless warrior. At some point he seems to have been taken prisoner by the Saracens and held for several years, although he may have joined them voluntarily. But there is no doubt that when he came back to Christendom, he made no more pretense of hiding his evil nature. He is reputed to have given caravans of pilgrims into the hands of the infidel for no reward other than the pleasure of seeing those unfit for slavery put to the stake. He hated women especially, and—could be most cruel in his treatment of them. Your pardon, madame.

"At last his reputation was such that the Templars themselves were forced to take action. Whether for fear of scandal or fear of the man himself, they did not seek to try or imprison him. But by that time their influence in the Holy Land was nearly at an end anyway; and they sent him, with a small group of his followers, to Montsévrain, a holding which had come into their hands during the Crusade against *les Albigeois*—the Cathars. Here, they told him, he would not be interfered with as long as he remained. In short, they threw the people of the region, like sheep, to this wolf.

"This was in 1299, not long after the completion of the cathedral of Saint-Bertrand. Soon the ugly stories began. It was said that the castle was lit by strange fires on certain nights, that chanting was heard that had no part in Christian ritual. Groups of unwary pilgrims were occasionally taken to the fortress, supposedly to be sheltered until their further passage to the Holy Land could be arranged. None of them were ever seen again. Perhaps worst of all, a number of children disappeared."

"Children," Linden murmured.

For a moment none of them spoke; then, as if by signal, each turned aside to some evasive activity, Linden taking out a cigarette, McTell moving to light it, Boudrie finishing his cognac once again. Firmly, McTell refilled the glass. Boudrie watched him almost with reproach.

"Whether these things actually happened or not, we will never know. Almost certainly, there is some truth to them. There were wilder accusations yet: that the worship of the demon Belial was open, that the Master had entered into a pact that gave him magical powers, and that to sustain these powers, he celebrated rituals that included human sacrifices. It is said he held a belief I think was not uncommon among primitives, that drinking blood would increase his strength."

"Do you realize," McTell said slowly, "that you still haven't used his name?"

Boudrie smiled, a mirthless tightening of the lips.

"Perhaps I share an unconscious superstition of peasant blood. His given name, Monsieur McTell, was Guilhem de Courdeval, but he was called by his brother knights Guilhem *suloy*."

It was the same word the sacristan had used, but it seemed not to be a proper name after all—a nickname, or label of some sort. McTell wondered if it could be Arabic, or perhaps related to the French *soleil,* sun—although there seemed to be nothing about the man suggestive of light.

"I'm sorry," he said, "I didn't catch that word."

Boudrie gazed blankly at him, torn from thoughts of his own. "Monsieur?"

"This Courdeval. Did you say his nickname was soleil?"

They stared at each other in mutual incomprehension. Then Boudrie sighed.

"Forgive me, I fall easily into the accent of Marseille. *Seul oeil,* monsieur. Single eye." McTell watched Linden shift uncomfortably in her seat, and felt a slight prickling of his own scalp. Perhaps there was something to the business of not speaking the name.

"... a game played by the youth of that age," Boudrie was saying, "a cruel and foolish one. They would nail a cat to a post through the loose skin behind its neck, then try to butt it to death with their heads. It seems that Courdeval, in a mark of his early savagery, participated in such a horror. He took the cat's life, but the cat took his left eye; and in a further embellishment, it was claimed that he came by the power to see from that socket, which he always left uncovered—but to see things that ordinary men could not."

McTell got up again, restless, and paced. "So that's the end of it? His execution?"

"Not quite. The story becomes more fantastical yet. You have heard of the curse of Jacques de Molay?"

McTell nodded, and turned to Linden's questioning look.

"De Molay was the Grand Master of the Templars when they were seized. The king kept him and his second-in-command in chains for seven years, then promised them freedom if they confessed to all the charges leveled against the Templars. They agreed until they found out that Philippe le Bel planned to go back on his word and imprison them to die. So they recanted in front of the entire population of Paris, and Philippe, in a rage, had them burned over a slow fire the next day. The story goes that de Molay roared out a curse–summons might be a better word–for both the king and pope to meet him in judgment before the throne of God within the year. Both died of mysterious causes in the next several months. A lot of historians think that's another fiction, made up to vindicate the Templars."

"Or to seek to prove that they did indeed possess supernatural powers," Boudrie said. "In any case, the business attributed to Guilhem de Courdeval is in some sense similar. Though his voice kept silence at the stake, he is said to have spoken most clearly with the wrath of his gaze. Even the strongest men–war-hardened knights of the king, and the Inquisitors who had accompanied them, well versed in torture–were afraid and shielded themselves from it. And those peasants it fell upon–well, we will get to that shortly. But here is a most curious addition, if there is any truth to it. Normally, of course, the bones would be at least partially consumed during such a fire."

He paused and drank. Though the room was cooling in the twilight, McTell saw that the priest was sweating.

"Courdeval's skeleton, it was said, remained un-marred by the flames. The execution took place in front of the fortress, late in the day, and by custom the bones would have been buried soon after. But no one could be found who was willing to touch them. So they remained there, in full view of the village, for weeks.

"At this point, the villagers began to die mysteriously."

"Ah-hah," said McTell, snapping his fingers. "I begin to see. The deaths were attributed to old One-eye's ghost."

"Precisely, monsieur. Guilhem de Courdeval's reputed practices and powers naturally inspired revulsion and fear. Besides the Satanism and blood-drinking, he was said to be able to order spirits around like houseboys; and the trials of his companions include alleged eyewitness accounts of him literally raising the dead—not merely summoning ghosts, as necromancers sought to do, but animating corpses. Of course these accounts, given under torture, are hardly reliable; even if they were truthfully intended, we must consider the possibility of some form of mass hallucination.

"But by far the greatest source of fear among the local populace was a particular servant which Courdeval was reputedly able to summon at will. This being was in the nature of a familiar spirit, but not a dog or cat, such as a witch might have. It was more like something dragged from the darkest parts of the imagination, like the creatures of Bosch or Goya."

"The figure in the carving," McTell said. The pieces of the puzzle were whirling in a tightening spiral, maddeningly close to snapping into place.

Boudrie nodded, face wry. "*Celui*—the one—it was called by the peasants. It was believed that, of the many journeys Courdeval made in his life, he made one of a very unusual sort, to a place that is on no map; and that it was from this place he brought back his companion.

"At any rate, according to the legend, Courdeval's spirit lingered on after the destruction of his body, and was able to take a ghostlike shape. Together with *celui,* he was believed to roam the night, taking revenge on the villagers who had betrayed him. At last a small group took refuge in the cathedral itself, but even this sanctuary could not stop the evil powers. The peasants were horribly murdered in the very aisles of the church, while the priest may have fared worse yet. He was found days later behind the altar, still alive–in a sense. His eyes were round as coins; his face held a look that troubled even the bravest knights. Trembling violently, he stared without sleeping at something only he could see, and his hands never stopped making the motion of pushing it away from him. He was taken back to Avignon and cloistered, and there he died before long, without ever speaking again."

"And the carving?" McTell said.

"It was done by a man named Peire Dupin, a stonemason who claimed to have witnessed certain of these goings-on, but escaped. There is little doubt that he did experience something shocking, though doubtless, too, his mind was primed to make a supernatural occurrence out of an entirely natural one. We must remember that he watched helplessly while his lifelong friends and his family were butchered. In any case, it seems that afterward he had but one wish: to finish that carving before he died. As with the unfortunate canon, this was not long after. Dupin was said to have lost his will to live,

81

declaring that a world where such things could happen was no place for him. Before that, he was a healthy man in the prime of life."

D. f. descripsit, McTell thought: *Dupin fils,* the son, hath drawn this.

"Who or what was in truth responsible for those deaths is one more thing we will never know. Perhaps other escaped Templars, hiding out and killing for revenge; perhaps bandits taking advantage of the general confusion."

Boudrie's voice dropped off; his eyes seemed to lose their focus.

"The sacristan mentioned some kind of grimoire," McTell prompted.

"Ah yes, "Boudrie sighed. "The agency by which Courdeval was said to work his magic. It was purportedly bound in the skin of a heretic flayed alive–a pretty embellishment. This book has always been a popular part of the legend, perhaps because it is an actual object, something concrete instead of mere hearsay. I suppose it would be a species of proof that the whole sorcery business had some basis in fact, if only in the mind of Courdeval. Unfortunately, if it existed, it has not been found."

The priest began to dig in his pocket, and McTell saw with chagrin that he was taking out a watch.

"Monsieur, you can't leave us hanging like this," McTell said, trying to put a lightness he did not feel into his voice. "How did it all end?"

Boudrie's thick finger tapped his knee. "Very well, Monsieur McTell, a few minutes more, and then I must leave you to your rest and go take mine. Your hospitality is most pleasant, but there are three or four old women who must hear Mass at a distressingly early hour each morning, and they would fare badly if I overslept." This time he filled his own glass.

"Here, then, is the final measure of both the superstition of the times and the fear in which Courdeval was held. When the massacre in the cathedral was discovered by travelers, a messenger was sent immediately to Avignon. With a swiftness unheard of for the times, a group of soldiers and churchmen were dispatched back to Saint-Bertrand with the object of laying Courdeval's spirit to rest. After careful preparations, they accomplished this, and then hurried back to Avignon, glad to be done with such an unpleasant business."

"And it worked?" Linden said.

"Apparently so, madame. Courdeval faded from history, leaving only an ugly record of murder and savagery. His companions were tried and burned, and the doors of the cathedral were for a time sealed under interdict, because evil had penetrated them. At last the memory grew dim, and the traffic of pilgrims and such began to populate the area once more. Like the grimoire, Courdeval's tomb has never been found."

"No skeleton, no book of magic, not even a leftover demon or two?"

"I fear not, madame," Boudrie said gravely.

She leaned forward to stub out her cigarette. "You were right, the original story was better."

Boudrie smiled and waved a hand. "Like most villages, this one is very dull. During the winter months,

83

life centers around the kitchen fire. A bottle of wine comes out, perhaps even absinthe, and a dog that ran loose and killed some chickens turns within a few years into the *loup-garou,* the werewolf. An owl someone sees beneath the full moon is a witch on her way to sabbath; and should that person fall sick soon after, why, clearly, it is the work of that witch. A horned goat silhouetted on a hill becomes the devil himself. Think what several centuries of this can accomplish."

"I suppose the proof is, to some degree, in the pudding," McTell said. "If Courdeval had really had such powers, the soldiers would hardly have been able to take him."

"An excellent point, monsieur, one that any intelligent look at this legend must include. Although there are of course counter-arguments. It has been speculated that Courdeval was taken because be had grown so arrogant, so confident of his own invincibility, that his vigilance was relaxed. Also, that because he was unsuspecting, his grimoire was hidden in the secret place where he kept it, a place only he knew. Without it he was relatively powerless; and as for his companion *celui,* it could be summoned only at night. Thus the haste to burn him before darkness fell."

"You talk as if this were a well-known legend, with fan clubs and discussion groups—like Sherlock Holmes," Linden said.

McTell agreed. "For all the research I've done, I've never even heard Courdeval's name."

"As I said, monsieur, this is not a story that does credit either to France or to the Church—or to mankind, for that matter. I have reason to believe that the trial records were suppressed. Through some strange circumstances, this parish possesses a fragment of one copy, and it is the only copy I have ever heard of. Most of the legend, as well as the speculation that surrounds it, has passed from *curé* to *curé* over the years; there is rather a great deal of time for that sort of thing here. And while the local people are familiar with distorted versions of it, there has never been enough tourist traffic to make it widely known. Nor is there anything so really unusual about it. Travel to any village like Saint-Bertrand anywhere in Europe, buy a round of drinks for the old men in the tavern, and soon your ears will ring with stories of the great and the evil nobles who once lived in this or that castle–yes, and their ghosts, too–which you will never find in the pages of any history book." He finished his cognac with a slow, appreciative swallow, then gripped the chair arm to rise. "But I think I have spread enough fairy tales myself for one evening. I am as bad as little René."

Though McTell's curiosity was still mainly whetted rather than satisfied, he realized that he had learned all that he was going to from Boudrie, for tonight at least.

"I'll get the car," he said.

"Monsieur, please believe me, I look forward to the exercise. I do not get nearly enough of it."

"But in the dark–" Linden said.

"After telling such gruesome stories, madame?" She laughed, blushing. "I will keep my hand on my rosary the entire way. It is not two kilomètres."

They walked with him to the door. "Monsieur *le cure*," McTell said, offering his hand. "It's been a great pleasure. I hope you'll come back again soon."

"Monsieur McTell, the pleasure was mine. I fear you may be in danger of finding me on your doorstep with regularity. Madame." He raised Linden's hand to his lips, eyes ardent. Priest or no, McTell thought with amusement, a Frenchman is a Frenchman. "Thank you for a so lovely evening. I hope you do not grow too bored with the poor society of our little town." He started away; with his lumbering gait and thick shoulders, he looked less like a priest than a laborer.

McTell hesitated, but then he called out: "Monsieur Boudrie."

The priest stopped and turned, face inquiring.

"May I ask you one more question?"

"By all means."

"I'm curious as to how you yourself look at the whole business. The Church still accepts the existence of hell and the devil and evil spirits, doesn't it?"

Moths fluttered helplessly in the soft porch lamplight; the song of crickets rose and fell. The night air was like a warm caress. McTell felt Linden's hand tighten on his arm.

"You don't have to answer of course." he said.

Boudrie shook his head slowly. "I have no objection to answering, monsieur. I am only trying to collect my thoughts. Such a question is more difficult to speak to in this day than it would have been a few centuries ago.

"Well, then. With regard to the Templars, I believe that, in the main, many innocent men were cruelly

86

treated for the basest of motives. As for the rest—if any of it were true, it would point to the existence of forces we can hardly imagine. The consequences of tampering with them would be beyond comprehension. Those charges that were leveled against the Templars of Montsévrain seem laughable to us today. But just as some men seem born to be saints, is it not conceivable that others come into the world as agents of evil? Certainly, to anyone with his eyes open to the world around him, it is too often easier to see the presence of evil than of good, is it not? I think anyone who accepts religion and yet uses his mind must at some point ask: If I believe in the power of God and His saints and angels to do works upon the earth, then does the other not follow?"

For seconds his gaze held McTell's. Then Boudrie's face creased into a wry smile.

"You ask me a simple question and I give you another lecture. To answer you succinctly, Monsieur McTell, I believe as Holy Mother Church instructs me to; and while spiritual agencies are not yet in complete disfavor, such credulousness as the fourteenth century knew is no longer fashionable even in the Roman Church."

McTell bowed. The answer had really told him only one thing: He had been right in thinking the priest a shrewd man. Once again, they exchanged good-nights.

"You were right," Linden said as they walked back inside. "The inner man is a great deal more impressive than the outer one."

"Does that mean I should be jealous?"

"He doesn't strike me as the fooling-around type. Although I'm sure that if he hadn't become a priest, there'd have been no shortage of applicants."

"I wonder if a donation to the church would be seen as condescending."

She shrugged. "I'm sure he'd be glad to have it, but he'd probably send it right on to the diocese."

"True enough," McTell said. "But I'll bet he'd hang on to a bottle of good Scotch."

He moved around the living room collecting the glasses and cups—none the wiser, he admitted, in spite of a most entertaining story. And reluctantly, he was coming to the conclusion that his mind was playing tricks. The girl obviously existed in the flesh, lived right there in the village. It was entirely possible that he had seen her previously, when he and Linden had first visited Saint-Bertrand, and that she had registered on his subconscious and come back in that sudden, inexplicable fashion.

There remained, then, only two choices: put it out of his mind, the intelligent thing—

Or climb again to the ruin and see what happened.

"John!"

Startled" he turned to see Linden in the kitchen doorway, fists on hips, and he realized he was standing motionless in the center of the room, his hands full of glasses.

"I asked if you remembered about the liquor," she said.

Guests! Linden's half-sister and her husband, due day after next.

"I'm sorry, honey, I blanked it out completely. I'll drive to Grasse in the morning."

"Plenty of Tanqueray. You know Skip."

He did indeed know his brother-in-law, and it was more with resignation than with pleasure that he looked forward to the visit. But there was a bright aspect: it would keep Linden entertained.

But that was a hell of a way to look at it. He set down his load of glassware and walked quietly up behind her, suddenly burying his face in her neck and growling:

"I am the ghost of the evil Courdeval, and I've come to drink your blood!"

"What, again?" she said. She held up her soapy hands. "You'll just have to wait until I've finished the dishes,"

"No respect," he muttered and, looking appropriately glum, went back into the living room. He poured a little more brandy into a fresh glass. Tomorrow, he supposed, he would begin the laborious and thankless job of getting his mind back to his work, and he tried to organize his thoughts in that direction, to choose a place to begin and a course of action.

But his mind rebelled, and instead, he fell back into the persistent dream image of the black mailed hand scraping at red soil, the visual equivalent of a snatch of song that played unendingly in some perverse and defiant chamber of the brain.

FIVE

It was past ten when Étien Boudrie arrived at the dark and empty rectory. He closed the door behind him, flipped on the light, and walked straight to the brandy. McTell's fine Rémy had tickled his appetite for liquor; the walk home through the night had honed it to an edge. In a few minutes he was comfortably settled in his study, a decanter at his elbow. The bootleg brandy he got by the keg from old Docre the vintner was a far cry from the Rémy, but it would do.

He had not been altogether truthful in what he had told the Americans. Mainly the sins were of omission. The story was grotesque enough as he had downplayed it; the parts he had left out stretched it to the ludicrous.

But that was not all. He had sensed again that strange longing in McTell, this time in the form of a too intense curiosity–and a conscious effort to conceal it. Boudrie had no real reason for thinking this; it was only a feeling. But it had caused him, almost instinctively, to take a stance perhaps more skeptical than he truly felt.

This, to be sure, was in accordance with a world view evolved during a youth in the brutal orphanages of Marseille, a young adulthood at war, and a lifetime since of dealing with human vice in its most mundane forms. But McTell had raised a good point. Such things as spirits and demons may not have been exactly fashionable in the Church anymore, but officially, at least, they still existed. Boudrie knew men who had performed exorcisms. It was not a joking matter. And there was certainly nothing amusing about the way the Church had dealt with such as Courdeval and his knights.

How heady it must have been to delve into the occult, he thought; how pale the everyday world must have seemed in comparison to the pursuit of the ultimate mysteries—not through the saint's patient forbearance, but through grim, impassioned struggle with the forces of darkness, imaginary or not. Small wonder so many people in superstitious times had turned to the worship of powers they believed could aid them on earth. When their lives were little but misery, how much worse could hell be? Such circumstances could lead to desperate acts, Boudrie knew well. The peasant crying out for relief from his oppressors had received no help from heaven.

Restless, he rose and prowled the room, examining familiar objects as if seeing them for the first time: the rather lurid portrait of his namesake, Saint Étienne, kneeling beneath a savage volley of stones, face aglow with the holy light of forgiveness; a more restrained Madonna and child; a rosary blessed by His Holiness John XXIII many years before on one of Boudrie's few journeys to Rome; and setting it all off, an entirely secular calendar with photos of the Côte d'Azur, most of which exposed a scandalous amount of female flesh. There was also his single keepsake from the war, a German officer's stiletto; but though Boudrie refused the frequent urge to put it out of his sight, it was not something he cared to let his gaze dwell on. Keeping it there was a form of penance, but not to be overdone. Grumpily, he turned to the bookshelf. Most of the tomes were devotional, unbearably ponderous texts of the sort read during mealtimes at monasteries.

But at last he admitted the truth, that he was looking for a particular volume wedged among them, a slender folder bound in cracked ancient leather. With a grunt, he stretched and pulled it down. His fingers came away thick with dust. Inside was a tantalizing fragment of an old *Register* of the Inquisition, which dealt with the trial of Courdeval's knights at Nîmes. It had come to Saint-Bertrand through the agency of a seventeenth-century canon named Somaize, who had apparently discovered it in a chapter house somewhere and purloined it as more properly belonging to the parish where the events had actually taken place; he had eventually become interested enough in the whole affair to add his own account of the legends he had been able to collect—including the pre-dations on the villagers after Courdeval's death.

As Boudrie paged through the handwritten Latin text, he remembered his almost physical sickness at the fanatic idiocy of the Dominican Inquisitors, their gloating concern for the spiritual welfare of their agonized victims. Although some part of him had been aware that such things had taken place, to be faced with the firsthand accounts had brought them home with terrifying force. Nothing else in his life had so tested his allegiance to his faith.

The pattern of the trials quickly became repetitious, almost to the point of dulling their horror. For each prisoner, interrogation followed by torture, even if he confessed outright; a day or two of rest; the process repeated often through one or more recantings. For those who stood by their confessions, sentence might be as light as wearing the yellow cross of the heretic. For those who recanted and remained firm, the stake was certain. For those few strong enough to maintain their innocence, death on the strappado or some other device was common. Failing that, they could expect to say good-bye to the sun, and lie broken on the cold, wet floor of some gloomy *cachot* until sickness or old age took them.

What must have gone through the minds of those lost souls, Boudrie thought, as they lay chained to stone walls in cellars where the time was eternal night, where background music was the clank of iron and the shrieks of the tormented, where every effect was calculated to raise terror to its extreme pitch—where, as in Dante's hell, hope could not exist? They must have known that nothing, even innocence, could protect them from the hooded monks, with their flickering torches and solicitous questions. Even suicide was forbidden, by the Church's decree that it was the one certain path to hell. What better way to control men's actions on earth than to convince them that if they did not obey, they would burn forever in a lake of fire?

He shook his head angrily and paged on. The section he wanted was at the end; it contained part of the preliminary accusations in the trials of the Montsévrain Templars. The rest of the account had been removed—deliberately, Boudrie was sure, but by whom, or when, he would never know.

The recorder, a monk who signed himself only as Johannes, began with the usual accusations of crimes against God. But the allegations became more specific—and intriguing.

"*Item,* that this Courdeval had entered into a knowing pact with the Enemy of Mankind, to be his servant and do his bidding, and was granted in return the power to command the spirits that ride the air;

"*Item,* that this Courdeval possessed a book said to be the agent of his evil powers, and that in this book he kept a record of his abominations against mankind;

"*Item,* that he consumed the blood of humans, to propitiate the powers he worshipped and to strengthen him and prolong his life;

"*Item,* that he subscribed to the pagan belief of Hermes Trismegistus that the spirit of the mage need not die, but could move from shape to shape at will; and that furthermore, if the accident of death should overtake his body, his spirit could gain another by means of a secret ritual. Such was the wickedness of this man, he was heard to declare that by causing some mortal to slay that which he loved most, the mage could then have that mortal in his power forever."

Which would have been yet another reason to account for Courdeval's carelessness, Boudrie thought.

Why should one worry overmuch about death if he believed he could change bodies like suits of clothes—and further, that his spirit could do so even after the death of the body it then occupied? It was a most sinister notion, one Boudrie had never encountered before: like demonic possession, but by a human spirit, a ghost; disturbing both in itself and through the implication that, in some unexplained fashion, it required a living human to slay a loved one.

But unfortunately for you, my evil friend, Boudrie thought, something went wrong. He smiled grimly. At McTell's, he had glossed over the account of the interment of Courdeval's bones. But according to the information Canon Somaize had gathered, the procedure had been highly unorthodox—perhaps a reason for its subsequent suppression by Church authorities.

The party of soldiers and clerics sent from Avignon had first consulted a noted Cabalist there—no doubt offering to pull his teeth if he did not cooperate, Boudrie thought. This Rabbi Eleazar had pointed out to them something they had certainly not wanted to hear, but could not deny: that the supposedly unbreachable sanctuary of the cathedral had not prevailed. They were dealing with a force much older than Christianity, he said, and they must resort to an accordingly more ancient belief: that a spirit could be rendered powerless by water. The best thing would be to take the bones to the sea, weight them down, and throw them in; but such a journey could not possibly be accomplished without dusk overtaking them in the skeleton's vicinity—and that of the companion it was purportedly able to summon. The next best thing would be to find a stream or spring, immerse the bones, and dam the water so it would forever surround them.

The party planned their journey carefully to arrive at Montsévrain at dawn. The spring they chose was the source of the fortress's water, somewhere on the mountainside below. Working frantically, they had dug back in to discover a natural vault. And it spoke volumes that the labor was done by noble knights, who under ordinary circumstances would have died before touching a shovel or pick. The bones were chained with silver to the floor of the vault, the water was blessed in perpetuity and sealed in with a great stone, and the party returned hastily to the village to pass a sleepless night, praying unceasingly that their remedy had been effective.

And so, seemingly, it had. A little more leisurely, the men devoted the next days to carving a warning into the stone in case it should ever be discovered, and then concealing it to prevent that from happening. The warning was in the form of a curious misquote from the Vulgate: *He maketh me to lie down in running waters;* and a more pointed: *Quiescentem ne moveto*—Disturb not that which rests.

Well, they had apparently done a good job of the concealment, Boudrie thought. No sign had ever been reported of either tomb or spring, although it was not as if anyone had ever gone looking. That part of the story was known to few except the village *curés*. In all likelihood, the entire business of spring and tomb had been fabricated long after the fact, to bolster the supernatural element of the story.

He paged on through the manuscript, gleaning bits of the Latin, remembering passages from more careful readings he had given it. Near the end, a loose sheaf came away in his hands. He looked at it blankly before recalling what it was. Decades before, on a visit to his alma mater, the *Grand Séminaire* in Marseille, he had been rummaging through the library and had come across some old texts on exorcism and demonology. One of these had contained a section of a book of magic purportedly written by the biblical King Solomon. Boudrie's eyes scanned the page: a description he had taken from the *Key of Solomon's* commentaries on all the mightiest of the fallen angels, along with their attributes, emblems, and the sorts of services they were prepared to perform for men.

The demon Belial, it said, had been created "next, after Lucifer." He gave excellent familiars, and must have sacrifices made to him. Belial's emblem was reproduced beneath: a curious design of looping lines, something like a boat seen broadside, with antennae.

Excellent familiars. A muffled figure neither man nor beast, seen only doing the work of gruesome death. Preposterous, of course. But like the blood-drinking, the belief in the possibility of bargaining with supernatural powers was as ancient as time. Boudrie was forced to admit that, given such an element of credulity, the pieces all fit together–to form a most unpleasant picture.

Had the same thought occurred to his curious predecessor, Canon Somaize? He had ended his account with a cryptic quote: *Some spirits there be that are created for vengeance, and in their fury, lay on sore strokes.*

Boudrie tossed the manuscript on the desk and filled his glass once more. It was past midnight, and he was suddenly aware of his fatigue. As he stood, an odd line of thought flitted through his mind. If it were true–if a spirit could be held in check by running water, or by anything else, for that matter–then rules for some sort of bizarre cosmic contest were implied; which, in turn, implied that something more powerful had made those rules.

Canon Boudrie's modest contribution to theology, he thought, and smiled: a proof sinister of the existence of God.

But his amusement died as he walked wearily down the dim hallway to his bedroom. Such stories might be for old women, but men burned alive were another matter. He thought again of the stiletto hanging on his study wall, and began to undress, mumbling a prayer.

SIX

McTell switched off his typewriter and slumped back in his chair, wondering if the sentences he had just written were really as fiat, the ideas as pretentiously mundane, as they seemed. In spite of his successes, there were times when in his heart of hearts he was certain his books were destined to fall into that immense body of work gathering dust on the shelves of libraries throughout the world, perused only by students with metaphorical guns to their heads. He had wasted the morning, his best time, driving to Grasse to buy a case of gin for his hard-drinking brother-in-law, and his mood was not now improved by post-lunch drowsiness and midday heat.

But none of that was the problem, not really. He stood and walked to the window. The sky had changed overnight, with a first portent of autumn. Though the air was still hot and muggy, a haze had entered it. Thin restless clouds moved over the mountaintops, over the hidden Mediterranean, perhaps all the way to Africa and long-dead Carthage. The world felt swollen, ready to burst. His gaze lingered on the ruin. The haze had drawn the sparkle from its stones and darkened its outline.

The problem was that here he sat, planning a dull academic book about events he had never witnessed, for an audience that for the most part could not have cared less, while the only real mystery that had ever touched his life hovered in the forefront of his mind, unsolved. The dream of the gauntleted fist had pervaded his sleep so insistently that the last time, he had lain awake for seconds before he fully understood that it was not his own hand scraping through the soil.

His restless gaze moved to the decanter of Scotch. He hesitated, but then poured two fingers into a glass. He had always disliked beginning projects in the afternoon, anyway. Drink in hand, he walked again to the window. Last night, another hike to the ruin had seemed sensible, almost obligatory. But in the clear light of day, the absurdity of the whole business had reasserted itself.

Footsteps moved briskly past the study door—Linden, preparing for the guests, carrying sheets and towels from here to there, planning meals, organizing excursions. He marveled at her contentment, at how her life seemed like a lake whose surface was often rippled but whose depths remained forever calm.

And suddenly he saw his own future spread out before him like an endless not-unpleasant suburb, with long sunny streets named Routine and Productivity and Modest Success, sloping gently down the Parkway of Retirement in Comfort to the darker cul-de-sac of Oblivion. And he would pass from this earth without so much as a taste of the passions that had moved the giants of his imagination: Coeur de Lion, Simon de Montfort, the Black Prince—yes, even the villainous one-eyed Guilhem de Courdeval; men of iron will and tremendous capacities, who had never retreated from life, never waited for circumstances to come to them, but who had acted to change the course of history—who, to satisfy their vanities, had not hesitated to burn cities, massacre thousands, savage entire continents—

Or to strike a bargain with the devil himself.

McTell raised his eyes to the ruin and admitted it. He wanted it to be true. He wanted a wrench thrown into the well-oiled machine of his life. He wanted there to be a connection between what had happened to him on that mountain and the young woman he had seen in town.

He wanted there to be magic in that empty hole in the ground.

It was midafternoon. He looked at the drink in his hand, knowing he should exchange it for coffee, sit down again, and wrestle with his typewriter for another two hours.

He drank off the liquor in a swallow. Feeling resigned and a little foolish, he went to find his rucksack.

The fortress's empty courtyard was restless and gray, wind tossing the nettles and skittering dry leaves across the paving stones. The sky was a streaked and moving tapestry of clouds. McTell approached the iron grate of the dungeon slowly and stopped a few feet back from its rim. He felt strangely, even frighteningly, alone. Not sure whether he was more nervous about something happening, or nothing, he inhaled and stepped forward.

101

His lips twisted wryly. The dungeon was just as he had last seen it—rocks and debris. This time he took a good look. The narrow crumbling steps led down to blank walls; whatever chambers might once have held prisoners were long since filled in. It was a flight of stairs to nowhere.

He raised his eyes to the gray nothing of the sky. There was no motion but the shifting clouds, no sound but the wind. And with a sudden bitter rage of disappointment, of frustration, of feeling that he had somehow been led on and then cheated, he turned away.

And took three steps before he stopped, stunned. He spun and strode back, gripped the iron grate, leaned close.

The riser of the bottom step was crusted with hard red soil, and as he stared, his mind supplied the image of the mailed fist scraping patiently at precisely that configuration of rock and earth. A little dizzy, he straightened up, clamped down on his excitement, and began to plan.

The grate was rectangular, perhaps two and a half feet wide by five long, mortared at several places into the stone—but not so securely that a little work with hammer and bar would not break it free. He had seen the tools he would need in the gardener's shed. What remained was a pretext to return. He thought, and then carefully hid his camera in a crevice of the great stone walls.

The heat of the day had fallen off, and he hurried back down the mountain, lost in anticipation. But when he at last looked up, his surroundings struck him with such force that he stopped. Nothing had changed—and yet, the air that filled his lungs was soft and heavy with the fragrance of pines, carried on the gentle breeze. Colors were muted in the waning light. The hillsides swelled, rounded and nude, while trees lifted slender red-tipped branches like fingers in supplication to the sky.

The mountain slopes drew together in dark secret crevasses, converging to the ancient sea.

McTell paused on the patio steps. Inside, the lights were on; the house looked alive with pre-dinner activity. Through the glass door he saw Linden setting the table. He glanced back at the path leading from the grounds, where he had already hidden the required tools–skulking in and out of the shed, feeling like a schoolboy. Why the secrecy? he thought. Why not just tell her?

He slid open the door and stepped inside. Brilliant crystalline piano music, a Mozart concerto, blended with the sounds of Mlle. Perrin in the kitchen. Linden was wearing a powder blue summer dress. Gold flashed at her ears and neck.

"You look absolutely ravishing, my dear," he said.

But when she turned, be understood that there was trouble. Her gaze was cool, moving deliberately over his hiking clothes and rucksack.

"You could at least have told me where you were going," she said. She turned away again, making needless adjustments to silverware and glasses.

McTell kept his voice carefully light. "I wasn't aware that I was supposed to punch in and out every time I left the house."

"I've been breaking my back all day trying to get ready for Mona and Skip. If I'd known you were going to be playing mountain man instead of working, I'd have asked you to help."

McTell's own anger flared, but he bit off saying the words—They're *your* goddamned guests—and waited until he had calmed down.

"For heaven's sake, Lin, I wasn't gone much over an hour. I was feeling restless and walked up to the ruin. I'd have been happy to help you, but I thought you had everything under control."

"What is it with this ruin, anyway?"

"What do you mean?"

She shrugged. "I just don't understand the attraction. Is there that much to see?"

"There's a wonderful view," he said. "It helps me think. That's what I get paid for, remember?"

"Huh."

For a moment neither spoke. Then he said, "Well, I'm ready for a drink. Want one?"

"My glass is on the counter."

As he crossed the room, he unslung his rucksack. He paused, hefting it.

"Oh, for Christ's sake," he said. "Don't tell me—"

"Now what?"

He unzipped the pack and ran his hand around the inside.

"I can't believe it."

"Whatever are you talking about?"

"My camera. I took some shots and laid it on a rock, and then walked away without it. All the way down the mountain without noticing a thing." He shook his head in exasperation

"Well, it'll be all right, won't it? No one's likely to go up there tonight."

He walked to the door and looked outside critically. "I'm a little worried about rain. I left it sitting right in the open."

"I don't think it's going to rain, John."

"You're probably right. Still, I may run up there after dinner. Bet I can make it back in forty minutes."

"In the dark?"

"There'll be plenty of twilight."

She glanced at him sidelong, but said nothing more. McTell poured himself a Scotch and freshened her martini. As he handed it to her, their gazes met. Hers was still cool and distant, and he suddenly understood that the real source of her anger had nothing to do with work, either his or hers: It was, simply hurt at being left alone– jealousy, almost as if she had sensed that in a strange ethereal way, another woman had come into his life.

He set his glass down, circled her waist with his hands, and pulled her, resisting a little, to him.

"Sorry," he said. "You're absolutely right, that was very inconsiderate of me. Whatever chores are left to do, I'm all yours."

"It's all done," she said, and at last, to his relief, smiled. "But next time, give a yell before you disappear, okay? I looked all over the house for you."

"Done," he said. He kissed her and went back to his drink.

"Can I come with you?" she said.

He stopped, the glass halfway to his lips. Excuses flashed through his mind.

"I don't think you'd be able to see enough to make it worthwhile," he said slowly.

"Oh, I don't mean tonight. Next week, after Mona and Skip leave."

He smiled, letting out his breath. "Of course. You can't say I don't know how to show a girl a good time."

"I'll pack a *pique-nique* lunch. And on the way up, I'll tell you about a fantasy I've always had. It involves performing oral sex in a scenic setting."

"Most intriguing," McTell said. "But I have to warn you, the battlements are in full view of the entire city of Cannes."

"Hah. As if it would shock them."

"What about the ghost of old One-eye?" he said lightly.

"He hasn't shown his face in six hundred years."

"For a scene like that, he might come up."

"Besides, he liked boys."

"Precisely my point. Although I'm not exactly a downy-cheeked youth."

"Closer than me, lover," she said. Her fingers quickly caressed his groin. "I'd better see how Mademoiselle's doing."

McTell carried his drink to the glass doors and leaned against the jamb, gazing out into the deepening evening.

For the first time, he had lied to his wife.

Perhaps an hour of daylight remained before the quick, almost tropical fade into night. The moon was on the wax, behind the clouds like a streetlamp in fog. McTell strode into the fortress.

He retrieved the camera first thing and stuffed it into the rucksack–it would not do to come home without that–then arranged the tools beside the dungeon's stone rim. He wrapped a handkerchief over the head of the cold chisel to avoid a clinking sound that might carry. Then he began to work, hammering swiftly, gouging at the mortar that held the crossbars. It was old and crumbled easily. In a few minutes he could shake the grate with his hands. He inserted a prybar under one end, braced himself, and heaved. With a cracking sound, the edge broke free. Exultant, he dropped the bar and threw the grate clear.

The sky darkened perceptibly as he descended; when he reached the bottom, it seemed almost night above. He crouched, flashlight playing on the step. His breathing was harsh and loud in the tight space. Carefully, he began to scrape, making the same motion as the hand in his dream.

Beneath the soil was solid rock.

He tapped it with the bar, then again harder, and then drove the point against it with all his force. Chips of stone sprayed his hands. He threw down the bar and stood, panting. He was a fool, a child, a madman, allowing himself to manufacture an elaborate fantasy–to *believe* in it–and finally coming face to face with the inevitable result: dust in his mouth. He raised his eyes. The rectangle of light above had grown so dim he could hardly distinguish it, and his anger was suddenly lost in a surge of claustrophobic panic. What if he saw hands replacing the grate?

He fought the urge to claw his way up the steps, and took several slow breaths, forcing himself back to calm. Then he crouched again and carefully examined the joint of the bottom riser with the tread above. It was packed with dirt. He inserted the cold chisel and gave it a tap.

It went in a quarter of an inch.

He tapped again. Another quarter.

Quickly, he inserted the bar's flat edge beside the chisel. Wiggling first one and then the other, he worked both in a full inch.

And felt the stone block beneath them move.

With excitement amounting almost to nausea in the pit of his stomach, he levered the block until it fell, with a soft thud, between his knees. Thoughts whirled in his mind: a nest of snakes, about to boil out over his hands, or the carcass of some long-dead animal, writhing with maggots and corruption.

He realized he was whispering, "It's nothing, there's nothing in there—" With the point of the bar, he probed the small cavity.

It touched something, with a dull metallic clink.

The flashlight beam shook with his hands. The object was flat and square, the size of a cigar box, wrapped in some coarse fabric rotted nearly to dust. Through it he could make out a greenish hue: oxidized copper, he realized, the metal the bar had touched. Gently, he lifted out the object. His fingers told him it was a small cask, with hinges and a clasp.

He fought the urge to tear away the cloth and break it open. Quickly, he swept the flashlight beam through the cavity. There was nothing else. He set down the light and gripped the stone block to push it back into place. For the first time, the beam caught the inner surface.

On it was carved an unmistakable rendering of the creature depicted in the church--*celui*. It was facing out, as if emerging from the stone.

Scalp prickling. McTell glanced hurriedly over his shoulder. The daylight above was gone. He shoved the block back into place and tamped dirt against it, then stood and scraped his feet to obliterate my tracks he might have left. Carefully, he tucked the copper cask inside his shirt. It was heavy, a cold dead weight.

When he reached the top of the stairs he was panting. With huge relief, he stepped into the open air. The sky was a little lighter than it had seemed from below. He moved quickly, replacing the grate, smoothing the crumbled mortar, collecting the tools. A final pass with the flashlight assured him that a casual visitor would notice nothing.

He had scooped up the rucksack and tools and was turning to leave when his gaze caught the big stone slab that had puzzled him on his first visit. Abruptly and certainly, its purpose struck him. It was the pediment of an altar. But it was nowhere near any foundation that might have been a chapel. It was facing the dungeon.

McTell moved swiftly through the ravine, the cold solid weight of the package against his chest, his senses electric with the surrounding gloom. It was only the moonlight through the branches, he told himself, casting the shadows that seemed to move of themselves; only the wind making the sound like voices, sighing and whispering in the treetops. He burst through the brush at the far edge and stood, slowing his breath.

The great walls loomed like the tombstones of fallen angels. Far below, he sensed the vast black void of the sea. He turned again and hurried on, imagining that he could almost understand the voice of the wind, speaking a language that was ancient when men first walked the earth, yet achingly familiar, whispering to something undiscovered in his depths—wooing, coaxing, promising.

Powerless to move, with vague, numb dread rising within, Mélusine Devarre watched the silent scene unfold. She could feel rather than hear the booming dirge of the cathedral bell from the village below, the clank of armor, the clopping of hooves. The air was gray and heavy with twilight; the stake driven into the ground before the fortress gates cast no shadow. Half a dozen men mounted on palfreys conferred in a tense cluster, whispering to each other in silent pantomime. Behind, them, a crowd of perhaps a hundred, peasants by their dress, waited in an expectancy of anger and fear. Black-robed monks hurried around the stake, arranging bundles of wood like mothers tucking in children.

From the fortress a procession began. Two lines of mounted knights in armor, flanked by foot soldiers in leather hauberks and mail, escorted a single man in their midst. He was a head taller than the others, his shoulders an axe-handle wide; his tunic revealed the massive corded forearms of a swordsman. His wrists were tightly bound. A single eye stared out from a face that was arrogant, grim, above all defiant. It was wide across the cheekbones, seamed and scarred, with the nose thick as a small fist, the mouth a taut line utterly without pity. Where the left eye should have been was an empty socket, uncovered by a patch.

Soldiers chained him quickly to the stake, and a man wearing the dark robe of an Inquisitor reined his horse forward. He shook a parchment from his sleeve and made a show of unfurling it. His hood fell back to reveal a white tonsure and a thin ascetic face with eyes the color of fog. With the parchment raised, he began to speak.

But under the bound man's gaze, the old monk faltered and stopped. It took him a visible effort to keep his attention on the parchment. But again, his eyes rose to meet those of the accused. The answering stare was mute, implacable, cold with contemptuous rage. The monk swallowed, tried to speak, failed; the parchment slipped from his fingers and fluttered to the ground. He sagged, nearly falling from his mount. Other horses began to stamp and rear; the crowd moved in agitation, a single body with a thousand limbs. No one seemed willing to approach the condemned. Confusion reached the edge of panic. The crowd seemed about to stampede.

Then from its depths a thickset monk lunged forward with a blazing torch. Three long strides took him to the stake. With a sweep of his arm, he hurled the torch into the woodpile and leaped back. The branches flared, then burst into a thunderous blaze, blurring the profile of the unmoving victim behind a sheet of wild red flame.

As if a dam had burst, the crowd surged forward, shaking fists and throwing rocks at the burning man. A woman dropped to her knees, face contorted, mouth stretched in a soundless shriek of fury.

The monk who had thrown the torch was still running, but his motion became slower and slower, as if he were fighting a torrent of invisible viscous liquid. As he forced his way through the mob, his cowl fell back, revealing his terrified face.

Recognition snapped Mélusine free.

Étien Boudrie awoke with a violent start, staring around him. Gradually he realized he had fallen asleep in his chair. With a groan, he sank back. His head throbbed and thirst raged in his throat. He closed his eyes and squeezed the bridge of his nose between thumb and forefinger.

For the first time in years, a dream of fire.

He struggled to his feet, angry with himself. The cloudy afternoon had made a drink seem fitting, even advisable. With no obligations for the evening, it had been too easy to take a second and third. Now the brandy decanter, full when he had started, was nearly half empty. His stomach burned, his throat demanded water. Thank God, no images remained from the dream—only a bursting, unbearably intense sheet of flame. In the kitchen he rinsed his face and filled a pitcher. When he got back to the study, he felt a little better.

The electric light seemed harsh. He lit candles instead and settled back. When he looked out the window, the restless clouds showed a gibbous moon. The clock said a little after nine. But sleep was hours away now; it made no difference whether he drank coffee or liquor, lay in bed or sat up in a bright room. He would remain wide-eyed and unfocussed until just before dawn. Then, when he must begin preparations for Mass, weariness would sweep over him like a wave from the sea.

The sleeplessness had not begun until after he had become *curé,* as if it were a part of his new burden of responsibility–as if his postwar days in the seminary had been a time of innocence, a gift he had not known enough to appreciate. At first he had prayed that his nights might remain uninterrupted. But finally he admitted that it was not the insomnia itself which was terrible, but the flood of memories it would not let him escape; and from those, he did not dare pray to be delivered.

The *maquisards* had called him Tien–an orphan boy, fearless, cunning, strong enough to have lifted the front end of a jeep off the ground on a bet, and once, to have carried a badly wounded comrade on his back eleven kilometers, over rough terrain, at night. But his courage had been illusory. He had been too young, too brittle. The day-to-day, night-to-night fear had finally broken him, and it had broken him the wrong way.

Over the protests of his insides, he reached for the decanter. At least, thank God, those dreams of fire had dwindled some years ago, as mysteriously as they had started, as if it had been a matter of processing a concrete amount of guilt. Until tonight.

The night breeze through the open window made the candles flicker. Boudrie stared at the moon–hanging over the earth like the eye of a pagan god, demanding obedience out of darkness. He rose and leaned against the sill, put his cheek against the cool glass. Clouds sailed past, turned the moon to a pale frosted orb, moved on to let it shine again. Diana, mistress of women, he thought.

There remained the other great sin of his life. But dwelling on that was not a way of expiation–it was a guilty, bittersweet pleasure, one he allowed himself only in his hardest hours.

Perhaps, after all, this was such a night.

Mélusine's eyes were open, her heart pounding like a fist hammering at a door. Her hands clenched the chair arms. The book she had been reading lay at her feet. She had pushed back so hard her heels had left marks on the rug. Pulling herself up, she limped quickly to the kitchen, threw on the lights, stood with her back to the sink, sucking in lungfuls of air. The first dizzy grasp of what had happened was coming to her. She was once again herself, safe in her own home, in the twentieth century. But for a few awful minutes, she had been somewhere else–a very long time ago. It was not as if she had drifted into a doze. One moment she had been reading. The next, she had been *there*.

Not only that, but someone else had been there with her: the priest, Étien Boudrie, whose terrified face had been revealed, when his cowl fell back, as that of the monk who had thrown the torch.

"Roger?" she called hoarsely, then remembered that he had gone to his office to get some sort of book. The air around her was still thick, almost vibrant with a sense of menace. Fighting panic, she made herself breathe deeply, then paced, willing the unseen presence to recede.

In a moment she was able to turn on the tap, run water over her wrists, fill a kettle and put it on the stove, more for something to do than because she wanted coffee. What she wanted was brandy, but not badly enough to go back into the parlor. She waited, listening to the comforting sound of the water heating, setting out the coffee things in measured movements, forcing the dark energy to dissipate—remembering the dry, soft voice, almost a whisper, of Tante Mathilde.

Do not be deceived, little bunny. The devil never sleeps, but walks the earth in ten thousand guises, searching for souls. The priests will tell you one thing, the professors another; but this has been true since the beginning of time, and will be true until the end. I know little of books, or of what people think is important these days. But I know that this battle for our souls goes on at every instant, unseen and unfelt through it may be. No passing of time can ever change it.

When the coffee was made, she poured a cup, steeled herself, and walked quickly back into the parlor. She stopped in the room's center and stood, testing. It was going to be all right, Her shoulders sagged with relief.

All right until next time.

It would be nice to have the company of a fire, she thought, but the nights were still too warm. Music, then. She put on a record of Chopin Études, bright, sparkling pieces free of the deep bass and minor chords that seemed to summon darkness. She poured a glass of brandy and took that and coffee back to her chair.

It had been going on for a week now. Little things, mainly, beginning with the knife seeming to twist in her hand. A pan moving by itself in the kitchen, ever so slightly, but enough to make her whirl and spill scalding soup. Waking in the night to the sound of a baby's soft weeping. Worst, the increasing sense of presence, sometimes pleading and cajoling, sometimes threatening, always unpleasant. Now this dream—except that a dream, it had not been.

All the air is full of good and evil spirits. They surround us endlessly. The weak ones run in terror from the others. If a man died in Paris, and it was raining, his spirit could run to Ploiesti and not three drops of rain would fall on him—that is how fast they run. The evil ones burn as punishment for the bad works they have done in life, and they crave to enter a human body, to stop the burning. Sometimes if a spirit is very, very strong, it can make the soul of a living person leave its body, and go into that body and own it. Sometimes that is what happens when people who are not bad, but weak, commit crimes. Because of your gift, spirits will be attracted to you. If you ever feel one threaten you, you must be very strong and keep it away.

How will I know if that happens, Tante Mathilde?
You will know, bunny. Believe me, you will know.

If only the old lady were alive now, Mélusine thought; if only there were someone to bolster her. Her husband was the kindest man on earth, intelligent and wise, but steeped in the automatic skepticism of the scientist. If she told him, he would sympathize, do his best to believe her, but then deal with the situation in the

116

only way he knew: watch her, surreptitiously and clinically and with agonizing concern, for signs of mental instability.

And Monsieur Boudrie? She hardly knew him—certainly not well enough to dream about, she thought, and almost smiled. She had not been a practicing Catholic since childhood, and never in her heart; she had learned a very different view of the world from the cradle.

The religion I believe, little bunny, goes back much further than the birth of Jesus Christ. It is the ancient and true faith, before men dressed up their different gods and used them to cause so much trouble. There are two gods, a good one and an evil one, who are equally powerful. They battle unendingly for our souls. Our lives are like the board of a game, and we move with each act we make: a step toward the good, a step toward the bad. Each step toward the good makes us stronger. Each step toward the bad puts us more in the power of the evil god and the spirits who are his soldiers. Fools spend their lives trying to gain money, or power, or luxury. They have no sense of what life is truly about. Our earthly time is only a tiny step in the journey of our spirits. The years that sometimes seem so long to us are only an eyeblink in eternity.

The old lady had died when Mélusine was six, just beginning to get a grasp of what lay within her. If Tante Mathilde had lived another ten years, Mélusine thought, even five, the education might have gone far enough for her to complete on her own. As it was, she had foreseen things: had known the moment of her great-aunt's death, even though she had been in another city at the time;

had known that she would marry Devarre when she first glimpsed him; had known that she would bear a child, and of which sex, the moment each was conceived. But she had never learned to control events in the way her aunt had hinted was possible.

When I was a child traveling with my mother and father in the caravan, many of the old people had power. The village girls would sneak to the camp at night for a spell to attract a lover, or to make a rival look ugly in his eyes. One night I saw a rich lady pay gold to be wrapped in the skin of a wolf and become the loup-garou. I watched her sleep, yelping, her hands and feet twitching; and when she awoke in the dawn, her hair was snarled, her skin scratched and bleeding, her eyes wild. The old people could bring a dead husband back to comfort his widow in her bed, as if he had never gone. I do not lie, bunny. You have this power too, and you must learn to use it, or it can be turned against you. But these are sad times, there is no one left to teach

The truly disturbing thing about this vision tonight was that it had none of the irrational leaps and bizarre connections of dreams. It had been a straightforward, cohesive drama, with the overwhelming sense of having actually happened, and she almost felt that she had been intended to see it. To what end? By what? What could the priest have to do with it?

The priest. Would there be any profit in talking to him? Clearly, he was a man of intelligence and ability: Rumor had it that he had been a hero in the war. And while it was common knowledge that he often smelled of brandy, there was no doubt of his humility and kindness.

Thank God for that weakness, she thought. She had no use for a pious, dried-up ascetic.

She sipped the coffee and sharp armagnac. The piano music was soothing. But suppose, she found herself thinking, it hid the shuffling approach of footsteps? Suppose a touch came at her shoulder. with a low laugh sounding in her ear? Or the door began to silently close itself, and as she whirled, an unseen hand switched off the light?

She shook her head and quickly stood, refusing the creeping, insinuating darkness that begged for her attention. Perhaps Roger would not be so far wrong. Perhaps she was on the edge of some sort of breakdown.

Well, she would wait a few more days, and if her unrest continued, she would think about a visit to the *curé*—a cautious call, perhaps in the confessional, to sound out his sympathies. After all, it seemed they were somehow in this together—whatever it was. Although she did not think she would tell him of his role in her dream.

Meantime, there was nothing to do but wait, and hope that when she heard steps on the walk outside, they were those of her husband.

Her name had been Céleste Giroudoux. Widowed by the war at the age of twenty-three, she was lovely and delicate, but never free of a darkness far back in her eyes. That darkness Boudrie had seen, and done his best as a priest to lighten; but he had sternly kept himself from seeing her as a woman.

And then one dusky afternoon in the confessional, when his heart was full and weary with the weight of the village's petty sins, came her sudden, passionate declaration from the other side of the screen:

"I think of nothing but taking my own life."

There could be no absolution without contrition, but her murmured apology lacked conviction. Still, Boudrie had pronounced the words Christ had used to the harlot He had saved from stoning.

From there had evolved the gradual awareness, the almost unnoticeable transition from a purely spiritual relationship to something more: the overpowering need to satisfy the hunger of two young, strong, lonely people—the hunger of one for what she had lost, of the other for what he had vowed never to know.

When had he first realized it would happen? It was impossible to say. Such an awareness was a fragile, delicate thing, seeking to bloom like a tiny flower under a vast blanket of thou-shalt-nots. He must have known, somewhere in his depths, long before the moment they first touched. Christ, the sweetness! Though he had rushed home and thrown himself into agonized penance, had himself shriven, sworn never to be alone with her again, some part of him knew all along that he would not give up what he had found.

Perhaps if he had moved to leave the priesthood at that very moment, Boudrie thought, instead of enduring three years of deceit and nearly two decades of despair, many lives would have been changed for the better—and one, at least, saved. But that he could not bring himself to do. His need to seek salvation, to atone, was too strong.

And so he hedged, unfaithful to both his lover and his God, and they went on, miraculously maintaining secrecy, caught in an unbearable position. At last he realized that even to pretend to stop seeing her was only piling sin upon sin; that the true basis of human life was not isolation in a musty church with the relics of an incomprehensible deity, but the mystery he shared with her.

Until the day she was gone.

Even after these nearly twenty years, his jaw still clenched at the memory of walking slowly, uncomprehendingly through the night, careless of who might see him, reading the letter again and again. It gave no indication of her whereabouts and few of her reasons. In time, he learned she had gone to stay with relatives in Normandy, and he warred with himself to keep from abandoning everything and following. It was not fear of what he would lose that finally held him back, but the determination to obey her wishes, whatever the cost to himself.

Five years passed before the real reason for her disappearance arrived in Saint-Bertrand: a bewildered, frightened little girl named Alysse; and with her, the news that her mother had drowned in the swift high tide at Saint-Malo.

It could have been an accident, but Boudrie knew the truth.

The child was said to be the offspring of a hasty marriage, but in his heart he knew the truth of that, too. The question was only whether there had been another man—hard though the possibility was for him to accept, it existed; she was, after all, a beauty—and the need to be sure nearly drove him mad. But the only person who could have told him was dead.

And while, at first, not even the fear that he would burn in hell forever was enough to keep him from joining her in death, something else was: his responsibility as a man, a priest—and perhaps as a father. That was when he began to replace Céleste with another woman, who lived in a keg or bottle, whom even Mother Church winked at, who was always there when be needed her.

From then on, added to the agony of his guilt was the sweet torment of the child, the loveliest creature he had ever seen. He himself had been an orphan; there were few things worse. And though he was helpless to claim her as his own, he had done everything in his power to see to her upbringing. It was impossible, he told himself often—she was far too exquisite to have sprung from his rough loins. But every time he saw her, fierce hope and pride flared in his heart, along with the dread that she might be the living proof of his sin.

He sat heavily in his chair and drank off the brandy in his glass. The hands of the clock said ten-forty. Long hours yet remained before dawn. His conscience tossed and heaved like the clouds around the moon. Was it not yet another great sin to remain in the priesthood with one's vocation so tarnished?

Yet his weakness in love, like his drinking and occasional rages, he could almost forgive himself. He knew, as he knew few other truths, that her passion had been as great as his. And even if the child were the incarnation of his transgression, how could he feel remorse for taking part in the creation of such loveliness?

But there were sins and sins, and with a groan he at last gave in to the memory of the night that had finished him as a soldier and begun him as a priest: when, at a village named Vézey-le-Croux, he had cut the throat of a sentry, barred the door of a wooden horse-barn, splashed gasoline on the walls, and set it afire–along with the nineteen German soldiers billeted inside. The *maquisards* had numbered only four, and were poorly armed; they could not possibly have otherwise taken the Nazi post, would almost certainly have been captured next day and tortured into betraying other comrades.

But never would he lose the stench of burning flesh in his nostrils, the shrieks of flaming bodies bursting through the collapsing walls. Nor would he forget the thirty-eight citizens of Vézey-le-Croux, two for one, shot the following week in reprisal.

Lives lost in the course of war were one thing, but fifty-seven souls were waiting for him as a direct result of the work of his hands, and whether it was heaven, hell, or something he had never imagined that lay on the other side of death, Étien Boudrie was certain of one thing: that he would be called upon to render an accounting. Sweating, he filled his glass.

And then slowly, reluctantly, he emptied it back into the decanter. There were times when drinking would not suffice.

He stepped coatless from the house into the windy night. Heavily, numb with anticipation of the remaining hours of darkness, he walked to the church. He entered through the apse, lit a candle, passed through the sacristy to the nave. There he stopped, gazing with an awe that

123

had never left him at the soaring vault above, the slender fluted columns, the precisely arched windows aglow with the faint moonlight–the physical evidence of man's struggle since the beginning of time to come to terms with his God.

"*Introibo ad altare Dei,*" he murmured, and felt peace coming into his heart. Through thirty years of days heavy with the weight of human folly, of nights too endless and black to support, he had come at last to understand that there was a single immense compensation: the terrific power, the wild, exultant freedom, of absolute loneliness.

It was the heart of the Passion of Christ.

He knelt, the rustling of his cassock echoing through the empty vault as if others, unseen and intangible, knelt with him. Hands clasped, he leaned his elbows on the communion rail and bowed his head.

"Forgive me," he whispered into the darkness. "I have been a man. I have loved a woman, and I have murdered my enemies."

The glow of the television screen flickered in the living room as McTell climbed the patio steps. Night had long since fallen. Through the glass he could see Linden, curled on the couch, dividing her attention between the TV and a book. He unslung the rucksack and held it carelessly against the bulky lump inside his shirt.

She looked up at the sound of the door.

"Forty minutes, huh?"

"Christ," he said disgustedly. "It started to get dark and I decided to try a shortcut. Needless to say, I ended up lost as a lamb."

"Far be it from me to say I told you so." She seemed amused rather than annoyed.

"Next time, I'll bow to your judgment. Let me grab a quick shower, then let's have nightcap. I need one."

Upstairs, he closed the study door silently and hurried to his desk. Carefully, he placed the copper cask on it. The crumbling cloth wrapping had disintegrated further during the hike; he could feel the spot where it had rubbed off against his sweating skin. With unsteady hands, he stripped away what was left. The clasp was oxidized nearly to dust, and suddenly his scholar's instincts warned him to stop, to take it to the proper authorities before he risked destroying something priceless. His hands hovered, his mind raced, torn with indecision.

But he gripped it angrily. The hell with authorities—it was he who had found the cask, who had risked and triumphed. If nothing else, that entitled him to the first look at whatever was inside. His penknife easily broke the thread-thin metal.

The object inside was wrapped in a sort of waxy parchment, bound with a black cord that might have been silk. Like the other fabric, it was too badly decayed for him to be sure. It came apart, almost dissolving in his hands.

Inside, as he had suspected, was a book.

It was about the size of a standard Bible, and bound in dark fine-grained leather that had a slick, greasy feel. The symbol on the cover, unlike any design he had ever seen, was barely visible, with the rust-colored ink—if ink it was—faded almost to match the leather. He could only make out that it looked something like a ship, with loops like antennae around it.

Slowly, cautious of the brittle parchment, he opened the book.

The leaves were of vellum, yellowed with antiquity but in good condition, no doubt from lying dry and undisturbed for who knew how many years. At the top of the first page was a pentacle enclosed in a circle. Inside each of the design's compartments was a symbol or words. He turned the page and, with his heartbeat steady in his ears, leaned close to the several lines of print. The words were in Latin, the characters clearly rendered in a strong, firm hand; and though most of the ink was faded black, at the bottom, on a separate line, several words were scrawled in a rusty color like that on the cover.

It did not take him long to make them out as: *Guilhemus Cordevalis, Magister Templi.*

McTell walked straight to the Scotch decanter, poured a stiff shot, and downed it. Then he went back, and with his hands braced wide on the desk, leaned forward once again.

Qui servum sibi fidelem velit, qui velit inimicorum sanguinem haurire, quique manum velit evitare mortis, adeat urbem oportet____, quo Belial Dominem salutet.

The missing word had been painstakingly blotted out, and he could not recall the meaning of *haurire*. But in three or four minutes he closed his dictionary and stared down at the translation he had scratched on a pad:

If a man wishes a faithful servant, if he wishes to drink the blood of his enemies, if he would cheat the hand of death, it is necessary that he go to the city of_____, that he may there salute Lord Belial.

The line above the signature read: *Factum ut faciendum. Guilhemus Cordevalis, Magister Templi ann. mcclxxxix.*

Done as was to be done. Guilhem de Courdeval, Master of the Temple.

The year was 1289.

Though his longing to continue was almost unbearable, he forced himself to close the book. Linden was waiting. In any case, it was his now, to examine at his leisure.

As he stood before it, marveling at the impossible series of events that had led him to this impossible find, the images that rose and fell in his mind gave way to a single one: the face of the girl stepping out of a bath, at the instant their eyes had met. Again he experienced the overwhelming sweet shock of that moment. Almost in a trance, following some instinct he could not name, he let his left hand move forward, his palm coming to rest on the book and covering the strange looping symbol.

But he quickly pulled it back, swallowing, remembering the priest's words: *bound in the skin of a heretic flayred alive.*

He wrapped the book again in its parchment, hid it in the bottom drawer behind a clutch of papers, then took a two-minute shower and changed into fresh slacks and shirt. As he passed the ball mirror, he paused. His face seemed firmer, somehow–the look in his eyes calmer, more resolved. There was a strength in the set of his mouth he had never before noticed.

Whistling quietly, he walked on downstairs to spend a little time with his wife.

SEVEN

Ramona Sumner Talmadge, prone on a lounge chair beside the swimming pool, rose up on an elbow to take the vodka and tonic McTell offered. She was wearing only the briefest of swimsuit bottoms, a tight thin vee of a startling pink; as she reached, her breasts swayed and then flattened. They were tipped with nipples so nearly the same color as the suit that McTell could not help wondering if she tinted them.

She was younger than Linden, about thirty; small but not petite, supple, with a body that would have been chunky had it not been so firmly muscled. Her skin was tawny and flawless, her hair blonde and tousled. Her green eyes met McTell's over the top of her sunglasses and crinkled at the corners when she smiled thanks. An almost visible aura of gold surrounded her, and he had thought many times that she seemed to have been purposely created for things of the flesh, and never meant to be concerned with those of the mind and spirit.

A few feet away, Linden watched, silent. Though dark glasses hid her eyes, her mouth was a line. She was wearing both pieces of a rather more modest swimsuit.

Mona caught McTell's left hand and examined it.

"What in the world have you been doing?"

"Oh, I must have scratched it when I was thrashing around in the brush last night," he said.

"It looks more like a burn."

He glanced at the palm she still held, and his offhanded smile froze on his lips. The mark *did* look like a burn rather than a scrape–a faint red discoloration of an indeterminate shape. He freed his hand from her lingering grasp and pressed it gingerly with his other. There was no pain.

He was still staring at it when another voice said:

"You Americans are such an intrepid lot. I should have hired a boy to fetch that camera." The guest who had accompanied the Talmadges was a tall cadaverous Englishman of late middle age, with a large bony face that seemed incapable of smiling, and dyed pomaded hair parted in the middle, in the style of the 1920s. Mona had introduced him as Robert, Lord Ashton, but called him Bertie–a name McTell found himself unable to say. Bertie was apparently employed by Skip in some vague capacity of manager or secretary. Though the midafternoon sun was fierce, he wore a navy blazer, white flannel slacks, and an ascot. But if he was in fact a lord, his house had seen better days; McTell himself had carried his shabby luggage inside. And he had already gathered that Bertie's interest in boys might not be limited to running errands.

130

The party was completed by Mona's husband, Arthur Murchison Talmadge IV–Skip to his friends. He was a reddish blond, leonine, handsome man, with a carefully trimmed mustache and the generally amused manner of the wealthy sportsman–although McTell had seen it turn ugly under the influence of drink. Skip was in his mid-thirties, and seemed to have spent most of his life involved in competitive yachting; there were frequent references to his career, past and future, though nothing was said about the present. It was not a field McTell knew, or cared, much about. Coming from a solid blue-collar background, he could not suppress a touch of contempt mixed with resentment for pastimes he associated with the idle rich. Skip made clear in turn his boredom with any topic not directly related to sailing, horses, or women. The two men were politely cool to each other.

As usual when entertaining guests he was less than delighted to see, McTell busied himself playing host, serving drinks and hors d'oeuvres. He drifted among the group, listening with half an ear to the sisters catching each other up on the past months, and to Skip's occasional remark about some sporting event.

But it all seemed unreal, even ludicrous, compared to the previous night. The copper cask waited in his study, hidden in the bottom drawer of his desk; a glance this morning had assured him it had not all been a dream. And annoyance though the guests might be, his triumph was too fierce and sweet to be undercut. He felt a smugness, almost a pity for them, as they chattered on about the trivial doings of their mundane lives.

131

"I understand you're a medievalist, John." It was Bertie's clipped voice. "I went down in history myself, you know, at Cambridge."

"You don't say," McTell murmured.

"You've come here to write another masterpiece?"

McTell might have imagined the faintly mocking edge to the voice, but in any case, he had no intention of discussing his work with this group.

"I'd hesitate to call it that. What was your area of interest?"

"Oh, modern British, that sort of thing. I wasn't much of a scholar."

The sisters' conversation had drifted off; they were listening. Then Linden said:

"The village priest told us quite a story the other night. It seems we had a real-life magician living in the ruin up there a few centuries ago. A Templar."

Bertie's eyebrows rose politely. "Don't know much about them, I'm afraid. Although in my university days I did run into a few modern dabblers in the black arts."

"Really," McTell said, suddenly interested.

"Oh, yes. Fashionable thing to do in certain circles, you know. Never amounted to much in my case. I did meet old Aleister Crowley once. Wreck of a man by then, ravaged by heroin and drink. Still, there was something about him. He'd seen some things, no doubt of it. They say he faced off with the devil himself one night."

"You're kidding," Mona said. "We're discovering a whole new storehouse of information in you, Bert. What happened?"

"Crowley came out second best, of course. One of those things where he was supposed to have gone mad, his hair turned white, all that."

For a moment no one spoke.

Then McTell said casually, "Do you believe it? The devil, magic, all that?"

Bertie shrugged. "No one's ever proved any of it to my satisfaction, but no one's ever disproved it, either. I was privy to a couple of rather odd events, although a skeptic could doubtless have made a good case for fraud.

"But someone once pointed out to me an interesting way of looking at the whole business. We think of it these days as something that was practiced by naive souls in a pre-scientific era, or else by outright charlatans. But then, we only hear about the failures. After all, a successful magician was hardly going to noise it about if he knew he'd be tortured and burned alive for it, what? The smart ones stayed underground, and who knows? Maybe some of them had some luck. Of course it seems like a bunch of mumbo jumbo—eye of newt wing of bat, graveyards and pentacles and all that. But to use an example, does any-one here really know why an automobile starts up when you turn the key?"

The women exchanged glances. Skip stared into space, boredom etched upon his features.

"There is a rational explanation for it, of course, but only up to a point. Further, only a few people—engineers, that lot—truly understand it, and, it took thousands of years of civilization and study of natural laws to reach that level. Even so, we only know causes and effects. I mean really, finally, a car's starting depends upon certain

133

facts, to wit, that some molecules are volatile enough to explode when a spark hits them, that a potential difference between other molecules in a battery can create enough electricity to generate that spark, and so on. Much beyond that we can't take it—we come to the point where we simply have to accept that those are the rules in this universe of ours, and work within them. Precisely why those molecules behave like that—what the *essence* of the whole business is—we can't know.

"So isn't it possible that what we call magic is simply another science—one that was viciously discouraged instead of encouraged—that has its own rules, its own causes and effects, which are just as logical within context as the rules for building an engine? And you can bet that if there are any people who have discovered those rules, they've damned well kept it a secret."

He finished with a little bow and settled back in his chair, crossing his legs.

"I say, old boy," Skip drawled, in an obvious parody of Bertie's accent. "What does a chap do around here for excitement?"

There was a pause. Then McTell said:

"We've been too busy settling in to worry much about it."

"Been to the beaches at Saint Trop yet?"

Mona shifted slightly in her chair.

"No," McTell said.

"Topless," Skip said, "and bottomless, and young. Enough to make you remember what the whole business is about." He turned to the women, grinned, and said, "Not to worry, darlings. Just idle curiosity on the part of a couple of old married men and one—confirmed bachelor."

Bertie raised a nostril and turned away, stony profile gazing off into the distance. Though Skip was generous with his money, McTell knew that he exacted a price, and it became heavier the more he drank. He had obviously started before they arrived, and in the hour since, had put away half a dozen Tanqueray gimlets with smooth, well-practiced ease. The drinking helped to explain, too, what Linden had intimated, that all was not well in the marriage bed. In spite of the Talmadges' wealth, McTell could almost feel sorry for them. But only almost.

Bertie gave Skip a glance of unveiled contempt, then leaned toward McTell.

"I'll leave you with this thought, old boy. Someone once said that the smartest thing the devil could do would be to make us stop believing he exists." His finger tapped the chair arm significantly, and he leaned back, satisfied at having had the last word.

Mona was swirling her drink, staring into it, mouth turned down—pouting—and McTell found himself suddenly weary at the thought of several more days caught in the sniping game of a marriage going bad. Then her gaze rose and shifted; she snapped her fingers.

"Pepin," she called.

A shuffling movement came from the shade near the house, and McTell realized sardonically that he had forgotten the final member of the party. Pepin the Short, Mona's new toy poodle, got to its feet and stood panting in sharp staccato. McTell was a little surprised that either Mona or Skip had ever heard of Charlemagne, let alone

135

his father. Perhaps the name had been Bertie's suggestion. The dog wandered over to the pool, sniffed the water, touched a tongue to it, then sneezed and looked around with bright, though slightly glazed, black eyes.

"There's drinking water right over there, silly," Mona said, pointing to the bowl that had been set out. "See?" Pepin remained where he was, tongue out, chest moving in quick jerks. "For God's sake," she said, standing. As she led the dog to the bowl, all eyes followed her. It was clear she was aware of this; and McTell understood the real object of the exercise: trying, on some barely conscious level, to get back what Skip had taken. When she sat again, she raised her knees; the narrow vee of the bathing suit exposed smooth folds of skin at the joining of her thighs.

"Darling, what are you going to do with that dog when you travel?" Linden said. "The quarantine laws are impossible."

"Leave him with you, of course," Mona said with a lazy smile.

McTell closed his eyes briefly, then stood.

"If you all will excuse me, I've got some letters to write. I'm afraid if I put them off any longer. I'll get home to find I don't have a job. I'll see you at dinner."

As he crossed the patio he heard Mona say:

"Well, I'm ready for a swim. How about it, sis?"

It seemed to take Linden a long time to answer.

"You go ahead. I'm sort of off swimming just now."

The coffee maker was still on in the kitchen, with two inches of thick dark liquid on the edge of scalding,

136

smelling and tasting burnt. But it was hot and strong, and McTell did not have the patience to make a fresh pot.

At last he was free to enter the world of Guilhem de Courdeval.

The tomatoes were a deep rich red, almost the color of blood—the result of Mélusine's patient hoarding of precious water through the dry summer. She stood at the garden gate, surveying with satisfaction the results of her efforts. The plot had been there when they bought the house, although neglected for several years. But it was good rich earth, and she had tilled and fertilized and harvested a crop that had turned out very respectably for a first season. Next year she would expand, perhaps add snow peas and peppers. But for now there were squash, cucumbers, romaine lettuce, and carrots, far more than she and Roger could eat; a little plot of herbs, for fresh basil and parsley and mint; and her pride, the tomatoes. Barefoot, with a basket over her arm, dressed in one of her husband's old shirts knotted at the midriff and a big floppy hat, she took pleasure in feeling like a country girl. She went through the gate and limped toward the bunches of bright red fruit.

Abruptly, a fly buzzed into her ear. She shook her head. It circled and drove immediately back in with a startling determination. Annoyed, she slapped. The fly zipped round and round her, as if angry itself.

The hum of other insects mounted swiftly, until it seemed an organized buzz of menace. Face stinging from her own hand, she hesitated. Tiny shapes hovered, more and more of them, rising in a cloud. She glanced up. The

137

treetops seemed to be closing over the little plot of ground; the vines and shrubs that surrounded her were oily-looking, hostile, pressing in to suffocate. A dread that nature was turning against her swept like nausea through her insides.

"*Merde alors*," she declared aloud. "I will *not* be pushed around by a bunch of bugs." She stepped determinedly forward, only to leap back with a cry at a sinuous movement beside her foot. She stared down at the snake. It was not much over the length of her forearm, black with red lateral stripes, certainly not poisonous.

But she would have sworn under oath that it was staring back with a more than reptilian intelligence: an evil intent. She was suddenly dizzy, aware of the stifling heat, the sweat on her temples and neck.

And I will put enmity between thee and the woman.

Then anger flared. It was a snake, she was a human. Its job was to run. She stamped her foot.

The snake wriggled closer, lifting its head nearly half its length off the ground, tongue flickering, malefic obsidian eyes locked with hers.

She threw the basket at it and in the same motion whirled and ran, clawing at the gate, slamming it behind her. She did not stop until she was in the house. With her back against the wall, she let her shoulders slump. In a minute she was better, but as she started to walk, she was suddenly aware of her naked, unprotected feet. She shivered, and quickly put on shoes. Then she marched into the parlor and poured a healthy slug of Calvados. The routine was becoming familiar, she thought. Whatever was going on, it threatened to turn her into an alcoholic.

Nerves? Imagination? Vapors?

None of those. It was *something,* and the time had come to find out what. Never before had she sought such information; Tante Mathilde's education had not taken her that far. But she had been toying with the idea for days now, and this last incident was enough. She gulped the rest of the brandy, and with her throat still burning, started upstairs.

The attic was a large room with gable dormers opening out of a gambrel roof; probably it had once been used as servants' quarters. The heat was suffocating. She picked her way through the trunks and extra furniture, stored there after their move. The small light the dusty windows admitted was strangely dim. Cobwebs hung from the rafters and walls like great thick clusters of evil fruit; dust motes circled lazily in the muted sunlight. It alt needed to be washed, aired, organized. Could snakes climb? She limped forward slowly.

I had an uncle, little bunny, one of the old, true Rom, a fine tall man with a great hooked nose and black mustache. One night in the country he got caught in a storm, and came to a farmhouse all boarded up. There he thought he would stay dry until morning. He made his way inside—locked doors and shutters are no trouble for the Rom—and built a little fire in the grate, and ate some food he had, and settled down to rest in comfort.

But before he could sleep he began to hear a voice calling. It was a small voice, coming from the upper part of that house. He thought perhaps some child had found its way inside and become trapped. My uncle was a brave man. He took a pitchy piece of wood for a torch and began to climb the stairs. The voice grew louder, calling for help. He climbed and climbed, and still the voice was above him, far up in the attic. He finally made his way up there, and reached for the attic door, when just in time, he understood.

It was a rat, calling with a child's voice. Only it was not really a rat. It was an evil spirit that had entered into that rat, and it was trying to get my uncle up there so it could frighten him out of his body. But my uncle was too clever for it. He quickly hung a talisman on the attic door to trap that spirit there. He could hear it howl with rage as he ran back downstairs and out into the rainy night.

If no one has come along and moved that talisman, that spirit might still be trapped there. That was in Hungary, bunny, but evil spirits know no boundaries.

She had stopped walking, she realized, and made herself begin again. Though she had not touched the amulet in years, hardly ever thought about it, she could always call its whereabouts instantly to mind—and from some instinct she had never understood, always kept it as physically far as possible from the room where she slept. She also kept it well enough hidden so that no one, particularly her children, would ever stumble upon it.

It was right where she had left it, in a shoebox inside another carton at the back of a shelf. She set the shoebox on a dusty table and took out the small wooden cask inside. It was of a deep, rich reddish hue—mahogany, she thought. The symbols engraved on the lid looked vaguely Eastern. Slowly, she opened it.

The inside was lined with black velvet. A thin silver chain with a pendant attached lay inside a silver dish. Both were tarnished with age; her aunt had not been certain, but had thought at least four hundred years. Chased letters rimmed the edge of the dish—an entire alphabet in an archaic Roman script. In the dim light, Mélusine's eyes could just make them out.

The promised lesson in the meaning of the symbols and the powers of the amulet itself had never come; she had been too young before Tante Mathilde's death. But she had watched the old lady use it more than once. It had frightened her then, and it frightened her now. The chain lay coiled in the dish like a tiny serpent writhing through the letters.

Swallowing, she picked it up. This was not the proper place, she thought, she should take it downstairs to the light. But her elbows came to rest on the table, her hands poising the pendant over the dish. It swayed, slowed. She cleared her throat.

"Come, spirit," she whispered. "Why do you trouble us?"

For thirty seconds the pendant moved only with the twitching of her hands, swinging in smaller and smaller circles.

Then it started, and though she had never felt it before, she understood instantly what it was. A mild thrill, an almost pleasurable current, tugged the chain gently. She was so startled she almost dropped it, and had to nerve herself to begin again.

This time the sensation began immediately. She stared as the pendant twitched this way and that, with sharp unmistakable tugs to indicate different letters. When it stopped, her shoulders sagged a little, as if she had been suddenly cut off from a life-giving drug. With trembling fingers, she quickly copied the letters onto a pad: P-E-C-C-A-T-A-P-A-T-R-U-M. She gazed blankly; they meant nothing.

But then a distant pull of memory took her back decades, to endless gray afternoons with pleated skirts and knee stockings and white-coiffed nuns who rapped one's knuckles with rulers. Of its own accord, Mélusine's hand made a quick, firm slash on the pad, separating the letters to: PECCATA PATRUM.

Sins of the fathers.

By what process she had resurrected that long-forgotten biblical phrase, she could not imagine. But this was not the time to wonder. The tension hovered around her, waiting; the flow of it must not be broken. Again she gripped the chain.

"What do you, want?" she said hoarsely.

Again the current and tugs; again she scrawled a dozen unconnected letters: S-A-N-G-U-I-S-F-L-O-R-I-S Her hand made a slash:

Blood of a flower.

The sense of presence was growing quickly, and now it was no longer thrilling and benign, but sinister, menacing. Sick with fear, she poised the chain the third time.

"Who are you?"

The jolt was instant, wrenching her with a painless but awful electricity. She watched, eyes and mouth wide, unable to let go, as if she were holding a live wire. At last it ebbed, hovering, waiting.

She dropped the chain like a hot coal, clapped down the lid of the cask, and fled. Visions of the door swinging shut in her face crowded her mind; what kind of fool was she to toy with such a thing in such a place? The journey through the looming shrouded furniture was endless: the thump-*thump* of her feet, the cobwebs brushing her face, the menace hovering behind her—whispering wordlessly but obscenely, threatening, sneering. She reached the ground floor, on the verge of shrieking. Staying inside was unbearable, but going back to the yard, out of the question. She scooped up her purse from the hall table and rushed out into the street.

There had been nothing cryptic about the final message, in French: L-E-N-O-Y-É.

The drowned man.

A quick look behind told her she was not being followed, at least by anything visible. She walked as fast as she could toward the center of town, wishing for nearly the first time in her life that she were a man, just so she could step into a bar alone and sit unquestioned, safe, surrounded by other humans, while she drank herself into oblivion.

A tap at the study door made McTell react with violent swiftness, sweeping papers over the book on his desk, tearing the sheet out of the typewriter. The door was opening as he tossed it with seeming carelessness, but face down, on top of the others.

"It's almost six, lover," Linden said. "Time to become a social animal again." She handed him a drink. "I hate to interrupt, it sounds like you're typing up a storm."

He shook his head to clear it, jolted by the too-abrupt transition from the world where he had spent the past hours.

"My muse descended and wouldn't leave," he said.

"Well, give her a big tip to make sure she comes back." She bent to kiss the top of his head, then leaned closer to the desk. "What's with the Latin?" She nodded at the still-open dictionary.

"Oh, I was translating an epigraph a while ago."

"Let me know when you're ready for me to do some typing. See you in a bit." She left the door half-open. When the sound of her footsteps faded, he rose and quietly closed it. Then he took the glass of Scotch to the window and rested his hip on the sill, gazing up at the ruin. For the first time, the full flood of marvel at what he had discovered swept through him.

There was absolutely no doubt: The book was the legendary, but authentic, grimoire of Guilhem de Courdeval.

But it was a marvel with a very forbidding edge. There was no doubt either that both priest and sacristan had been right about this much: If a tenth of what McTell had already translated was true, then Courdeval belonged in the front ranks of history's terrible men.

The book appeared to be a combination journal, autobiography, and recipe manual for magical incantations and rituals. While it was highly unusual for a warrior of those times to have been so well-lettered,

Courdeval had obviously been a most unusual man: an uneducated northern knight, he had realized, upon joining the Templars and being introduced to the luxuries and sophistication of warmer lands, that he was a barbarian, and that the way to power was not through force, but knowledge. This he had set out to acquire with the same ferocious tenacity he displayed on the battlefield, keeping company with monks and scholars while his brothers-in-arms roistered about; and in not too long a time, he came to regard his fellow soldiers as little better than animals, as he himself had once been. His contempt soon extended to other magicians of the time. Most, he declared, were nothing but frauds and cowards, playing games with charms and spells, trying to cheat the devil of his due.

But just as Courdeval had demonstrated an almost superhuman arrogance and pride, he had possessed a will to match it, and he had marched consciously and without wavering into the service of evil. His practice of the black arts had begun in Asia Minor, at the court of a Saracen prince with whom the Templars were friendly. Here, the arcane knowledge of the Arab world was available; and here, Courdeval stated, he had first learned of the possibility of making the hazardous pilgrimage to the unnamed city—a place, McTell had gathered by now, that was not on any map, but that Courdeval, at least, had considered very real. Nor did the journey resemble any melodramatic medieval scenario of signing a pact in a graveyard some midnight, in return for seven years' power to perform tricks. Courdeval stressed that it was an unimaginably dangerous undertaking, requiring years of study to learn the pitfalls that must be avoided, the proper ways of appeasing certain beings the traveler would encounter—and some of the preparations he listed had made McTell's mouth go dry.

But the Templar had persevered and triumphed, or so he claimed, and been found worthy of acceptance into the service of mankind's enemy. In return, he was granted the power to command spirits—including the muffled familiar the peasants had called *celui*—and the secret, as he had written, of cheating death.

This last intrigued McTell particularly. The immortality in question was apparently not the sort of unchanging aspect given to, say, the Wandering Jew, but rather some form of renewal of the flesh. It seemed to involve a specific ritual that had not yet been described. But Courdeval stated with authority that there was no longer any more need for him to be burdened with an infirm body than with a shabby tunic. Obviously, this did not jibe with his fate, and the apparent answer was that the book was the elaborate fantasy of a madman. But if so, the insanity had not affected his powers of communication; the tone was measured, clear, and above all, authoritative.

McTell had read only thus far some half-dozen pages of the text. He thought distantly of his own book, the work he had come to this place to do. It seemed the most frivolous, ridiculous thing he had ever heard of. There was no question that he would spend the next days translating the grimoire in its entirety. He was becoming familiar with the hand, and his Latin was beginning to flow. He picked up the book to count its pages and estimate how long the task might take.

There were perhaps a hundred written pages. Many of the margins contained arcane symbols, jottings, comments. Another two dozen leaves at the end were blank.

McTell was about to close the book when his gaze was caught by a few lines of writing on one of these.

At the top of the page, there seemed to be a heading or title: *Liber Viatoris,* Book of the Pilgrim. A little below that was a sentence, written in Courdeval's unmistakable hand: *Incommodum veneficae viatori lilium tribuit.* McTell had encountered the word *venefica* in other contexts, but he checked the dictionary. It meant witch or sorceress.

"The witch's misfortune brings the lily to the pilgrim," he said.

There was no telling what Courdeval might have had on his mind, writing such a cryptic statement nearly seven hundred years before–who could the "pilgrim" have been?–but of this McTell was certain: He would have done anything humanly possible to have avoided any "misfortune" stemming from Guilhem Seul Oeil.

He realized that a quarter of an hour had passed since Linden's visit. Hastily tucking his typewritten sheets into the grimoire, he hid it in the bottom drawer, then hurried down the hall to wash. He had not quite gotten over his queasiness at handling the book's cover.

In the bathroom, he again noticed the strange mark on his left palm. Although it was not tender, he decided that it must be a bruise.

As he walked down the stairs, Linden was crossing the dining room.

"I forgot to mention," she said, "we have a little surprise. Mademoiselle Perrin has come down with some kind of a bug. Apparently it happened very suddenly, just an hour or two ago. She sent her niece to take over; a sweet girl, but I'm sure she's not the cook her aunt is. Wouldn't you know it, just when company comes." She turned to the kitchen and called, "Alysse!"

The girl came to the doorway. She was shy, coltish, her eyes downcast, and she seemed to be trying to shield herself behind the silver soup tureen she held.

"This is my husband, Monsieur McTell," Linden said in French. The girl dropped her knee in an awkward curtsy.

McTell's hand found the banister and gripped it tightly. From a great distance, he heard his own voice say:

"*Enchanté, mademoiselle.*"

PART TWO

Like one, that on a lonesome road
Doth walk in fear and dread,
And having once turned round walks on
And turns no more his head;
Because he knows a frightful fiend
Doth close behind him tread.

Samuel Taylor Coleridge

EIGHT

Étien Boudrie closed his breviary and made the sign of the cross as the first clods of dirt hit the coffin.

"In the name of the Father and of the Son and of the Holy Spirit," he murmured. In the vague, absurd hope that just once he might escape the inevitable, he turned from the grave; but the sound was already there, a long low moan of grief that threatened to rise into a wail. He closed his eyes briefly, sought strength from his leaden spirit. Then he turned to the group of raven-clad women clinging in support to Thérèse Taillou–the widow Taillou now. Her husband, Henri, who for two decades had monopolized the business of providing Saint-Bertrand with its water, lay in the coffin beneath those clods of earth.

For a moment Boudrie stood still, the scene imprinting itself upon his mind as funerals never failed to do: the cluster of gray-haired women in mourning; the two dozen other visitants moving, with a silence that seemed furtive, away from the gaping hole in the earth; the sexton and his assistant in coarse black suits, berets tucked politely under their arms, waiting for the widow to leave before finishing their work of filling the grave. The heavy, restless sky sent gusts of wind through the grass of the little hilltop cemetery, bringing a twilight that had lasted all through the afternoon. If only it would rain, Boudrie thought. He stepped forward, opening his arms to the new widow. Her face was twisted with shock.

He patted her shoulder, murmuring sympathy, promising his prayers, urging her to be strong in the faith that Christ had called her husband to his eternal reward. Privately, he was not so sure, and he knew she was not either. Henri Taillou had been a man short of intelligence and mean of spirit. Suspicious of all he did not understand—which included nearly everything beyond the confines of his nineteenth-century life-style—and envious of those he considered better off than himself, he had also been possessed of a rapacity that had mushroomed beyond control during this summer's drought, earning him the deadly enmity of those neighbors forced to pay his exorbitant fees for the water upon which their lives depended. It was common knowledge that he beat his wife and son—a tradition Philippe would be likely to pass on—and that the chances of finding him sober at any given time had dwindled in direct proportion to the passing of his years. Something in Boudrie marveled that the woman was capable of grief for such a man, but he knew that it was real. The one thing people could not bear was loneliness, and if their only companionship was hateful, they learned to thrive on that hate.

152

The death had come as a shock. Old Taillou possessed the constitution of a bull, and despite his drinking, had shown no signs of giving out. Boudrie, called to the deathbed, had seen the corpse's face unaltered by the mortician. It had been contorted in rage or fear—no doubt the former, knowing Taillou, a man who would have faced even his own end with indignation. But it clearly had not been a pleasant death.

Well, Boudrie thought, see what good your new money will do you now, poor man.

At last he managed to disengage himself. He could not help feeling that mixed with the outward sympathy of Mme. Taillou's companions was a certain grim satisfaction. Many were widows themselves, and the image of vultures welcoming a new member to their flock lodged itself disturbingly in his mind. Although he had seen and felt the gamut of human emotions through the years, funerals, especially those that left women bereaved, never failed to penetrate his armor of numbness.

He walked heavily to the old 2CV and wrestled his body into the seat. As he reached for the ignition switch, his glance caught Taillou's son, Philippe. The young man had skulked at the edge of the crowd in his usual furtive way, but now he was looking at Boudrie strangely, almost imploringly. Boudrie hesitated, but then decided that Philippe knew well enough where to find him. He had had enough of funerals. The engine coughed, missed, reluctantly caught. Gauthier *père* had removed the broken spark plug, not disguising his irritation, but typically had replaced only that one. Well, what could you expect when you could pay only a pittance? There was a time when such things were done purely for the love of God, but the need for money had undeniably replaced that. And who could blame the poor lilies of the field? If it was true that Christ cared for them, Boudrie had witnessed precious little of it in his lifetime. The hood rattled and bounced where he had wired the broken hinge.

As he drove the three kilometers back to the village, he wrestled with his conscience. Amalie Perrin had been sick two days now, some sort of fever, and he had not yet visited. The thought of doing so filled him with unease. It was not a house he cared to enter; memories of his three years with Céleste lurked there like ghosts. His craving for a drink was terrific. Too soon, he reached Saint-Bertrand. His watch told him the hour was not as late as the sky made it appear. With a sigh, he yielded to conscience.

But as he made the turn into town, he thought of Roger Devarre, and brightened. The business would be infinitely more bearable if the doctor accompanied him. Though Devarre was an agnostic, Boudrie was anxious to cultivate his acquaintance; there were few people in the village with whom he could converse on a more than mundane level. He swung the car up the Rue du Maréchal MacMahon and stopped in front of the building Devarre used as a combination office and studio.

The waiting room was antiseptically clean, and probably the most modernly furnished place in Saint-Bertrand. Framed diplomas and certificates lined the walls, magazines were scattered on a table. There was no receptionist, and only rarely a patient. Through one door Boudrie could see a surgical table covered with white

154

muslin, stainless steel cabinets and sink, a scale, and other medical paraphernalia. Boudrie tapped on the door across the hall. Ajar, it swung open.

High ceilings, a skylight, and a large bay window filled the room with the Provençal radiance that painters had acclaimed for centuries. Frames and canvases lined the walls—models of earnest, painstaking effort unaided by talent. Devarre turned, surprised, palette in hand. He wore a white smock that looked suspiciously like a physician's rather than a painter's, smeared with colors like Joseph's coat. A dab of violet on the end of his nose added a finishing touch to his habitually good-humored expression. Boudrie stepped forward, hands behind his back, and examined the work on the easel, vaguely recognizable as a reproduction of the sloping village street outside. For all he could tell, it was intended to be impressionistic.

"Dreadful, isn't it? Devarre said cheerfully.

Boudrie glanced out the window at the actual scene and closed one eye.

"Perhaps," he said diplomatically, "you're not quite sure yet which style you're working toward. These things take time to mature."

Devarre laughed. "The truth is, I haven't a shred of ability. Let me assure you, Étien, it's rough to have a huge passion for something nature denies you." He hung up his smock and quickly washed at the sink, then took from a drawer a leather-covered flask and two small glasses. "An ugly day, isn't it?"

"I have just come from burying Henri Taillou."

155

Devarre had written out the death certificate; a stroke, with no mention of liver and kidneys drastically deteriorated from decades of determined alcohol abuse. He shrugged, a gesture Boudrie repeated. They touched glasses and drank.

"Your wife is well?"

Devarre shrugged again. "A touch of the *cafard,* I think, though she says nothing. It's hard for her to be so far from the children; the house is very empty. I know Mélusine loves the freedom of this place, but she misses Paris too." He smiled wryly. "I try, but I'm afraid I'm not as much company as I should be. Perhaps she needs a lover."

Boudrie smiled too. Then, bluntly, he said:

"Do you regret coming here?"

Devarre's face went thoughtful. He filled the glasses again.

"Quite simply, no. I could give you any number of reasons: the weather, the peace, the fact that I'm free to do what I love–even the light, pretentious as that may sound. But perhaps the real truth lies elsewhere; I'm not sure myself. Let me ask you the same question. If you were free to choose your own curacy, would you leave?"

Once again, they touched glasses.

"I have come to ask you a favor. "Boudrie said. His own voice sounded stiff, formal. "I'm just on my way to visit Amalie Perrin. I thought perhaps–if you're not too busy . . ."

"But of course. I've been meaning to look in on her again myself. The patients cramming the reception room will just have to wait." He reached for his bag, scanned its contents, seemed satisfied. "It's not raining?"

"Not when I came in."

"Then I'll trust to luck and leave my coat."

"We can take my car," Boudrie said, feeling a little magnanimous, a little self-conscious. Devarre drove a Citroën sedan.

Learning forward into the rising wind, Boudrie led the way to the 2CV. The smell of moisture had come into the air. Perhaps, after all, it would rain.

It might have been the gray afternoon light filtering into John McTell's study, or the restless warm wind, or just the absence of another human being, that made the house seem so empty. Only the shrill yapping of Pepin the Short broke the silence, and even that seemed to underline the solitude. The dog was tied up outside the gardener's shed; Linden and the guests had gone out for lunch and a drive. McTell supposed he could not blame Pepin, but that did not ease the irritation.

He had stayed home on the pretext of working on his book, but the truth, he admitted, was that he had wanted to be close to Alysse. She was gone now too, home to take care of her aunt, and perhaps that was the real reason he felt forlorn. At least he had had a precious hour alone with her, finding excuses to linger in the dining room while she went about her work–watching her, this shy slender girl with the strange flat nose, as he had watched her from the moment she had entered his sight, with a fascination that verged on obsession. It was best when she did not know he was there; she would skip about her

157

chores, humming, occasionally breaking into a few steps of dance. At such moments her loveliness made his head light.

But it was not just her beauty. He had never been even slightly interested in the seduction of young girls, even if he had been fool enough to think she would be attracted to a man three times her age. It was the sense of connection, of sharing a mysterious bond deeper than the rational mind could grasp.

Did she sense this too? Had she seen his face during that instant when, through some inexplicable psychic warp, he had watched her step from her bath and their eyes had met? Had it even happened?

Above all, what impossible coincidence had brought her from his imagination into his life?

The need to know, to try to get some hint, had spurred him to approach her. But careful though he had been to keep his demeanor easy, to maintain a physical distance, the barrier that sprang up was instant and impenetrable. Her face had darkened, her gaze dropped.

"How is your aunt?" he had asked.

A little shrug. "Not bad." When he lingered, she added in a voice hardly above a whisper, "It is nothing. She'll be better in a day or two." With another apologetic shrug, she hurried back to her work, leaving him a touch annoyed. Her thoughts had been poisoned against the Americans by Mlle. Perrin, he suspected, and he found himself thinking meanly that the old witch's illness served her right.

And while his obsession was less with the girl herself than with her part in the inexplicable events that had

158

pervaded the past days, he could not deny a moment or two of fantasy of having met Alysse years before under similar circumstances—of discovering that strange magical bond when he, too, was beginning his life.

How different it might have been.

At any rate, it was a relief to be free of Skip and Mona for a few hours. The sophisticated but empty conversation laced with Mona's unending sexual innuendoes, the brittle company, and the aimless drinking had begun to get seriously on his nerves.

Pepin barked and paused, barked and paused, seeming to measure precisely the time it took McTell to forget about him before giving forth with a new burst of complaint. The sound had a particularly grating, aggravating quality, and he remembered, not for the first time, that Linden had agreed to keep the dog while the Talmadges continued their travels—which might be months. There was something to the notion that dogs reflected their owners, he thought wearily as he rose to shut the window. As if in response, the barking seemed to rise in volume.

He sat again and went back to the translation of the grimoire of Guilhem de Courdeval, which was accumulating page by page on his desk. It was another reason why the afternoon and its solitude seemed oppressive.

Whether the events described were factual or the fantasies of an impossibly twisted mind, the cold-blooded clarity and viciousness of their telling had shaken McTell so badly that half a dozen times he had closed the book with the intention of never opening it again. Most of the rituals were ostensibly for the appeasement of beings whom Courdeval named; the means of pleasing them seemed to be the destruction of human life in various appalling ways. Here, too, was corroboration of the vampire legends. Blood had been consumed like wine. Perhaps worst of all, Courdeval seemed to have possessed a grotesque sense of humor. Three nuns, for example, were impaled upon stakes to which cross-members were added to fashion rough crucifixes.

But one ritual in particular stood out from the others. It involved a peasant, a widower, whom Courdeval had courted with bribes and favors, but then turned on and forced by some unspecified means to murder his only daughter. McTell had not elsewhere encountered this third-person aspect; Courdeval had apparently taken no part in the proceedings except to direct the man's actions. Further, instead of his usual knight-attendants, he had been alone. The gruesome object was the young woman's blood; this was then prepared by means of a crucial incantation, which, he made clear, was a secret he alone knew and with which nothing could cause him to part. It was not committed to writing in the grimoire.

When the ceremony was over, Courdeval announced with clear triumph that he had demonstrated beyond doubt that he no longer needed to fear death. With a display of his ferocious humor, he added that out of concern for the unlucky peasant's grief, he had dispatched the man to join his daughter. But there was no further explanation of the event's unusual features; the grimoire shifted to other doings. It seemed only that Courdeval, at the cost of two lives, had proved his immortality to his own satisfaction.

So you may have believed, my friend, McTell thought. But if there is a devil, he cheated you, too; and while you boasted enough of your rewards, you neglected to mention the possibility of your punishment. And mercifully, your secret incantation died with you. No one else would ever be tempted to try such madness.

Grotesque though it all was, McTell could not deny a fascination—even a grudging admiration—for the man's boldness, his twisted but enormous courage. He could almost see the grim one-eyed visage that was becoming fixed in his imagination, and this time even fancied he caught a glint of humor in it. But his reverie was shattered by a stream of wild, nerve-fraying yelps. He realized that the dog had literally barked itself hoarse. The hell of it was that there was nothing he could do; released, Pepin would ran away, and McTell was damned if he would bring the dog into the house. He was simply stuck until Mona came home. His resentment flared. The idiot animal seemed a perfect emblem of the people who had invaded his life at this delicate time. What would Guilhem de Courdeval have thought of a man who could not keep his house free of annoying guests, or even pets? No doubt he would have dispatched one of his unseen "servants" to take care of so trivial a matter; and for a moment, McTell allowed himself to reflect on the substantial, if underhanded, satisfaction of being able to remove such a nuisance as a small, stupid, noisy dog simply by an act of will. If he could, he decided wryly, he would.

The afternoon light was deepening. A glance at his watch told him it was past six—time for a drink and a shower. With Alysse gone, they were on their own for dinner; Linden was bringing groceries. He stood, poured a little Scotch neat into a glass, and was raising it to his lips when he realized the barking had ceased. He cocked his head, listening, then hurried downstairs.

Outside, the gray early twilight spoke of the onset of fall. Pepin's rope hung, broken, from where it was tied to the shed. The door was partly open. McTell glanced quickly around, then strode forward and stepped inside. In a few seconds his eyes adjusted to the fading light that came through the single dingy window; then he saw with relief that the dog was there, a small white blur crouched in the farthest corner. The other end of the rope still hung from his collar.

"Too dumb even to run away, huh?" McTell said. He set his drink on a shelf and started forward to pick up the rope.

A low hard growl rose in Pepin's throat.

McTell stopped. The dog was not just crouched. It was backed into the corner as tightly as it could get—body arched, hackles standing on end—and staring at McTell with a beady-eyed intensity that raised the hair on his arms.

"What in the hell," he said. The growl continued, deep and steady. "Pepin," he said sharply, and took a firm step forward.

The dog leaped at him, snapping savagely, spraying saliva, with a sound that was almost a scream. McTell sprang back. In the dim, musty little shed, man and animal glared at each other. The only sound was the dog's frantic panting.

"All right," McTell said softly.

He took a spade from its hook on the wall. Holding it before him like a sword, he advanced step by step. The dog's sounds rose sharply in pitch; it backed against the wall until McTell was nearly touching it with the spade.

Then it flung itself forward, teeth ripping at McTell's calf.

"You little bastard!" he yelled, flailing with the spade. But the dog was gone, a white streak of speed, rope streaming behind. McTell ran several steps, shouting hoarsely, realizing the futility of pursuit even before Pepin disappeared into the brush.

He stood still. Silence closed around him like a presence; then, tentatively, birdsongs started. He knelt to examine his leg, and saw, with relief that the bite had not broken his skin—only torn a long rent in his fifty-dollar pair of slacks. He rose, walked slowly back to where his Scotch waited, and drank it off. His hand lifted the frayed end of the rope. It did not look chewed.

How had it broken?

Why had Pepin run back into the shed, instead of away?

What had gotten into the dog to make it behave with such obvious terror?

But the real question was one McTell did not want to consider: What had gotten into *him?* He picked up the spade and hung it on its hook.

As he walked to the house, an odd, high, mournful whistle rose in the distance, a sound like nothing he had ever heard. He waited, but it was not repeated. Children, perhaps; perhaps they would catch the dog. Or perhaps the rope would snag on something and hold Pepin. McTell scanned his surroundings; but he had had enough experience of this brush-choked terrain to know that even a daytime search would be difficult and likely fruitless, let alone with night coming on. Besides, the truth was that he would be quite content never to lay eyes on the little cur again. In short, he supposed that he was sorry—but not very.

Abruptly the twilight was ripped by a howl, perhaps a hundred yards off: the sound of an animal in terror or pain. It rose to a shriek that was almost unbearable, until McTell's shaking hands clapped themselves over his ears.

Just as suddenly, it ceased.

He was still standing motionless, perhaps three minutes later, when the BMW pulled into the drive. Doors slammed, voices approached. With an effort, he composed himself and turned to face them. Linden was holding the car keys and a net sack of groceries. She looked a little weary—and the others looked as if they had not stinted on the wine.

"Who do you have to suck off to get a drink around here?" Skip said jovially, and walked past McTell without pausing, headed for the bar.

"How about your wife?" Mona murmured, with the words slightly slurred.

But Linden was watching McTell's face, and concern came into her own.

"What happened?" she demanded.

McTell folded his arms and nodded toward the shed. The broken rope told the story. Mona took several half-running steps toward it, then stopped.

"When I came downstairs, he was already loose," McTell said. "I tried to catch him. He attacked me."

Mona whirled on him, fists clenched.

"I'll just bet he did." she said harshly.

Stunned, McTell stared at her furious face.

"You hated that dog! You think I didn't see it? You turned him loose, didn't you."

McTell exhaled. "I don't know where you came up with that little fantasy," he said evenly. "But I wish you'd have the courtesy not to call me a liar"–he knelt, and elaborately displayed the rip in his trouser leg–"in my own house."

Tears sprang into her eyes. She swiveled to face Linden and in a choked voice said:

"Christ, how can you *stand* him?" She shoved her fists in her pockets and walked rapidly away.

Shoulders stiff, McTell turned and climbed the patio steps, leaving silence behind him: Linden uncertain which of them to follow, Bertie moving discreetly off into the garden. McTell ignored both, along with Skip's glib offer of a drink as he crossed the living room.

The grimoire and translation were still on his desk. They were not things he wanted anyone else to see. He closed the study door behind him, got a fresh glass and poured more Scotch. Then he went to the desk.

His hand stopped in midair.

The grimoire, on his typestand, had fallen open to the page titled *Liber Viatoris,* Book of the Pilgrim. He blinked, trying to remember turning to it. The passage he had been translating came many pages before.

But that was not all. There were now, not one, but two sentences written on the page.

Slowly, in disbelief, he leaned forward. The new line read: *Liberatio parvuli viatori potentiam tribuit.*

The room was deadly quiet. He straightened, took a step back, gazed aimlessly around. His gaze fell on his drink. He reached for it, but then glanced uneasily at the decanter, checking its level. Was that what was going on: had his drinking caused him to look right at the second sentence previously and not see it? He bent forward again and examined the text carefully. There was no doubt; only one page was titled Book of the Pilgrim, and the first sentence remained the one about "the witch's misfortune." He could have nudged the book open to that page, he supposed, in his haste to check on Pepin the Short. But the second sentence . . .

He read it again. Only the word *parvuli* was unfamiliar. He reached for the dictionary.

The little one's release brings power to the pilgrim.

He put the grimoire and papers back into their drawer and, with creased forehead, walked down the hall to wash. The mark on his palm was not going away, but it had still not begun to hurt. If anything, it seemed to give a mildly pleasant sensation when touched, like an itch being scratched. Was that what it was, then? Poison oak, or an insect bite? He stared at it, imagining that its shape was becoming more clear.

But then, he seemed to be imagining a great many things these days. One thing he was not making up, however, was an angry and irrational sister-in-law. For a moment he paused while the scene replayed in his mind—the dark shed, the hard solid feel of the spade in his hand, the panting dog's fear—and beneath his guilt flared a tiny ember of triumph at having bested this insignificant but otherwise unassailable enemy.

But what was that shrieking he had heard in the woods?

Slowly, he walked downstairs, bracing himself for an evening of thinly disguised anger and further obligatory half-truths.

Boudrie drove slowly along the narrow potholed street. The row of housefronts was continuous, like a block-long masonry wall, yellowed with age, broken only by iron gates of uniform green that led into each small courtyard. The row was grim and silent, like the rest of the town, like the deepening afternoon. He parked and briefly closed his eyes, remembering with sudden terrible clarity how he had once hovered in this darkened doorway at night, blood surging with guilt and passion, waiting tensely for Céleste to let him in.

With the satchel that contained the tools of his trade—breviary, holy water, eucharist—he climbed out of the car. He wondered if Devarre could sense his reluctance, if perhaps, for reasons of his own, he even shared it. Without looking at each other, carrying bags that almost could have marked them as members of the same athletic team, they walked to the door.

The cousin who had come from Fayence to nurse, a Mme. Durtal, let them in. To have the doctor and priest both in the house flustered her; button-eyed, frumpy, she hurried around, arranging chairs and chattering.

"Alysse went to shop, she'll be back soon. I'll make tea."

"Perhaps," Boudrie said. "First . . ." He nodded toward the stairs.

"You don't want to wait for Alysse?" she said, surprised.

Only to get it over with, Boudrie thought.

"I think the less it is brought to her mind, the better." Blood rose to his neck at the transparency of the excuse. Mme, Durtal only shrugged.

"As you wish, monsieur. Amalie is probably still sleeping." Her tones seemed to underlie the futility of the gesture.

"There'll be no need to wake her," he said, a touch too quickly.

Mme. Durtal led the way. Devarre, after a glance at Boudrie, followed. Boudrie waited in the dark, sparsely furnished room for the count of ten before he, too, stepped onto the stairs.

The bedroom was small and stern, with a squat heavy dresser and chairs. The single touch of femininity was provided by a silver jewelry box that had belonged to Céleste. Several oval portraits were arranged around a mirror. One was of a woman perhaps in her early twenties, with rich chestnut hair, a straight fine nose, hollow checks, and the faintly haunted look that told of a despair which never entirely left her.

Unpinned, that hair would fall below her waist.

Boudrie turned savagely from the memory, from the portrait that seemed to mock him. Devarre looked at him with a glint of interest, but said nothing. The disheveled gray-haired form on the bed moved only occasionally, tossing in a way that suggested had dreams. Mme. Durtal opened the heavy drapes on the two windows that gave onto the courtyard. The gray light only seemed to make the chamber gloomier.

Devarre took out a stethoscope and reached under the covers. He took the pulse, checked blood pressure, began to shake down a thermometer.

"She has eaten?"

"A little broth yesterday. Mostly she sleeps."

They waited in silence until Devarre withdrew the thermometer from her mouth, tightly compressed even in sleep. He exhaled, looking perplexed and a little angry.

"Normal."

"Then she's improving," Mme. Durtal said, relieved.

Devarre did not reply. He began to repack his bag.

It was his turn, Boudrie knew. That there was a proper procedure for caring for the semicomatose, he was aware, but it escaped him. He opened his breviary, paging through it blindly. Devarre stepped back and watched in silence, hands folded before him. Mme. Durtal knelt, adding embarrassment to Boudrie's burden.

"Hail, Holy Queen!" he read. "Mother of Mercy! Hail!" His voice was too strong for the little room. He dropped it to a whisper. "To you do we send up our sighs, mourning and weeping in this valley of tears . . ."

He finished hastily, then uncapped the vial of holy water and lightly crossed her forehead–a gesture

169

terrifying in its ineffectualness. But what else could he do?

Abruptly, he found that he was looking into her open eyes. At first they stared through him, but gradually they cleared and focused.

"*Bonsoir,* monsieur." Her voice was a thin, reedy whisper, eerily disembodied in the twilit room. "Am I dying?"

Boudrie forced his face into a semblance of a smile.

"No, Amalie. Monsieur Devarre says you're fine. You just need to sleep."

She smiled back faintly and nodded. Her eyelids flickered.

"That's all I seem to do."

For half a minute no one spoke. She appeared to have dropped back into slumber. Boudrie was about to step away when the whisper came again.

"Monsieur *le curé?*"

He reached for her hand and held it between both of his. It was warm, dry, without substance–like a fragile bird. He leaned close until his ear was near her lips.

"Do you miss her as much as I do?"

Stunned, Boudrie stared at her closed eyes, his jaw sagging stupidly. Had she said what he thought? The words had been barely audible. Neither Devarre nor Mme. Durtal seemed to have caught them, or at least their import. But the realization hit him like a weight slamming into his chest. When he had crept into this very house at night, making love to Céleste while her sister, Amalie, slept–or so they had supposed–how had he allowed himself to believe that she was ignorant of what was going on? Did she know, had she known all these years? And about Alysse . . . ?

Her hand had relaxed. He stroked it, let it go, and backed away, almost stumbling over Mme. Durtal in his anxiety to get out of the room.

"You see, she's better," the woman said excitedly, following him down the stairs. "Now I will make tea." She hurried to the kitchen. Boudrie longed to stop her, to insist that they must leave; but he reminded himself unhappily of his duty.

Devarre's face was wry. "You are close to her?" he said.

Boudrie hesitated; but there was no way Devarre could know, even if he had heard.

"To her sister," he mumbled. "Long ago."

"Alysse has been helping my wife around the house, until this. Mélusine misses her already. She's a surrogate daughter, I suppose."

Boudrie nodded stupidly, without words.

"This is hard for you, isn't it?" Devarre said. "I always thought the job of visiting the sick could not be worse than for a physician. Now I see that I'm only expected to heal them, or at worst pronounce them dead—not share their grief."

"It goes better when something stronger than tea is offered afterward. But I don't mean to keep you. If you have another engagement—"

"Not at all. It's too late to abandon you, anyway."

Relieved, Boudrie settled back to wait. After what seemed like hours, Mme. Durtal emerged with a tray of tea and lemon-flavored cakes. Dutifully they sat, sipping

171

and listening to her chatter, which verged on the desperate. Her husband had not wanted her to come, even though he knew perfectly well that there was no one else to take care of Amalie. Poor Alysse, already working all day, and now coming home to an invalid at night–only seventeen, hardly more than a child.

As if Mme. Durtal's speech were a hailstorm of tiny blows. Boudrie lowered his face closer to his teacup. Another long time passed before his watch registered the obligatory polite interval. The woman's face fell when the two men rose.

"I can't understand where that girl is," she said as they stepped out the door. "She should tell you how those Americans live. The wines, the finest cuts of meat each night." Her little eyes were bright, her voice gathering momentum like a train leaving a station. "And a swimming pool, when the rest of us hardly dare to bathe–"

Devarre coughed into his hand.

"With regret," Boudrie said loudly, overriding the squirrel-like chatter, "we must leave you to your supper. If there's anything I can do . . ."

Deflated, she said, "You'll come again soon?"

They assured her they would.

Beside the car, the two men paused. Night had come early with the clouds. Boudrie cleared his throat.

"I've been thinking about your fee. There's a little extra money allotted by the parish–"

"Don't talk foolishness," Devarre said curtly. "You can see I'm of no use."

"Not true. But fortunately for me, I'm spared such certainty." He searched for a delicate phrasing. "Then it's not a fever?"

Devarre gazed past him toward the lights of the main street.

"That it should baffle me is not so strange. I'm an internist, and an indifferent one."

To be sure, Boudrie thought; that explained the half-dozen framed awards on Devarre's office walls.

"But yes, it's very odd. Outwardly she shows the symptoms of fever–sleeping, not eating, and so on. But her temperature is normal, her pulse rate and blood pressure both a little down, but acceptable. I'm just hoping it's not something truly serious–meningitis, or some obscure disease only a specialist would recognize. It started off seeming so harmless. She really should go to the hospital. Perhaps the neurosurgeons . . ."

"If she gets any worse," Boudrie said. "You have my word. We'll find the money somewhere." For a moment they stood in silence. Then he said, "Well, I don't suppose you'd care to join me for a drink."

"Another time, thanks. I think what I need is a walk home to clear my head."

"A better idea," Boudrie agreed.

"Tell me: Mademoiselle Perrin cooked for you, did she not?"

"Two or three times a week she would make something extra and drop it by. I was able to pay her a little."

"And now?"

Boudrie shrugged. "I'm not so helpless. I've been a bachelor many years."

173

"Mélusine's been wanting to have you over, but she's too shy to ask. This is the perfect excuse. I'll talk to her and give you a call." They shook hands. In the deep dusk, Devarre's shape became indistinct after a few steps.

Boudrie lingered beside the car, telling himself he was savoring the crisp air, the first touch of autumn. But in truth, he was reluctant to go home to the lonely rectory–and spend the rest of the evening, and probably the next several besides, pondering obsessively the implications of *la Perrin's* words.

Then he beard approaching footsteps.

"*Bonsoir, monsieur le curé,*" Alysse called. It simply never stops, Boudrie thought, but his heart swelled as always at the sight of her. Cradling a net sack of groceries, she bobbed her head and bent slightly at the knee–her way of greeting him since she was a child, as if she were going to genuflect. It touched him and annoyed him in about equal parts.

"*Bonsoir,* Alysse. It's late. I fear you have an angry cousin at home."

"I took a walk by the river."

"Thinking great thoughts?"

"Just thinking." Her tone was serious, but she had always been a serious child; her bearing was grave; her face already beginning to show the lines of thoughtful maturity. She had grown up poor–and, he reminded himself sternly, without parents. That the young suffered from great impatience, Boudrie knew well, especially when their home life was not all that could be desired. He had seen too many girls leave Saint-Bertrand with boys as equally unfit for the world as they–often pregnant, and off to repeat the cycle of poverty and desperation that was their heritage. An uncomfortable twinge touched him. Paternal jealousy? Guilt? He looked at her face, so much like her mother's, but with that broad peasant nose. Impossible, he assured himself weakly.

"How does it go with the Americans?"

She shrugged. "Not bad. Madame and Monsieur are very kind. Some guests have come—"

"Who are not so kind?"

She hesitated, then conceded, "It's more work."

"You're going back tomorrow?"

"There's nothing I can do for Tante Amalie. I saw Monsieur Devarre; did be say anything about her?"

Without hesitation, Boudrie answered:

"He believes the fever will run its course in another day or two." Jesus, Mary, Joseph, forgive me, he thought.

"I'll pray."

He nodded. "What will you do then?" he said suddenly. "After your aunt is well, I mean. A job, or go on with school? Surely you can't stay here forever keeping house for tourists."

"I'm not good in school," she said matter-of-factly.

"There's a young man?"

She lowered her eyes, then shook her head.

"So—?"

"What else can I do? There are no good jobs here. I could go to Grasse, perhaps—work as a waitress or in a store. But it doesn't seem like much of an improvement."

"A hard life for a girl," Boudrie, agreed thinking of smooth, elegant city men and their promises.

She looked at him with something like resentment.

175

"I'm not such a 'girl' as everyone seems to think." Her posture shifted subtly as she spoke; there was a sullenness to her tone. Boudrie's eyes widened–the combination was nothing short of sultry. Christ! There was a woman growing out of this child he had known all these years. Her defiance suggested that she knew a good deal more about the world than he had suspected, and was even prepared to tell him about it. He quickly decided he did not want to know.

Her face relaxed into a smile.

"No need to worry, monsieur. I'll probably grow old cooking and keeping house, like Tante Amalie."

Her mockery made him grumpy, but then he smiled, too.

"At least until you marry a handsome young man and move away?"

"It's possible," she said.

Loss hovered in the air between them.

"Well," he said, "it might do you good to get the fresh air of a bigger place for a while. If you do want to try to get a job, let me know. I can't promise anything, but no old priest is without his ways and means."

She cocked her head a little to the side–pride that would not give way to the obligation to show gratitude. Abruptly, he remembered the identical expression on her mother's face from a long-distant night when, for the first time, he had dared to take her flowers.

"Go home," he said, waving his hand. "I don't need your cousin's anger aimed at me." Eyes stinging, he fumbled for the car door handle.

"Monsieur?"

He stopped.

She hesitated, then said, "Do you ever–dream while you're awake?"

Boudrie turned to her again. The breeze had blown loose strands of hair across her face. She ignored them.

"I'm not sure what you mean," he said slowly.

For long seconds, he felt her on the edge of speaking again. Then she gave a little laugh.

"I'm not, either. Sometimes I think I daydream too much. But see, I'm holding up dinner. *À bientôt.*"

He watched her walk quickly to the house, almost called her back. Had he sensed trouble in her voice, or only imagined it? The door opened; he could hear Mme. Durtal's scolding break into the thick night, then go quiet with the closing door.

Well, Christ knew the girl had reasons enough to be troubled, he thought, climbing laboriously into the car. His mind roved until it settled on brandy. He pressed a little harder on the accelerator.

McTell lay unmoving while Linden slipped off her robe and got into bed. They did not touch.

"Are you feeling all right?" she murmured.

Hands clasped behind his head, he gazed out the window at the restless night clouds, illuminated from within by the fattening moon.

"Sure."

"You seem–tight." She turned on her side and laid a hand on his arm.

He shrugged "I'm not angry. But it's a bit much to have that wretched mutt nearly tear my leg off, then get insulted to boot."

"Darling, I'm so sorry. She's always been like that—starts yelling at whoever's closest when something goes wrong."

"Nobody accused her of being the brightest woman in the world," McTell said.

For a moment neither spoke. Then Linden said:

"I noticed beside the pool that your opinion of her intellect didn't keep you from looking at her tits."

"God damn it," he said, heating up, "I can't help it if the woman won't keep her clothes on."

"Shhhhh–just teasing." Then Linden's voice dropped huskily. "I bet I know something that'll make you feel better." One fingernail drew a slow line down his biceps, then moved onto his chest.

He started to protest, but then lay still, staring out at the gently tossing black treetops, allowing his wife to believe that she could put things right. But it was like observing two actors at a distant remove; his mind stood apart, uninvolved.

And suddenly, with a chilling certainty that came deep in his guts, he understood that between the two of them what they called lovemaking had only been an exercise in sensuality, an exchange of pleasure without the far deeper surrender his spirit cried for; that the trouble was not fatigue or depression or aging, as he had tried to tell himself, that even at those moments when he drove his seed into Linden, hearing his own cries mingled with hers, it had simply never been right. It was as if he was forever seeking a warmth within her that he never found—not mere warmth, either, but heat, fire, the way he had once burned in the arms and body of his lost first love. He let his eyes close, remembering with startling vividness, for the first time in decades, nights when every touch seemed breathtakingly new, when their hunger for each other had been endless and they had spent hours shyly and silently exploring the marvels of their bodies counterparts—and always, that almost unbearable heat, which had dissipated through the years to a lukewarm acceptance of what would suffice.

He pressed his palms to Linden's cheeks and raised her face.

"Come lie down," he said.

"Am I not doing right?" she said anxiously.

He shook his head. "Fine. Come on." Reluctantly, she lay beside him again, one arm across his chest. "I suppose the run-in with Mona has me more upset than I thought."

"I feel helpless. I wish there were something I could do."

"I think I just need some sleep," McTell said.

She rose up on an elbow and looked into his eyes.

"I love you, you know," she said.

"I love you too, Lin." The words sounded dutiful.

She watched his face a moment longer. Even in the dark, he could see her unease, and he tried to find more words of assurance, to say them with greater conviction. But nothing came, and she slowly turned on her side, her back to him.

"Lin?" he said after a moment. "How long are they going to stay?"

He felt her shrug. "As long as they want." And then, as if it explained, "She's my sister."

Sleep was slow in coming to McTell, and while his rational mind protested that he was being unfair, a deeper and more powerful voice laid his troubles directly to the intruders in his house.

NINE

The sun had returned, and in the sluggishness of the afternoon heat, McTell sat at his desk and stared at the grimoire. His night had been restless, and the morning had not improved his nerves; while Linden and Mona wandered the grounds calling for Pepin, he had stood at the edge of his study window, watching uneasily.

But they had found nothing, and after lunch had gone out driving to inquire if anyone in the area had seen the dog. Bertie was taking his somewhat ostentatious siesta, complete with sleeping mask. Skip was doubtless getting a head start on the cocktail hour. Outwardly, all was well again; McTell and Mona had entered into an uncomfortably polite truce. But he could not concentrate, and he wondered vaguely at the numbness that had replaced his earlier shock at some of the material in the grimoire.

Or perhaps, in the light of day, he was grudgingly coming to admit that this preoccupation was really nothing but some sort of wish-projection, and a rather embarrassing one at that. He had been trying to turn a

181

series of odd events and coincidences into something more. Courdeval's book, he was sure by now, was only the dark fantasy of an unhinged mind like de Sade's; and like the partner in a *folie à deux,* he, McTell, had been drawn into the sinister game. While he might have become numb to the grimoire, his disgust for himself was growing.

He pushed back his chair and stood; wanting something but not sure what: a cup of coffee, a drink—

Or perhaps just the sight of Alysse. Distractedly, he started down the hall to wash.

As he passed the French doors to the upstairs deck, he heard voices drift up from the patio. They were indistinct—male and female, speaking French. Riboux the gardener, probably, in one of his rare appearances out of hiding, boring Alysse with some pompous drivel about how the estate should be properly managed. McTell did not care enough to take the man to task for his laziness, as long as the grounds remained in tolerable condition.

Then a husky masculine laugh split the air, and he swiveled so fast a muscle burned in his neck. He hesitated, then stepped quietly out onto the deck.

Skip was stretched out on a lounge chair beside the pool below, wearing only a brief racing-style swimsuit. Blond hairs glinted against the deep tan of his well-formed legs and chest. One hand held the ever-present Tanqueray; the other was gesturing in the direction of the Côte d'Azur. Alysse stood an arm's length away, dressed in the white print frock she had worn the day McTell had first seen her in the village. Both her hands were clasped around a fresh drink. She seemed poised on the edge of flight, but at the same time, her expression was one of frank admiration and amusement. Skip continued speaking, hand waving airily; the words were indistinct, but the accent was crisp, sophisticated. Alysse burst into laughter; Skip's well-polished chuckle joined in. When he exchanged his drink for the fresh one, his hand lingered on hers. Her face went shy, but there was a peculiar tinge to the look—dark, speculative. She said something timidly, laughed again, and backed away, followed by the empty mirth Skip so clearly summoned at will.

McTell walked inside and leaned against a wall, resting his cheek against the cool plaster. Spots danced before his eyes, as if he had stood up too quickly. His pulse was thumping like a locomotive pulling up a hill—slowly, steadily, and very hard. He imagined himself taking the girl by her shoulders, shaking her, shouting:

"Can't you see through him? He's a pretty wrapper with nothing inside."

But of course, she could not. Besides good looks, he possessed money, sophistication, and a confident patronizing air easy to mistake for importance. She was a teenager who had spent her entire short and impoverished life in this tiny feudal village.

He closed the study door behind him and poured a stiff drink. It was only a flirtation, he told himself; he was blowing up over nothing. Skip was playing his usual sort of game.

Or did this anger really stem from the answering look he had seen in Alysse's eyes?

There was no point in even pretending to go back to work. As he returned the grimoire to its copper cask, his glance fell on the strange cover design. He paused, staring. Slowly, he raised his left palm. The caul-like mark was a dark angry red, its outline at last clearly visible.

The two were identical.

McTell laid his palm on the cover and turned his gaze to the window. The ruin glowed in the sunlight like a rough jewel.

There had been no sign of Pepin, and dinner was strained; but Mona seemed subdued, even contrite. After the meal she and Linden cleared the table, while Skip fiddled with the television, maintaining a position close to the bar. McTell stayed in the background and watched for his chance. It came when Bertie stepped into the garden for his evening stroll, examining the flowers with a knowledgeable eye McTell quickly poured two snifters of brandy and joined him.

Bertie accepted the brandy with a gracious inclination of his head. He was wearing a dinner jacket, black tie, and ruffled shirt.

"I'm quite envious of your marigolds," he said.

"I'm afraid we're not very horticulturally inclined." McTell said. "There's a gardener, but I suspect he spends most of his time napping with a bottle of *vin rouge*."

"Shouldn't be surprised. By the way, couldn't help witnessing your little contretemps with Lady Mona yesterday. You have my condolences. I've been on the wrong end of that sort of thing with her myself."

McTell shrugged. "To tell the truth, I let her go in one ear and out the other."

"Best way to handle it, of course. Afraid I have to kowtow a bit more. Professional relationship, all that. Odd about the dog."

"He acted like he'd gone crazy. I'm just glad he didn't break my skin; I can't help but wonder about rabies."

"Possible. They only got him a few weeks ago, and kennels are regular breeding grounds for disease. Perhaps he'll turn up yet, and we can have him quarantined." Bertie glanced around, then, added in a lower voice, "Actually, I'd be a damned liar if I said I'll miss the little cur. I was against it from the start."

McTell smiled and raised his glass.

Nightfall was near. The songs of crickets and nightingales were rising. By unspoken consent, both men faced the vista of mountains to the south, dominated by the dark silhouette of the fortress.

"That business you were talking about the other day," McTell said suddenly, as if it had just come to mind. "Did you ever run across anything like a grimoire?"

"Once or twice. At least, books that were purported to be copies of the real thing."

"I happened upon one in the Bibliothèque Nationale not long ago, doing some research. I suppose it's on my mind because of the ruin there. You heard about the story the priest told us."

"Yes, Linden was regaling us with it on the drive yesterday."

"This book," McTell said, "had a very odd design on its cover. I've never seen anything like it." He took a pen and pad from his coat pocket and made a quick sketch.

Bertie held it up to catch the remaining light.

185

"Can't place it exactly," he said, "but it reminds me of the sorts of symbols you find in old works on alchemy and demonology. Those fellows had the demons all catalogued, you know, as if they were some sort of nobility: hierarchy of rank, attributes, even coats of arms. This could be one of those."

"Like Belial's?"

For the first time, Bertie turned to look at him.

"Maybe. Why him in particular?"

"Oh, I suppose I made the connection with something the priest mentioned," McTell said hastlly. "It seems that some of the Templars were accused of worshipping him."

"Yes," Bertie said after a moment. "I suppose they were." He turned away, taking out a silver case and opening it to expose a row of black cigarettes with gold filters. "Smoke?" McTell shook his head. Bertie's lighter flared in the dusk, illuminating his hollow cheeks and high bony forehead.

"I only glanced through it," McTell said. "What intrigued me were a number of references to a pilgrim. Very cryptic, though—no explanation of any sort. Does that ring any bells?"

Bertie dragged on the cigarette, exhaling a delicate cloud.

"Not specifically. But the obvious correlation would be with the adept who was using the book—making the metaphorical journey to, say, the philosopher's stone."

Behind them the door opened and closed. McTell's mouth tightened in annoyance.

"As I say," Bertie went on, "I really don't know much about the occult; just some dabblings. But I do know that it can be very dangerous, for a number of reasons, on a number of levels." He glanced at McTell again.

"Personally, I think that's all a bunch of crap," Skip drawled, coming up behind them. "People who think they're dealing with spooks are just digging up their own insanity. My wife, for instance. Now that she's upset about Pepin, there's no stopping her. She claims she's been having nightmares—one last night about soldiers in armor, impaling people on sword points. And one of the victims had Linden's face."

"I suppose," McTell said slowly, "that Freud would have had a ball with that."

"PMS, probably." Skip said. "Or those stories Linden's been telling. How about you, my lord? How've you been sleeping."

"Alone," Bertie said primly. Skip laughed, the husky chuckle that, briefly but vividly, brought to McTell's mind the image of his hand touching Alysse's. He smiled tightly and sipped his drink. The hum of crickets rose like an unseen orchestra tuning up. Moths battered themselves against the lighted windows with tiny fluttering sounds.

"I missed our little cook tonight," Skip said. "She's taking over for a sick aunt?"

Careful to keep his voice cool, McTell said, "Yes. Mademoiselle should be back any day."

"She's an orphan, I understand? No other family?."

McTell turned to him. "That's right. Why?"

"Just thinking that must be a tough way to grow up."

Bertie cleared his throat and murmured, "If you gentlemen will excuse me." He went back into the house.

Skip was staring thoughtfully toward the mountains, stroking his mustache. Then he said:

"Come on inside. I've got something that might interest you."

McTell doubted it. For another minute he remained, thinking about Bertie's words: *the adept who was using the book—making the metaphorical journey to, say, the philosopher's stone.*

In the light of the doorway, he stopped to examine his palm, making sure the makeup of Linden's he had smeared across it was not wearing off.

From the inside pocket of his sport coat, Skip took a leather case about the size of a pack of playing cards. One half held a mirror; the other, lined with velvet, had precisely fitted spaces for a small vial, a silver knife, and a slender glass tube. He spread the apparatus on the coffee table.

"A special treat to cheer us all up," he said, "in memory of our dear departed Pepin." Mona, sitting beside him on the couch with crossed legs and folded arms, rolled her eyes. They held an unreadable look, and flicked from time to time at McTell. She had been drinking more than usual.

Deftly, Skip's long tanned fingers tapped a sizable amount of white powder from the vial onto the mirror. With the knife he chopped and worked it, forming it into lines, then scooping them together and starting over. It was like a shell game, almost hypnotic—which, McTell supposed, was the point. Everything about the man was smooth. He wheeled, and walked to the sliding door. The nearly full moon was rising, lighting the sky, turning the slope of Montsévrain into a sea of sharp black shadows. From behind him came Skip's voice: "Ladies first"; then the sounds of long, shuddering inhalations.

"Very good, Linden." Skip's voice was faintly mocking. "You must have been practicing. My lord?" McTell watched Bertie reflected in the glass, stalking across the room stiffly for another crumb from the rich man's table.

"Come along, John," Skip said.

"I think I'll pass," he said, turning away.

"Ever tried it?"

He shook his head.

"Come on," Mona said. "It'll shake some of the lead out of your ass."

"Great stuff," Skip agreed. "Uncut Peruvian flake. We bought an ounce of it in London, and my darling wife got it through customs in a way that only a true woman of the world could."

"Really, Skip," she murmured, but did not look displeased.

"But I have to warn you, it makes you awfully randy, The ladies especially. If you won't try it, I might just have to take care of things myself tonight."

"Threat or promise, sweetie?" Mona said. "We both passed puberty long ago, remember." She rose, pulled a record from the shelf, and flipped up the cover on the turntable. Skip's eyes followed her, narrowing for just a second before the smooth look returned. The opening strains of a Charlie Parker cut jumped into the room like another presence. McTell liked the music, but it was too loud, discording annoyingly with his mood. After a moment, Bertie moved discreetly over to turn it down. McTell realized that he was appreciating the man more; dependent on Skip's charity and sexually out of his element, he was dignified, perceptive, knowledgeable.

As if reading his thoughts, Bertie turned to him.

"I've been thinking, old boy, about this occult business you seem to have on your mind. Remembered a story, an incident that happened to me long ago. Might give you something to chew on."

"I'm all ears," McTell said, trying to sound amused.

"I was just on the fringes of that sort of thing, you understand," Bertie began. "This must be more than thirty years ago now. There were a number of self-styled witches and occultists running around in those days. A Welshman with a wandering eye, I recall, who claimed to be a warlock; a widow who gave séances; that sort of thing." He took a cigarette from his case. As he replaced it, McTell noticed that the dinner jacket was shiny at the elbows.

"A man I knew in London arranged a little gathering featuring a so-called swami from India. You know, one of those chaps with the turban and caste mark on the forehead. Flowing robes, all that. You see them and think, nothing but a sideshow fraud.

"Well, this fellow was of a different stamp. I felt the minute he walked into the room that he was an evil man. You could see it in his eyes, sense it around him like an aura. When he spoke, there was a greasy, ingratiating quality about it—as if his voice was somehow trying to

190

creep its way inside you, to get control. Difficult to explain, but thoroughly unpleasant, take my word for it.

"Our host was a fellow named Parkins, I recall—sort of a silly, nervous type, always looking for some thrill or other. He was well-to-do, and had paid this swami to put on this show, you understand. Well, the swami came in and announced that he was going to summon a spirit. He arranged his apparatus on a table, some sort of wand, candles, various other gewgaws, and then spread a cloth on the floor. It had a circle embroidered on it, with various sorts of designs inside; I remember thinking that it must be a sort of Eastern version of a pentacle. He stood inside that circle and told us it would protect him from the spirit. The rest of us would be all right, he said, since we weren't dealing with it—as long as we didn't speak. If someone said a word, the spirit would turn on that person. Of course, we were all skeptical about the whole thing—jocular, even. I, at least, didn't take the warning seriously.

"The swami had Parkins turn out the lights, and lit the candles, and began to go through his mumbo jumbo, waving the wand, speaking some incomprehensible rot. We remained quietly jovial, thinking this was going to be your run-of-the-mill séance, that pretty soon the table would start thumping or something like that.

"Then it started to change,"

Bertie dragged on his cigarette. His forehead was creased. McTell realized the others had gone silent and were listening too.

"The temperature began to drop. In a couple of minutes it was very cold, a clammy, nasty sort of chill. At the

191

same time, the air started thickening. I don't really know how to describe it. There was an incredible sense of menace, as if this evil, insidious, terribly threatening presence were literally materializing in the room. I tell you, old man, never in my life have I experienced a sense of pure terror like that. Not fear for your body, or even of death. It's fear for whatever it is that makes you *you*—for the essence of your being. If you haven't experienced it, I don't think you can imagine it. The thing is, there's absolutely nothing you can do—you can't fight it and you can't hide."

Bertie glanced searchingly at McTell. He shook his head, not sure himself what he meant.

"It reached the point where it was really unbearable. I know I was on the edge of panic. The sense that at my second this thing was going to appear and—I don't know—tear one's soul right out of the body.

"At last Parkins leaped to his feet and screamed, 'Stop it, stop it this instant!'

"All that energy turned like *that*"—Bertie snapped his fingers—"into a sense of fury, of rage. Then it was gone. Poor old Parkins was pale and shaking—I imagine we all were—and the swami was absolutely livid. I remember distinctly that in the midst of the confusion, he pointed at Parkins and said something I couldn't hear, very rapid, very low, and then made some kind of sign with his hands. Then he gathered up his things and hurried off. Parkins was in quite a sweat, as you may imagine, and tried to stop him, but the swami refused to even look at him. I know Parkins tried to find him afterward."

"So Parkins was all right after all," McTell said.

"For a while, old man, for a while. We laughed it off with him, told him the whole thing was obviously a fraud–some sort of trick played by the swami to collect his money and get out before he had to deliver. There were some jokes about getting demon-proof locks for the doors, that sort of thing. We all went home, the days passed, the memory faded. At least, it did for the rest of us.

"I didn't know Parkins well, but from what I gleaned afterward, things got rather worse for him. He had a growing sense of being watched and followed by something he couldn't see. In a few weeks the poor man was a wreck. Couldn't sleep, couldn't bear to be alone for an instant. He searched desperately for the swami–ads in the papers, rewards offered, even went so far as to hire a detective–but the man had vanished."

McTell glanced at the other faces. Linden was watching with her mouth slightly open. Skip, as usual, looked bland and a little bored. Mona leaned against a wall, arms folded, unimpressed.

"So what happened to him?" she said.

Bertie exhaled a cloud of smoke.

"Fell off the roof of his own house. He'd been dining out, took a taxi to the door, went on inside, and apparently he kept right on going up the stairs, clambered out a window onto the roof, and fell. Or leaped. Three stories, head first. Turned out that his valet had snuck out for a pint, so Parkins was unexpectedly alone in the house. It seemed clear from the signs he left–doors flung open, some blood from his hand on the window latch–that he'd run up the stairs in a wild dash."

"As if he'd been running *from* something," Linden said.

"Precisely, my dear." Bertie shrugged. "Of course, the police tried to put it down to an intruder, but there were no signs of one. Then it was generally decided that Parkins was an impressionable sort, and the swami's threat had conjured up some imagined menace that finally drove him mad. Like they say voodoo works. It came out later that he'd gone to see his minister with the tale, and the minister suggested with some amusement that he try a therapist. That was enough to brand him as unstable as far as the police were concerned. Case was closed."

"How awful," Linden said. "That poor man"

"Yes," Bertie said, drawing out the word. For a moment no one spoke.

Then Skip said, "Just goes to show you." He sounded cheerful; his hand busily shaped more lines on the mirror. "Play with fire, you get burned, just like mama always said. By the way, what time are we leaving tomorrow?"

"That's an all-inclusive 'we,' John," Linden said.

McTell glanced up. His imagination had been vividly at work on Bertie's story.

"Again, please?"

"We're going to Nice, and you're coming with us. We took a vote and decided we're not going to let you be such a recluse."

Protest rose to his lips, but Skip said, "Now come on, John. I've been doing all the squiring and Linden all the chauffeuring. Be a sport."

"And Bert can go off to the sailor bars without leaving Lin third wheel," Mona said. Her gaze was bold and cool. Bertie smiled tightly and moved off toward the liquor cabinet.

McTell shrugged. "I'll bow to popular opinion."

Skip applauded ironically, then held up the glass tube and said, "Next round."

As the others gathered at the table, McTell walked quietly out onto the patio. Elbows on the railing, snifter in hand, he gazed out into the balmy Mediterranean evening. Can't fight it and you can't hide, he thought sardonically.

When the sliding door opened behind him, he did not turn. The footsteps were soft—the slap of sandals—and a little unsteady.

"I want to apologize for jumping on you yesterday," Mona said. She leaned a hip against the railing and settled on her elbow, facing him. Her head was tilted so her hair hung in a cloud.

"Forget it," he said wearily.

"I've been having bad dreams, not sleeping well. I think that's what's got me on edge."

He sipped his brandy, gazing straight ahead.

"Okay, then, I'm just a silly bitch."

McTell exhaled. "Mona—"

She pushed away from the railing, standing straight; her voice was harsher now, almost shrill.

"Professor John McTell, the great brain trust, patting the dumb blonde on the ass and waiting for her to go away. Christ, I'm not so stupid I can't see that."

"Maybe," he said, "you ought to take it a little easier on the booze."

She drank defiantly, her gaze not leaving his face.

"Bet I know something the professor doesn't. Something about that little twat of a maid you're so sweet on."

He swiveled, and triumph gleamed in her eyes.

"Not that stupid," she said again. "Not blind either. Unlike my dear sister. I see the way you look at that girl, just like I saw the way you looked at my dog–and the way you look at me. You may be a genius; professor, but you don't know shit about hiding things."

Gazes locked, they measured each other.

"What is it you know?" he said quietly.

Mona laughed, a throaty drunken sound. Her lips glistened with liquor.

"I know what's going to happen to her tomorrow."

"And what," McTell said with strained control, "might that be?"

"What's it worth to you?" she taunted.

He said nothing, but held her gaze, forcing her with his will. Her smile faded, and then softly, almost sadly, she said:

"What happens to all little girls. She's gonna get fucked."

McTell's breath stopped.

She laughed again, a brittle humorless sound.

"This trip to Nice? Guess whose idea it was. How about the guy who's going to beg off sick at the last minute and stay home. Alone with her. All day."

He said, "Skip."

She nodded, and he realized distantly that the darkness in her eyes was pain.

"It's all he cares about any more, young girls."

"Skip," McTell said, "is going to stay home tomorrow and rape Alysse?"

"Honey, you *are* naive. She's probably been fucking since she was twelve, and doing it for money since she was fifteen. She's a chambermaid, not a princess. Besides, when a rich man screws the help in this kind of place, it's not called rape. Especially when she doesn't have any father or brothers."

Skip's voice echoed in his mind, cool, disinterested: *She's an orphan, I understand? No other family?*

"And you," McTell said in disbelief, "aren't going to do anything about it?"

Her mouth twisted bitterly. "Why should I?" Then, softly, "Haven't you ever heard of an understanding?" Her fingers moved to the top button, of her blouse. "Sauce for the goose, honey. Grow up." She undid the button, then the next. "Let's take a swim," she said.

McTell stared at her. She was smiling again.

"What's wrong with that? They can join us if they want." Her blouse was open to the waist, and her hand moved inside, caressing one breast. Behind her the pool was a black pit, the moon's reflection like a shimmering streak on its surface.

But all McTell saw was a slow-motion kaleidoscope of Skip and Alysse, writhing in a tangle of limbs.

"I have to check on something," he said thickly, and stepped back, stumbling a little.

Her smile remained, but her eyes were hard.

"They're going to go out for a drink," she whispered. "Stay here with me."

As he reached the door, her voice followed, soft and mocking:

"If you're worried about your little girl, believe me, there's nothing a few hundred francs won't fix. It could be a sweet deal for you, too, after Skip breaks the ice. They say the French invented the blow job, darling." She paused, then added, "Just remember, my French is pretty good too."

He closed the door, shutting out the sound of her low laughter.

As he crossed the room to the stairs, Linden said:

"So, did you two kiss and make up?" The three of them were grouped around the coffee table; her eyes were bright from the cocaine, her smile almost frantic. Skip gazed at McTell, bland, sly—smirking with secret knowledge.

McTell stared back. "Yes," he said.

"Good," said Skip. "Then why don't we all shoot into town for a drink? We're feeling antsy."

"I just remembered a mistake I may have made," McTell said, "in my book."

He climbed the stairs, fist clenched against the deep powerful thrill in his palm that coursed to his shoulder with each beat of his heart.

Slowly, he crouched and opened the bottom drawer of the desk. Willing his hands to steadiness, he opened the book.

There were now not two, but three, lines of writing.

He counted his steps as he walked to the Scotch decanter, concentrating on every movement: lifting out the cut-glass stopper, taking a leather-covered tumbler from the shelf, pouring. He drank, paused to breathe, drank the rest. Then he turned back to the book.

The line read: *Solitudo auri viatori pacem tribuit.*

The golden one's solitude brings peace to the pilgrim.

He wheeled and walked to the window, staring out at the silhouetted ruin.

The obvious correlation would be with the adept who was using the book—making the metaphorical journey to, say, the philosopher's stone.

But another voice was speaking in his mind, a faint prudish whisper in the words of the priest Boudrie:

If any of it were true, it would point to the existence of forces we can hardly imagine. The consequences of tampering with them would be beyond comprehension.

McTell raised his hand before his face and gazed at the mark, half-covered by the fading smear of makeup. How long would his heroes, those men of iron decision and action, have hesitated? Of all the human beings who had ever dreamed of such an ability, how many had actually stood on this brink?

For a length of time he could not measure, he stayed rock-still while the two voices warred within him. When his mind finally cleared, he looked blankly around the room, as if it were a place he had never seen before. Then he put away the grimoire and walked downstairs.

The others were standing, waiting. Mona had come back in, and was off a little to one side.

"How about it?" Skip said. "Up for a drink?"

"I'm going to stay," Mona said. "The coke's giving me a headache." Her gaze met McTell's.

He smiled back at her regretfully.

"Since I'm the only one who hasn't been indulging," he said, "I suppose I'd better drive." Her mouth turned down into a pout. He shrugged imperceptibly–what could he do?–and with his own eyes said, Soon.

"Did you fix your mistake, darling?" Linden said as they walked to the car.

"No mistake," McTell said. "Everything was fine."

TEN

Mona walked back into the empty living room and stood sulkily in its center. The gambit had not worked; now she was stuck here, alone. Her head was spinning with alcohol, cocaine, and a welter of emotions that refused to sort themselves out.

She had never met a man who could make her feel so utterly inadequate. The worst of it was, he so obviously did it without trying. But in spite of that—or because of it—he was damned attractive, and all her instincts urged her in the same direction: Get hold of his cock, show him what she could do with it, and things would quickly change. Some part of her wanted his respect, or at least attention, any way she could get it; another, to draw him out in that most vulnerable way and then crush him, the way she had so often felt crushed by him; and still another, to prove to her brainy, condescending, cold-fish sister what the essentials of being a woman were really all about. Especially since her outburst over the dog, Linden had been treating her like a child—as if Mona had dared to trouble an Olympian.

But in fifteen minutes alone with him, she thought grimly, she could ruin him for Linden forever.

There was also the fact that Skip had not touched her in months, and in spite of their understanding, neither had anyone else. Her mouth twisted at the thought of Alysse. The girl made even her feel old, and she had lied to McTell: Alysse was a virgin if ever she had seen one.

She folded her arms and began to pace. She had tried to stop it at first, of course, this fixation of Skip's; but it became clear that the alternative was divorce, and she could not bear the thought of being alone. Besides, it would not exactly be rape—call it high-pressure seduction—and Skip would be more than generous in smoothing things over afterward. Offered more money than she could hope to make in months, even a year, the girl was sure to accept, and that would be the end of that. Anyway, it was bound to happen to Alysse sooner or later, that loss of innocence, just as it had happened to Mona at the age of thirteen. An eighteen-year-old neighbor home from college; a summer of furtive passion, playing games on hot afternoons in the empty rooms of her family's rambling summer house; and at the end, an abortion, and never seeing him again. A vague, distant regret touched her, a pang for another way it might have been, another person she might have become. She shook it off and finished her drink.

Well, this business with McTell was not over yet. She had seen the look in his eyes as he was leaving. He was thinking about it, and one thing she knew: When a man got to that point, it did not take much—a few well-placed touches—to push him over the edge. She could waylay him when he came home; Skip would undoubtedly stumble drunkenly to bed, and Linden was too naive to wait up and chaperone. A whispery voice in Mona's mind clucked its tongue, reminding her that McTell was, after all, her sister's husband. She shrugged petulantly, said "half-sister" aloud, and walked to the bar. Her head really was beginning to ache. She poured another drink, inhaled another line of cocaine, paced the room. The jazz on the stero was suddenly irritating. She went to turn it off.

As she walked back, she saw that the television was on. She frowned; it was odd that she had not noticed it, but then, no sound was coming out. The picture on the screen seemed to be an old black-and-white movie, a horror film from the looks of it. The scene was a nighttime landscape, lit by a nearly full moon; on a mountaintop in the background was a silhouetted ruin that looked vaguely familiar. Nothing was moving; either the shot was still or, in typical French fashion, something had gone wrong with the transmission. Yes, now there were words across the screen, an apology about technical difficulties, no doubt. But they were written in an odd Gothic script. She bent close, making them out as: *Qui est celui qui vient?*

"Who is this one that comes?" she said. The sound of her voice made her suddenly conscious of the silence around her, of her aloneness.

And now there did seem to be a shape moving on the screen—small, dark, barely visible, scuttling through the brush high on the mountainside. There was something about the way it moved that she did not like at all, even on film. Abruptly, the dreams that had been haunting her nights flickered swiftly through her mind. She straightened up uneasily and reached for the on-off button. When she touched it, she received a tiny shock, the way she might from a wall switch when in stocking feet.

But the set was already off.

She looked quickly back at the screen. The picture was gone.

Some sort of satellite ghost, then, creating static electricity. Who knew what they were doing these days with all the different kinds of waves? She laughed nervously, and went again to the bar to freshen her drink, ignoring the ever-weaker voice that warned her to quit. The lines of cocaine waiting on the mirror were irresistible. She prowled the room aimlessly, examining coffee table books, toying with a backgammon board, flicking through the record collection. Dancing couples in smoke-filled rooms intertwined on the album covers. A stunning black woman, her nude body adroitly shadowed by the photographer, appealed with gazelle-like eyes to a silhouetted clarinet player. The image brought a powerful charge of pure raw lust: the ache for a man who would not just fall into bed with a mumbled good-night, but hold her, talk to her, *fuck* her. She thought again of McTell by the pool, and how close they had been. Wet, slippery bodies brushing in the dark water. Secret touches, whispers, quick and sudden heat, the urgency in the fear of being discovered . . .

She stepped out into the sultry night. The water in the pool lapped faintly against the sides—a sexual, seductive sound. She kicked off a sandal and dipped her foot. It was blood warm.

In a few seconds her clothes lay on the deck. She stood posed in the icy, silvery moonlight, breasts thrust forward–filled with the awareness of her own sensuality. Not McTell, not any man, could resist her like this. A sudden breeze sent a rush of cooler air against her skin, stiffening her nipples. She gripped her hair, twisted it into a knot atop her head, and with slow steps descended into the pool. The water slid tantalizingly up her thighs. She pushed off, glided silently, dreamily into the night.

Then, from far away, came a faint haunting whistle.

She twisted to face it; it was like nothing she had ever heard–soft, piercing, infinitely mournful. Her gaze moved over a barren knoll perhaps a hundred yards away.

A figure stood on it.

She sucked in her breath. Her movement splashed water in her eyes; she shook her head to clear them.

The figure was gone.

She continued to stare, treading water. Moonlight fell full upon the bare knoll. Where could he have gone? The impression had been so clear: a big, tall man, legs braced wide apart, both hands clasped upon some sort of staff.

Her breath was coming quick and shallow. The water was no longer welcoming, but chilly, black, caressing her obscenely. She paddled hurriedly to the edge, pulled herself out. The rising wind gave her goose bumps, lifted the fine hairs on her arms. Clothes clutched to her breasts, she hurried inside, locking the door. But there were other doors, several, that were never locked—in her confusion she could not even remember them all. She started for the main one, but the hallway was suddenly endless and dark, the whole house vast and empty.

She stood still, calming the pounding of her heart. Well, what if it had been a man? He would probably not even have seen her, and in any case, there was no violence around here. Someone taking a shortcut home, or at worst, a poacher. She started for the stairs; she was cold and wanted a big fluffy towel. Abruptly she paused, swallowing hard at the image that had leaped into her mind, the television screen with its Gothic script:

Qui est celui qui vient?

A gust of wind rustled the shrubbery outside. She climbed on, bare feet making only a whisper on the thick carpet. Moonlight streamed through the octagonal panes of the French doors opening onto the second-story deck. From there she would be able to see the knoll again. Slowly, reluctantly, she moved toward the doors. Leaving them open, she stepped out into the wind. It blew her hair, tossed the dark treetops.

Who is this one that comes?

Timidly, she gripped the iron railing and peered around the building's corner.

Her mouth opened in an O. The man was back.

The moonlight glinted off the stick he leaned on—not a stick, but a *sword* as tall as his chest. He seemed to be wearing armor and a headdress of mail. His stance held an indescribable menace. Wind wrapped around her body suddenly like grasping fingers. Something clicked behind her. She whirled. The doors had blown closed.

She spun back. The man's head was turned to the side, strong profile clearly silhouetted. He was watching something. Dazed, she turned her gaze to follow his.

A choked cry broke from her lips.

The shape was squat and dark, moving with impossible speed—not directly toward her, but in a zigzag, as if following a spoor. It appeared briefly in a clearing, became a rapid blurred ink spot against the foliage, appeared again. At the sound of her cry it stopped instantly and straightened up. She choked off her breath in her throat. It stood waist-high, wrapped in some sort of hooded cloak. For seconds it cast its small head about, like a weasel sniffing the wind, stubby arms held rigid before it; and at last came the distant understanding of what the television had been showing her.

Then a shriek tore through her mind, soundless, awful, the cry of an unappeasable thirst to destroy. It echoed and swelled within her, blackening the world around until all fell away and she was plunging into a vast plain of fire. Shapes—thousands, billions—rose from the flames, reaching for her, joining the creature's scream until it was bursting her skull.

When it stopped, both her hands were clutching the sides of her face, nails digging into the flesh. Her clothes lay forgotten at her feet. The dark shape was crouched again in its rapid gliding search, moving steadily closer to the house. From a great distance she heard a gurgling sound and realized dimly that it was coming from her: the insane, overwhelming need to scream, barely held in check by the remaining thread of rationality that warned silence.

She ran to the doors, yanked the handles. They would not budge. She pounded, pulled, slammed herself against them, and at last threw back her head and screamed. The sound was answered inside her mind, echoed and amplified a thousand times. The doors gave way suddenly, with a rush of wind that jeered and gibbered in nightmare tongues, clutching at her hair and skin. She stumbled through, fell against the wall, raced down the hall to the stairway. Gripping the newel post, she swung herself around.

The lights went out.

In the blackness, she clung to the balustrade, straining to listen over her ragged breath, her hammering pulse. Something was rustling the bushes outside. There came a heavy thump against glass.

A dark shape was moving outside the sliding door. Hope glimmered—she had locked it—but as if reading her thoughts, the shape disappeared in the direction of the front of the house.

Her knees gave out.

The thought, *I must run,* repeated itself again and again in her mind with childlike simplicity. Kneeling, swaying, holding the balustrade tightly with both hands, she tried to make her legs move. They refused. From a distant part of the house, she heard another stealthy thump. Hinges creaked. Wind blew across the darkened living room below, scattering papers.

She began to slide backward: a push, a pause to draw her legs up, a push. There was another sound under the wind now, a sort of slithering. Mouth working silently, she slid and paused, slid and paused, until her back was against the wall. The sound changed tone as it shifted from tiles to the carpeted stairs. A thick, dark shadow was creeping up, coming slowly into view.

The last sound she heard before losing consciousness was the sort of noise a snake might make if it could whimper with anticipation.

The house was dark, the front door wide open.

"What the hell," Skip said, gripping the car seat to lean forward. McTell cut the engine and strode across the drive. The uneasiness that had been mounting in him rose to fill his throat. Eyes wide with the strain of piercing the darkness, he groped for the light switch and flicked it back and forth. Nothing. A lighter flared in the center of the living room. It was Bertie, his face looking ghostly and disembodied, tense with fear.

"John!" Linden called sharply. The sound made him whirl. She stood in the hall doorway, hands on hips, face stern. Skip was behind her, looking over her shoulder. "What in the world is going on here?" she demanded. "What's wrong with the lights?" And then, the question that had been hovering just below the surface of McTell's consciousness, that he had not dared let rise: "Where's Mona?"

He walked to the stairway. "Mona?" he called, hearing the strain in his own voice. "Are you up there?"

Not a sound issued from the inky darkness upstairs. Like a man climbing to the guillotine, choked with dread, he started up, Bertie following with the lighter.

He was first to see her shape: back against the wall, slumped and spread-legged like an abandoned doll.

209

He closed his eyes, certain that she was dead.

The doctor was named Devarre, a wiry, clean-shaven man of about fifty, with veined forearms beneath rolled-up sleeves. Moving quickly without seeming to hurry, he examined Mona's pupils, listened to her heart, took her blood pressure. She was not outwardly harmed, but nothing they had been able to do could make her regain consciousness. Skip had picked her up and taken her to bed; Bertie had ventured with a flashlight into the pantry and discovered the blown fuse. While they waited for Devarre, Skip continually wet her lips with brandy. Bertie paced-sternfaced, silent–going frequently to look out the window. Linden stalked from the phone to the room and back, chain-smoking. Twice, McTell caught Bertie looking at him with narrowed eyes.

It was Bertie who had discovered her clothes, scattered by the wind across the balcony.

Devarre unhooked his stethoscope from his ears, reached into his bag, and popped an ampule under her nose. She sputtered and shook her head feebly. For the first time, her eyes blinked. Hope leaped in McTell. He leaned forward intently, gripping the foot of the bedstead.

"How do you call yourself, madame?" Devarre said in quiet, clear French.

The world hung still for McTell. When the word "Mona?" broke wonderingly from her lips, he could have wept with relief.

Devarre asked her several more simple questions, receiving one-word answers in the same dazed tone.

Then he motioned them out into the hallway. His English was heavily accented but fluent.

"It appears this lady has sustained a great shock." he said, looking from one to the other. His professional manner did not quite conceal the curiosity in his eyes. "It is rare to see such a thing with no sign of physical injury. Have you no idea what could have caused it?"

"We were gone:" McTell said. "We found her like this. But the front door was open, and the lights had gone out—a fuse blew out. Maybe an intruder"—he glanced at Bertie and finished lamely—"of some sort."

"Such a thing is also rare around here," Devarre murmured. "There were other signs of a breaking in?"

McTell hesitated, then said, "No."

"She recently lost a pet, a dog, that she was very attached to," Linden offered. She rummaged nervously in her purse for a cigarette.

"*Eh bien*," Devarre said, closing his bag with a snap. "A lady so—how do you say? Strung highly?—who can suffer such a blow over the loss of a pet or a failure of electricity—a night of two of rest and observation would do her no harm. I will call for you the hospital in Grasse. You can take her yourself? Or shall I ask for an ambulance."

"We'll take her," Skip said.

Devarre nodded. "You will forgive me one more question. Is it possible that she had taken drugs? Barbiturates, perhaps, mixed with alcohol?" No one answered. With the doctor on the way, Linden had hurried to hide the cocaine.

211

Devarre shrugged. "They will give her tests at the hospital. She is in no immediate danger." He glanced around at them, eyes keen. "You must understand that I do not ask merely out of curiosity, and that such information would not go outside my profession. It's just that I could perhaps speed things." Again, a slightly shame-faced silence greeted his pause.

"I don't think that's the problem." McTell finally said.

To his relief, Skip agreed. "I'm not saying we've never done a little recreating," he said, not quite meeting Devarre's eyes. "But certainly not nearly enough to bring on something like this."

Devarre nodded. "You will show me the telephone, madame?" He shook hands quickly with the men, a Gallic, fingers-only clasp. As he followed Linden down the hall, he paused once more.

"Mademoiselle Alysse is in your employ, is she not, monsieur?"

"Yes," McTell said warily.

"A lovely girl. It is a sad thing about her aunt's illness. We can only hope she will recover soon." He bowed slightly. "*Bonsoir,* messieurs," he said, and continued down the stairs, leaving McTell certain that the doctor had meant more than he had said.

He turned back to the bedroom. To his amazement, Bertie moved swiftly to block him, swinging the door shut behind. He stood before McTell with an ugly, danger-ous-looking mixture of fear and fury on his big bony face. Uncertainly, McTell stopped.

"I thought I'd help pack," he said.

"Don't come another step." Bertie's voice was low and tense. His fear communicated itself like a hot wave crawling over McTell's skin.

"I don't know what the hell went on here," Bertie said between his teeth, "and I don't know what you have to do with it, but something is very wrong around this place, and I think you know what it is."

Eyes locked, they stood, and McTell felt something come unveiled in his face.

"I think you do," Bertie whispered. He backed into the room and closed the door hard.

Suddenly so weary he sagged, McTell walked downstairs. Linden came from the hall into the living room, and seemed startled at his appearance.

"Buck up," she said. "We have to drive her to the hospital."

"Bertie's gone over the edge, too," McTell said. He held out his hand to stop the question forming on her lips. His own voice sounded blurred and far away. "Go with them if you want, take our car. I've had enough of them."

He climbed heavily back up the stairs, closed the door of his study, and dropped into his chair. Long after Mona had been helped downstairs, after Linden had said an uncertain good-night and promised to call in the morning, after the car tires had crunched on the gravel of the drive; when at last the blessed relief of silence—of peace—had descended, he sat gazing out the window at the moonlit ruin.

ELEVEN

"A word with you, monsieur, if you please."

Startled, McTell turned to find Riboux, the gardener, standing in the driveway, twisting his greasy beret in his hands. His tiny mustache and button face gave him an almost comic appearance. But there was nothing comic about the look in his eyes; it made McTell feel suddenly queasy.

He had not passed a good night.

"There is something I must show you," Riboux said. He spoke slowly with exaggerated enunciation, as if to an idiot. McTell glanced around. It was early; Linden had not yet called.

He turned back to Riboux. "After you," he said.

The gardener led him through the grounds and down the familiar path toward Montsévrain. Clouds had moved in during the predawn hours; the day promised to be the coolest yet. The foliage was alive with the hum of insects, as if they sensed the onset of autumn. Perhaps fifty yards from the house, Riboux pushed aside a sort of hedge that concealed the entrance to a smaller path, one McTell had

214

never noticed. His uneasiness rose. They walked another thirty yards.

Then, without speaking. Riboux stepped aside. Mc-Tell found himself looking into a lovely small glade.

Lovely except for the thing that hung at eye level on a tree at the far side: a bundle of white fur, pathetically small and still. A smell like a packing house thickened the air. He stepped closer, then quickly spun away.

The dog had not been hung, as he had first thought. It had been impaled through the abdomen, on a branch snapped off to a point.

And then practically turned inside out. Blackening entrails crawling with insects spilled to the ground.

Riboux was gazing at him steadily. "I had been in the habit of coming here to take my meals," he said.

McTell pointed weakly. "The dog escaped two days ago. We looked—"

"I do not think this is a joke, monsieur."

McTell stared at the man, not sure he had heard correctly.

"A *joke?* God knows it's not a joke. What could have done such a thing? A bear?"

"I do not think this is a joke," Riboux repeated. His gaze was stoic now, revealing nothing. "I will bury this dog." A spade was already leaning against a tree. With a jolt, McTell recognized it as the one he had used to drive the dog from the shed.

"And then, monsieur, as I had been meaning to tell you for some time"—Riboux paused, in the delicate complicity of two men sharing a face-saving lie—"I fear I must leave your employ to attend to my own affairs, which I have let suffer too long."

McTell nodded dumbly. At the edge of the glade, he paused and took a bill from his wallet. Riboux was digging grimly, a man who wanted an unpleasant job done.

"Perhaps it would be as well," McTell said, "for Madame Mona to believe that her pet was picked up on the highway and taken to a good home." Riboux said nothing. McTell tucked the folded bill into the bark of a tree.

He resolutely held the matter from his mind as he walked back to the house. There he sat on the patio steps. The pool gleamed dull blue-gray under the gathering clouds; the trees were turning the cheerful colors of early autumn; scurrying ants and shiny black beetles moved purposefully along the ground.

Now he knew what the shrieking had been. Woodenly, he stood and climbed the stairs to his study.

He stood holding the grimoire in his hands, remembering his initial repulsion to the feel of it. Now its weight was solid, familiar, even comforting. It was, after all, his—or at least more his than it had been anyone else's for several hundred years.

There could be no more doubt about the identity of the pilgrim.

And though he had spent the night in feeble attempts to rationalize, the sight of Pepin had removed that doubt, too. For an instant, he pictured Mona as the dog had been. His stomach threatened to heave.

However it had all come about, whatever force was at work, he could no longer trust the book—or was it himself he could not trust? He glanced uneasily at his palm. And despite the fact that it had somehow connected him with the most extraordinary experiences of his life, despite his overwhelming sense of being involved in a drama that demanded to play itself out, he would have to be satisfied with trying to piece together the puzzle from a safe time and distance.

But what to do with the grimoire? His scholar's mind refused to allow the thought of destroying it. He could send it to the Sorbonne or his own university; but if he attached an explanation of what had happened to him, he would be considered mad, and if he did not, there was no telling what new evils the book might give rise to in unwary hands. For minutes, McTell's tired mind sought the least unacceptable choice.

At last he thought of Boudrie. Whether the priest in truth represented a power that could contain whatever was working through the grimoire, whether there was anything to the whole business, McTell did not know. But he was certain Boudrie would be a sympathetic, even if skeptical, listener, and most important, he was close by. McTell replaced the grimoire in its cask and wrapped the cask in newspaper, while his mind edited a version of the story to tell. He would not mention his part in releasing Pepin—or his decision to abandon Mona. He was not yet sure about the mark on his hand. Uneasiness grew, and he moved more quickly.

Holding the parcel, he paused for a final glance at the ruin. In spite of everything, the book was hard to part with. It was, impossibly but undeniably, connected with magic; it had offered him an undreamed-of power; in some sense, it represented what he had craved all his life.

217

And he shrank from the inner voice that sneered at him for abandoning it, for fleeing back to his timid, risk-free existence, his ivy-covered world and bone-dry books and secondhand longing for the miraculous.

He turned away from the window and hurried to the stairs.

A small purse rested on the dining room table. He recognized it as Alysse's; no one had thought to try and contact her, tell her she would not be needed today. He stopped, listening for her in the kitchen, but the house was silent. His steps took him to a window.

She was in the garden, stooped, knees together, a wing of hair concealing the side of her face. For half a minute he watched her move slowly down the row, remembering the smirking look far back in Skip's eyes, Mona's mocking laughter.

"You'll never know," he said softly, "but I did it for you."

He was nearly to the door when the phone began its harsh antiquated buzzing. He hesitated, but Alysse probably would not hear it. He walked back down the hall.

"They're checking out of the hospital now," Linden said. "They're going to Cannes, to a hotel."

"She's better, then," McTell said with relief.

"Yes." Linden sounded dubious. "I'm going with them, just in case, and I'll probably spend the night. Skip's nearly useless, and Bertie left for Paris."

"A shame," McTell murmured.

Neither spoke for a moment. Then she said, "John, she told us a little about what happened. She's still not very coherent, and she doesn't want to think about it.

They've got her on some pretty heavy tranquilizers. But it sounded just dreadful. Some sort of creature stalking her."

"Creature," McTell said sharply. "Not a man?"

Another pause. "She says not. She says it wasn't an animal, either."

"That doesn't leave much," McTell said.

"John, she said it was some kind of—of demon, or something. I know how that sounds, but she was absolutely insistent."

Abruptly an image appeared in McTell's mind: the figure carved on the wall in the village church. It faded into Bertie's pale bony face, frightened and enraged.

I think you know what it is. I think you do.

He swallowed, then said, "Now, wait a minute. Let's not forget that she'd ingested a substantial amount of alcohol, cocaine, and who knows what else. Skip's a regular walking pharmacy."

"I know, I know all that. But what was it, then? Bertie took me aside as he was leaving. He said, 'If I were you I should never set foot in that house again, and I would see to it that Professor McTell joined you elsewhere, immediately.' That was the only thing he said to anybody all night. I got the feeling he didn't even want to be in the same part of the country."

"I'm starting to think," McTell said slowly, "that what we had were several incipient nervous breakdowns, and they all picked last night to happen."

"That's reaching a long way for coincidences."

"Darling, neurotics are acutely sensitive. When one starts to go, the others pick it up and work off it. None of

219

those people is exactly a model of stability. Good God, they don't do anything but hang around and claw at each other."

"Now *you* wait a minute." Her voice was heated. "Mona is my half-sister, I've known her all my life, and she may be a little high-strung, but she's never shown the slightest sign of mental instability. Skip's just plain too lazy to have a breakdown, it would be too much work. And Bertie's, well, a lord."

"Lord, my ass," McTell said angrily. "He's a faggot *poseur*."

"How did that fuse blow?"

"How the hell should I know? It's an old house, the lights are probably all on one circuit. Maybe Mona plugged in a hair dryer. And as long as we're talking about instability, what was she doing running around on the balcony naked as a newborn fawn?"

In the tense pause, he pictured her lighting a cigarette. Nervously, he flexed the muscles of his forearm. It seemed thicker, brawnier, than usual.

"Maybe," she finally said. "Anyway, here's the point. I'm not going to feel comfortable in that house again. We're going to have to pack the rest of Skip and Mona's things and send them on; they're certainly not coming back. I think we should just pack our own while we're at it, and move on."

Irrational resentment surged in him. "What about the lease?"

"The hell with the money. John, this is serious. I don't know what went on, and you're welcome to think

I'm getting hysterical too, but I simply don't want to stay there anymore."

The weight of the book under his arm seemed huge. He thought of Pepin. And slumped.

"Okay," he said.

"Good," she said, clearly relieved. "I hate to stick you with the packing, but Mona won't stay in the hospital any longer and absolutely refuses to be alone for a second."

"I'll do the best I can."

"Unless you'd rather come down and join us in Cannes. Then I could help you when we get back."

"Honey, to tell the truth, I'd just as soon take my chances with the spooks," he said wearily.

"All right. I don't blame you. I'll call you when we check in. The Carlton."

"I'm not going anywhere."

"*À bientôt, chéri,*" she said. "I miss you." The line crackled when she hung up.

He put down the phone and walked back into the living room. So not just the book but the house, too, was leaving his life. It was strange how attached he felt to this place, how much like home it had come to seem in the short time they had been here.

But she was right. When sufficient time had elapsed, he would tell her the whole of the story. And at some point years down the line, an edited version would make good entertainment for guests–stored on some distant shelf of memory, to be taken down and dusted off from time to time, with the familiar streamers of unfulfilled longings and what-ifs that would accompany him into old age.

The tingling flared in his palm.

McTell stopped.

What could be hurt by one last look–at the only real mystery he would ever encounter?

He hesitated. The priest's voice seemed to sound in his mind, urgent, warning.

He turned and strode to the stairs. In the study, his fingers fumbled to tear the cask from its wrappings and the book from the cask.

A new line of writing had appeared:

Nomina florum viatori amorem tribuunt.

The language of flowers brings love to the pilgrim.

He closed the book and walked slowly back down the hall. Standing at the top of the stairs, he watched Alysse enter the dining room with an armload of freshly cut flowers and spread them on the table: mauve and yellow roses, daffodils, marigolds, lavender, other blooms whose names he did not know. Still damp, they dripped onto the glossy finish. Her fingers glided over the array like a gentle bird, suddenly swooping to pick stems. She placed them carefully in a vase, arranging their heights, pausing after every few additions to survey the whole. Her eyes never lifted. For minutes he stared, until the only sound he heard was the faint, soft brushing of stems against petals.

She grasped the slender vase with both hands, leaned forward, and set it at the table's head. For the briefest of instants her gaze rose to touch his. Her eyes were dark, unreadable–empty. Then, like a moving doll that had been unplugged, she folded her hands, bowed her head, and stood motionless.

222

Sweat beaded his forehead, blurred his vision. A faint metallic burning had risen in the back of his throat. He closed his eyes, but her image remained before him, floating like the evening star.

When his hand touched her shoulder, her body went limp, falling into his arms. For minutes, he held her. Her hands, doubled into fists, clung to his shirt, her face buried between them on his chest. As in a dream, he touched her face and hair, felt the beating of her heart through her slender back, the surging of his own blood, the roar in his ears that drowned out every other sound.

At last he raised her face with his hands. She gazed up through half-closed eyes, eyes that he knew saw nothing; and the tiny dying voice inside cried at him to take her home.

When he bent, her eyes closed and her lips parted. Trembling, he touched them with his own, and then lifted her in his arms and carried her up the stairs.

Warm misty wind tore like fingers at Étien Boudrie's cassock as he hurried out of the Church of Our Lady of the Flowers in Grasse. He had been shriven, all right, but instead of feeling that he had laid down his burden of sin, he felt it had been beaten out of him. Capuchins, he thought uncharitably; the old monk on the other side of the confessional screen had possessed the bearing, and the compassion, of an agent of the Inquisition. From now on, Boudrie vowed, he would make an appointment with a priest he knew instead of just walking into a church that happened to be close to where he had parked.

The *mistral,* he thought, eyes searching the cloudy sky. It had been trying to come on for days now, and had at last succeeded; early this year, but not unwelcome–yet. Though he had had enough of summer, by March he would be craving the warm Midi sun. It was all part of God's plan, no doubt. As he turned the key in the 2CV's ignition, he uttered an automatic prayer. The engine churned into what passed with it for life. He sat for a moment, a little dazed, trying to remember where he had to go next. Ah yes, all his errands were done–he could go home, thank God. He wheeled the little car around and drove through the narrow hilly streets as fast as he dared, counting on his clerical garb in case he was stopped by the *flics.* The breeze through the window was almost cool. At the city's outskirts he swung onto the highway and accelerated to 105 km/h, grinding the gearshift as if he were at Le Mans, taking a mean satisfaction in the little car's rattles and howls. Though confession might cleanse his soul in the eyes of the Church, it invariably put him in a bad mood–perhaps, he thought, because the sins of which he found himself capable at this point in life seemed either insignificant or too firmly established to combat. Someone had declared that it was not mortal sin which dragged down the soul, but venial. There were times when Boudrie secretly agreed. It could have been the full moon that had prompted him to confess–another remnant of peasant superstition–or perhaps waking to find the *mistral* to boot. Whatever insanity was simmering in the village, he thought, was a good bet to surface soon.

Then he remembered the odd confession of the previous evening. Grumpily, he slowed the car to a speed suitable to a man of the cloth.

He had been on his way out of the church, talking–or, rather, listening–to Mme. Durtal, the cousin who was nursing Amalie Perrin. While she knew that monsieur *le curé* was a busy man, it seemed a long time since he had visited the sick . . .

Only two days, he thought, wincing. He had shooed her off with promises and had been about to lock the doors when the figure rose from a bench in the square and walked furtively toward him. Boudrie understood instantly that whoever it was had been waiting until he was alone, and quickly identified the young man as Philippe Taillou. Mumbling, unable to meet the priest's eyes, he asked to confess. With interest sharpened, Boudrie led him back inside.

There followed the usual halting admissions about drinking, lying, petty theft, self-abuse, and mostly unsuccessful attempts of an adolescent male to channel his sexual desperation into the female complements God so clearly intended. But that He often made such consummation difficult in the extreme, at least for young men like Philippe Taillou, Boudrie could not deny. With a mixture of pity and amusement, he listened to the list of disappointments–nearly a year had passed since Philippe's last visit to the confessional, and the tale was a long one–mitigated only by a brief encounter with a young lady working the grape harvest in Fayence. Perhaps in an attempt to lighten the sin, Philippe had added miserably that she both outweighed him and had a heavier mustache.

When the recital ended, silence occupied the booth for the better part of a minute; Boudrie was in his element, and he waited, knowing that the object of this visit did not lie in the commonplaces he had just heard. At last, slowly, the story began to come.

It was a hard-eyed priest who left the church a quarter of an hour later, watching a relieved, but still fearful, young man hurry home in the dusk.

As Boudrie drove, the urge for a drink on this misty day coincided with the sight of the hotel run by the Marigny family at the intersection of the road to Mandelieu. He swung the car in front of the building and vaguely considered taking off his Roman collar in order to appear unofficial, but it was pointless. Everyone knew him. Besides, what harm was there? Even a priest needed to wet his throat occasionally. He climbed out and made his way to the door under the sign that sought to dignify the shabby little establishment: *Grand Hôtel Marigny*.

The half-dozen men gathered at the bar were interchangeable with any such group in any rural tavern in France: berets, overalls, thin mustaches, shrewd faces. He nodded to them, the brothers Ticoutin, Grégoire Ariot, one of old Honoré Fragonard's sons, all evading whatever gainful employment might come their way, drinking up money they did not have.

"*Ça va, mes enfants?*" he said heartily.

The words roused them sufficiently from their shock at seeing him to elicit a mumbled chorus of, "*Oui, Monsieur le curé,*" and a general touching of caps. The men continued to stare as he lumbered to the bar. It annoyed him. Perhaps it was not so usual to see a priest in a tavern, but Christ had consorted with tax collectors and harlots, been crucified with criminals, had He not?

"I have only come in to use your WC," he told Paul Marigny loudly, "but I may as well drink a glass of brandy. God, but there's a dampness in the air." He turned to glare at the group at his elbow, received a hasty murmur of assent.

Boudrie watched with thirsty eyes as Marigny filled the glass. He downed it in three slow, strong swallows, not sure he had ever tasted anything so good in his life. With a thunk, he set the empty glass on the bar and surreptitiously motioned for another.

Then he turned to the small window beside him, gazing out at the brooding gray afternoon. So old Henri Taillou *had* had something on his mind the last weeks of his life, something that, stubborn old fool that he was, he had died too suddenly to confess. Though his communications about it had been mainly limited to drunken mumblings overheard by his son, Philippe had not required much detail. He had been feeling it, too: a sense of being watched, followed, even stalked; a foreboding of doom.

"It is impossible for me to take pleasure in anything, monsieur," he had whispered. "Now that Papa is gone. I can't help but feel that it's turned on me. I think I hear voices, speaking some language I have never heard; I even think I see faces. I can't bear to be alone in the dark. I know Monsieur Devarre did us a kindness by calling Papa's death a stroke, but . . ." His voice had trailed off, leaving Boudrie to remember the contorted look on the face of Henri Taillou's corpse–a look Boudrie had attributed to the recognition of Death.

And at last Philippe had told him about bootlegging water from the hidden spring, and passed through the confessional screen a piece of paper with the guardian stone's inscription laboriously copied out.

It matched precisely the one in the legendary account of Guilhem de Courdeval's tomb.

Legendary, Boudrie repeated: nothing more. If it was the actual tomb, it might prove to be a find of real archaeological significance, and he had already decided to walk up there as soon as time allowed, perhaps the next morning. Philippe himself seemed to have had no idea what the stone might connote–only that tampering with it had brought evil luck. A typical peasant superstition to explain away trouble.

As for the idea that there might be some real connection between the tomb and what had happened to Taillou *père*–

Boudrie turned back to the bar to find a full glass at his place. Absently, he drank it, and fumbled in his pocket.

"*Non, non,* monsieur," Marigny said. Palms out, he waved the money away. "Courtesy of the house."

The simple kindness took Boudrie so much by surprise that it brought a sting to his eyes.

"*Merci,*" he said hoarsely, and made his way to the door, barely aware of the respectful chorus of "*Au 'voir, monsieur le curé,*" that followed him.

Not until he was once again fighting his way into the car did he remember that his bladder remained full.

McTell awoke in the cool gray of twilight. His arm was draped across the shoulders of the woman beside him. Foggy from slumber, he sat up. He first noticed how hard and powerful his upper body seemed to have grown—not the chiseled structure of a weight lifter, but the thick, functional torso of a middle-aged man who used his body strenuously for most of every day. This change pleased him, but there was a bother, too—he seemed to have gotten something in his eye during sleep. He tugged at the lid, but the irritation went farther back, as if in the optic nerve itself. Linden was dug into the bedclothes like a burrowing mammal, her breath a tiny warm caress against his thigh. A wave of deep chestnut hair spilled across the pillow.

He blinked. Then the events of the afternoon flashed into his brain. With them came a surge of panic.

"My God," he whispered. Memories flicked with the speed of movie frames: the girl's lips tightening in pain, head twisting to the side; himself lying afterward with his face against her small breasts, breathing in the salty musk of her skin. And then, before grim reality could creep in, there had come sleep, irresistible in spite of his efforts to fight it off, so deep and absolute in the still gray house that he had awakened assuming the woman beside him was his wife. He twisted to look at the clock. It was almost eight. He swore quietly; Alysse was always home about seven.

"Wake up, wake up," he whispered. He intended his voice to be soft, but it was harsh and throaty. She did not stir. More sharply he said, "*Réveilles-toi*," and shook her. She moaned in protest, moving slightly. At last her eyes opened. He searched them with his, afraid of what he might see. Reproach? Accusation? But they were sleep-filled and vague.

"*Chérie,*" he said, pulling her to him. "You have to go, it's late." The feel of her skin against him was electric; his penis stirred, his hands moved. No time, he thought fiercely, and threw off the covers.

A patch of drying blood crusted the sheet beneath.

McTell squeezed his eyes shut briefly, then took her by the shoulders. She was limp, passive.

"Get dressed," he whispered. "*Comprends?*" He rose, gathered her clothes, gave them to her. Slowly, dreamily, she automatically began turning the tiny triangular panties to tell front from back.

Relieved, he picked up his own clothes, hurried down the hall to the bathroom, splashed water on his face, brushed his hair. His mind raced. When he came back she was dressed, sitting silent and motionless on the bed.

"Are you all right?" he said, kneeling to take her hand. She gazed at him without expression. Fear tightened around him. It was only the shock of lost virginity, he told himself, so sudden and unexpected.

But he knew it was a lie—had known it when they first touched. She had not been, and still was not, herself.

"I love you," he said, with desperation in his voice; "*Je t'aime.*" And this, he knew, was true.

Holding her hand, he raised her to her feet.

"You must say you stayed late to do some sewing for my wife." He quickly straightened her hair with one of Linden's brushes. The little bit of makeup she wore was smeared, and panic touched him again; but he steeled himself. It would have to do. Arm around her, he led her through the gloomy, silent hall and down the staircase. At the bottom he flipped on the wall switch–

To illuminate a sight that hit him like a sledgehammer in the chest.

Linden was sitting at the table, with Alysse's purse at her elbow. An ashtray full of half-smoked cigarettes sat in front of her; she held another, smoke curling from its tip, between her fingers. Legs crossed, arms folded, she looked almost relaxed–except that her face was bloodless white, a taut mask of fury stretched across a living skull.

"How touching," she said. Her voice trembled. She stabbed the cigarette into the ashtray. Through his filter of disbelief, McTell saw that there was something else on the table: the grimoire, which he had left lying on his desk. His notes and translation were scattered beside it. His grip tightened on Alysse's hand.

"In case you're wondering, I went upstairs and saw you two, curled up like a couple of kittens. You looked so sweet I couldn't bring myself to wake you." And then, in a shaking but measured tone, "You filthy, sneaking bastard."

McTell's arm circled the girl's shoulders protectively.

"Wait. I'll send her home. Then we'll talk."

"You're goddamned right we'll talk!" Abruptly she stood, leaning forward into Alysse's face. Her eyes were

231

hard and glittering. "Don't you ever set foot in my house again, you little bitch."

Alysse made no sound, registered no sign of upset, fear, or curiosity. Linden's eyes went uncertain. McTell turned the girl and walked her down the hall to the door.

"I'm sorry," he said in French, "I can't take you home. But I'll see you again . . ." She walked steadily and silently off into the twilight. Agonized, he strained to watch until she disappeared.

Then he turned back inside to face his wife, like a stubborn child called to task.

TWELVE

Étien Boudrie raised his hand in weak protest as the cheese and fruit tray came his way again. The meal had been rich: fresh oysters, bright tomatoes bursting with juice, *pâtés,* peppers in marinade, and a *gigot*–a heavily spiced leg of lamb that would have graced the table of a bishop.

"You must eat, monsieur," Mélusine Devarre said firmly. "I know how men live when they cook for themselves. Like this one"–she cocked her head at her husband, who sat with his hands folded on the table before him, looking vaguely pleased–"when I met him. A bit of bread and soup, perhaps twice a day, as he ran to and from the hospital. It was criminal."

Boudrie accepted a wedge of Brie, another of Gruyère, and half an apple. It was true that this was the first meal worthy of the name he had eaten in days.

They had talked mostly of the village, avoiding by tacit consent any topic like religion, though he suspected that Mélusine, at least, had been raised in the Church. He was content, even relieved to let the evening flow by

233

without being reminded each moment that he was a priest. He turned to Devarre.

"When you married, you were in medical school?"

"An intern." Devarre shook his head at the memory. "Eighteen hours a day in the hospital, often thirty hours at a stretch. Auto accidents, delivering babies–" He smiled at his wife. "I had no time to think of food. Or romance, for that matter. I was married to my profession."

"If I might ask, then," Boudrie said, hoping his voice betrayed no trace of jealousy, "how did this happy union come about?"

Her eyes were calm, almost stern. "First I saw him, then I met him, and then"–she seemed about to smile, but did not–"I waited." Devarre was gazing at her in simple adoration. A striking woman, Boudrie thought: dusky skin, features leaning toward the Moorish–almost harsh, but pleasingly strong. Even her limp served mysteriously to accent her presence. He suspected that she had done a good deal more during her courtship than wait. For an instant he imagined her as Céleste, and twenty years of a lost life–what might have been–opened like a void before him. Automatically he offered a silent prayer of contrition and groped for his wine glass.

Devarre, seeing, said, "Time for a liqueur."

"I'll bring coffee in a minute," said his wife.

The two men rose and went to the small, comfortably furnished parlor, with a fire laid and ready to light–the first of the year, Boudrie thought, the end of summer. Devarre motioned him to a chair and knelt with a match. When the flames were crackling, he opened a cupboard and read labels aloud:

"Grand Marnier, Calvados, Napoléon, Rémy Martin, armagnac—"

Boudrie cleared his throat. A minute later, each of them was settled in a fat leather chair, with a glass on the table at his elbow. Boudrie felt himself falling into a near trance, listening to the faint clatter of dishes. With the fire, the brandy, the sounds of the woman in the next room, he wondered if such contentment would be bearable.

But through the lethargy, something stirred unpleasantly far back in his mind. His forehead wrinkled, as much in irritation at being disturbed as with the attempt to recall. Then he had it. His frown deepened and peace slipped quickly away. First there had been young Taillou's odd confession; now this other thing, whispered at twilight as Marie Riboux was leaving the church. He was certain she had not been lying, but there was no telling how much her husband might have exaggerated in his drunkenness. Boudrie could hardly ask Riboux himself. Although every other man in the village had doubtless heard the story by now, only a woman would tell such a thing to the priest. Riboux would beat her if he knew. Boudrie's gaze flicked to Devarre, who also appeared immersed in thought. It would be a good thing to get off his chest; it was not a matter that violated the confessional, and he knew he could count on the doctor's discretion. Still, thirty years of keeping secrets was not an easy habit to push aside.

Devarre looked up and said, "You haven't been to the Perrin house again?"

235

A little ashamedly, Boudrie shook his head. "And you?"

"No." Devarre looked away again. His lips were tight, as if he were trying to keep something from passing than.

"But you have news?"

Devarre drank, then rose and paced, his face almost angry with concentration. Finally he said:

"Not about Mlle. Perrin—directly, at least. But something very curious happened last night. It's stepping past the bounds of my profession to discuss it, really, with anyone but another physician—or the police, if it should come to that."

"It could be said that priests are the policemen of the soul."

Devarre smiled, but the tense look came quickly back.

"It's none of my business, really. But—I'm suddenly not sure the Americans' house is such a good place for Alysae to spend time."

What remained of Boudrie's dullness vanished. He rearranged his big body straight in the chair.

"I don't want to get into moral judgments," he said carefully. "but if you suspect the girl's welfare might be in jeopardy, I urge you to tell me as much as you can." When Devarre still hesitated, he added coaxingly, "I myself was their guest at dinner not long ago, and I found them very pleasant. You'll have a job convincing me otherwise."

Devarre exhaled, then sat hunched forward, elbows on knees.

"I was called out there last night." he began.

Boudrie listened with the patience of his years in the confessional, his expressionless face belying the sour unease that rose in him at the doctor's flat, objective account.

"... could possibly have been brought about by, say, a large dose of barbiturates, perhaps compounded by alcohol. But her husband refused to allow urine or blood tests. He as much as admitted they use drugs occasionally, which probably explains his reluctance. At any rate, when I called the hospital this morning, they were gone, against my wishes. Of course, there was no way to hold them."

"The woman was unharmed?"

"Apparently. At least she was walking, speaking, and aware of what was taking place."

"You haven't called Monsieur McTell?"

"I considered it, but I was afraid my curiosity might be thought undue."

Boudrie leaned back, letting his gaze move to the ceiling. His hand went automatically to his glass.

"At any rate," Devarre said, with a touch of formality in his tone, "I thought such an environment might not be the best place for a teenaged girl."

"But that's not all," Boudrie said quietly.

"No." Devarre sounded resigned. "Even if there were some 'recreational' drugs around, perhaps for adults to play with them occasionally is not so terrible. Those people are nothing like addicts, not even heavy users. Certainly not the type to addict a young girl.

"But the look on the woman's face—she was like an exploded flashbulb. Her mind had been so overloaded with shock that it had simply shut down. I have seen that sort of syndrome a few times in people who have witnessed or survived horrible accidents; but to such a great extent, it is very rare. And what could bring such a thing about in a place like that? The environment is as safe as a playpen. The husband assured me she had no history of mental problems. Even if he lied—and why would he?—for her to go, in a matter of hours, from normal functioning to poof"—he snapped his fingers—"would require a shock of enormous force. I don't believe it could have been triggered merely by a memory, or some sort of hormonal imbalance."

"You have no ideas?"

Devarre shook his head. "Not really. It seems that a fuse had blown, putting out all the lights. About the only thing I an speculate is that she imagined some sort of intruder, perhaps under the influence of drugs. But she had not been physically touched, in spite of the fact that she was quite naked when they found her—apparently she had been swimming—and nothing in the house was disturbed." With a look of wry amusement, he added, "Madame McTell did say that she had recently lost a well-loved pet, a dog."

Boudrie's mouth opened. He closed it again.

"But I hardly think that could account for it." Devarre paused, then added, "This is where I overstep myself as a man of medicine, but I would swear there was something clandestine going on." He rose to pour more brandy. "But I'm doubtless reading something into nothing, and it's none of my concern anyway."

238

"I'm not so sure either of those things is true," Boudrie said slowly.

Devarre turned. face questioning.

"I'm not just being polite," Boudrie said. "Stories have come to me, too. One has to do with this pet—it could even, perhaps, explain the woman's shock." He hesitated.

It was Devarre's turn to coax. "It would go no farther than this room."

Boudrie nodded. "Do you know Anton Riboux?"

"Perhaps by sight."

"No matter. He worked until today as gardener for the Americans. He quit this morning suddenly and has been drinking since. His wife was angry with him: It was an easy position, it paid well, and now he has nothing. Naturally, she did not keep her feelings to herself. He reacted with anger in turn, of course"—he was about to add, "and threatened her with his fists," but caught himself—"and then blurted out an ugly story. The pet you mentioned—"

Mélusine walked into the room, carrying a tray with a silver coffeepot and white porcelain cups. Startled, Boudrie began to rise.

"*Non, non,* monsieur;" she said quickly. "Pay no attention to me."

More easily said than done, he thought; but he settled back. Mélusine poured cups of the thick black espresso, then sat in a chair near the fire. Fabric rustled as she crossed her legs.

Boudrie had been about to repeat the first thing Marie Riboux had told him:

"The blonde sunbathes shamelessly in the nude, not covering herself even when Anton passes by." Which, Boudrie was sure, he had taken every possible opportunity to do—yet another indication of how serious the fright must have been for him to give up the job.

But Mélusine's presence made him reluctant. Not that the rest of the story was pretty. Why was it easier to speak of violence than sexual matters?

"This dog," he said. "Riboux claimed that he found it this morning horribly mutilated, and that Monsieur McTell paid him extra for burying it—with the understanding of silence."

"My God," Mélusine said. "What could have done such a thing?"

"He seemed sure it was not the work of an animal."

"You're sure this is true?"

Boudrie shrugged. "Exaggerated, no doubt, but I think, essentially, yes. He has not enough imagination to make up such a tale, anyway."

"Could he have been fired, really, and be bitter?"

"It's possible," Boudrie admitted. "Although the dog did disappear."

Devarre leaned forward intently. "He said Monsieur. McTell paid him for silence—so the others did not know."

"I think that's the case, yes. It was the secrecy more than anything that disturbed Riboux, that drove him to tell his wife. As if McTell knew something that must be covered up."

"But if the woman who owned the dog did not know, this could hardly account for her shock."

Boudrie watched his theory crumble.

"I hadn't thought of that. Then instead of one unhappy occurrence perhaps explaining another, we're left with two that are independent."

Devarre nodded, but his wife said, "Independent as far as we know."

Both men looked at her in surprise. "You know something more?" Boudrie asked.

She gazed into her coffee cup, held in both hands.

"No, but I have a feeling." Then, with quiet emphasis, "And not a good one."

"A natural reaction to such unpleasantness." Devarre said comfortingly.

"It's more than that."

He turned to Boudrie. "Gypsy blood. How can I argue? She guessed immediately the sexes of our children."

"Knew," she corrected firmly. Out of delicacy, neither added that each time, she had announced to Devarre within hours after their lovemaking that she was pregnant.

"Will you tell us more, madame?" Boudrie said.

She rose abruptly and walked to the fire. There she knelt as if about to pray, rearranging the embers into flame.

"Dreams, partly," she said. "Only I'm not so sure they're dreams."

"*Clairvoyante?*" Boudrie said sharply.

She nodded. "Such things used to happen to me long ago. Now they've started again, but they're ugly and frightening. I'm sure–I *fear*–I saw some things that actually took place. Medieval, I think."

241

"You've told me nothing of this," Devarre said, almost harshly.

She smiled, but her worried look returned. "There was no point in upsetting you until I knew more." He seemed about to speak again, but then settled back, looking disturbed.

"And you do?" Boudrie said.

"I wasn't sure at first. Now I think, yes. You are familiar, monsieur, with the planchette?"

"A fortune-telling device, is it not?"

"Like the Ouija, yes. Well, I inherited one from my great-aunt, she from her grandmother, and so on. It's very old, three or four centuries at least. Instead of a board, there's a silver dish with letters etched around the rim. One holds a little pendulum, an amulet on a chain, and waits for it to move to the letters."

"You told me that was a necklace," Devarre said accusingly.

"And you believed me, *mon chou*. I had not paid attention to the thing in years, monsieur; when we came here from Paris, I put it on a shelf in the attic. But when these visions began, I decided to see if I could contact whatever was causing them."

"You succeeded?"

She nodded, mouth tight. "There's always the possibility, of course, that one is supplying messages from one's own subconscious, and I can't rule that out—at least in the minds of others. But in my own mind, I know the truth. It was something outside of me, a very definite presence: tremendously powerful and thoroughly evil. I

242

asked it three questions. It gave me three answers. The first two were in Latin."

Boudrie's hands gripped the arms of his chair.

"Of course, I'd had a little in elementary school and church," "Mélusine went on, "but not for many years. Consciously, at any rate, I remember almost nothing. I asked it first why it troubled us. It answered, 'Peccata patrum': sins of the fathers.

"It took me a moment to understand. I thought at first it was the sort of jumbled message that so-called spirits often give in séances. But the next time, I was ready. I asked it what it wanted. It spelled, 'Sanguis floris.'"

"Blood of a flower," Boudrie said.

She nodded. "Clear as the words were, their meaning still makes no sense to me. It's almost as if the spirit were deliberately teasing."

"And the third," Devarre said. The tone of his voice made Boudrie glance at him. The good-natured expression was gone from his face, and Boudrie quickly decided that whether it was human, spirit, or anything else that troubled Mélusine, it had in Devarre a grim and implacable enemy.

"The third," she said, "was in French. I demanded to know who or what it was. It answered, 'Le noyé'—the drowned man." She turned to Boudrie, concerned. "You are all right, monsieur?"

Boudrie coughed and waved a hand. "Nothing," he mumbled.

She stood and paced, arms folded. "The really horrifying part was what happened next. Whatever power it was suddenly opened up full force. I could not let go of the chain. It was like a terrible, loathsome sort of electric shock, only the agony was in my spirit, my being, rather than my body. It seemed to last forever. When it paused for an instant. I threw the chain down and ran. I was so badly frightened, I hurried to the center of town, just to have people around me."

"As if you were its enemy," Boudrie said softly.

"Worse. A if it had me in its power, then deliberately let, me go, like a cat a mouse." She shivered visibly. Devarre rose and strode to the liquor cabinet. Boudrie watched his profile as he poured: pale with fury. He caught Boudrie's gaze and tried to smile.

"I don't know who I'm angrier with." he muttered. "This spirit, or Mélusine for not telling me.

"One question," the priest said. "Are either of you familiar with the name of Guilhem de Courdeval?"

They looked at each other, then at him, shaking their heads.

"A passing reference, perhaps, during some talk of local legend?"

"You must remember we've only been here a matter of months," Devarre said. "What about this Courdeval?"

Boudrie hesitated, but the thought was too outlandish to voice.

"I'll explain another time. *Eh bien,* madame, is there anything else you can tell us?"

The lines in her face seemed to deepen. "This is very vague," she said. "For some days now, I have felt at times a fluttering, as of a moth outside a window, trying to get in. It comes to me at odd moments, when my mind is

244

blank. It's different from the dreams, from–the other. Now, suddenly, there seems to be a second fluttering of the same sort; I felt it just this afternoon.

"I know how insane this must sound, but I think they are spirits being pushed out of their bodies."

Boudrie swallowed.

"The new one is not as strong as the first, which makes me think it is young. It is bewildered, frightened, unable to comprehend what is happening. The other one is growing more distant; it is almost gone." Her voice dropped, and she said, "I'm certain both are women."

It cost Boudrie an effort not to crush the fragile glass in his fist.

"You must forgive me for leaving so suddenly," he said, pulling himself to his feet. "I have work yet to do tonight."

"Do they mean anything to you, monsieur? Those messages?"

Sins of the fathers, he thought. Blood of a flower. The drowned man.

He said nothing.

"I've tried and tried to make sense of them. What fathers? How can a flower have blood? If I wasn't so sure of what I felt, I'd be tempted to dismiss them as tricks of my subconscious."

Her gaze was intent, searching. Boudrie chose his words carefully.

"I don't believe you are playing tricks on yourself. But I must think this through before I speak further. If anything concerning this–matter–arises, please contact me at once."

245

They walked to the door. "Madame," Boudrie said, "I dined magnificently." He bowed, raising her hand to his lips.

"Then you'll come again soon," she said firmly.

"Yes, please do," said Devarre. "It's not every night I get an education like this. I've just learned you can live with a woman twenty-four years and suddenly find out that all the time she's been two people, one of whom you never met—and a witch to boot."

As Boudrie hurried off into the cloudy night, she suddenly called:

"Monsieur *le curé!*" He turned to see them standing in the doorway, arms linked, and again he felt a pang of regret for what might once have been his.

"It bas to do with water," she said. "Tainted somehow. Evil."

The unease in his spirit moved like a restless creature beneath the surface of the earth, one that would neither come up and show itself nor lie still.

For a full minute neither of them spoke. The only movements were Linden's trembling inhalations of her cigarette. Then she crushed the butt, rising in the same motion to lean toward him. Her hand slapped the grimoire.

"*This,*" she said. "is what you have been doing up there? Oh, yes, besides screwing the maid, I mean." Her glittering gaze held his, then dropped. " 'If a man wishes a faithful servant,'" she read contemptuously, "'if he wishes to drink the blood of his enemies, if he would cheat the hand of death, it is necessary that he salute

246

Lord Belial'—my God, have you gone crazy? This is the most disgusting thing I've ever come across in my life. Where did you get it? Why didn't you tell me?"

McTell stood unmoving, jaw taut, hands open beside his thighs. They felt as heavy as slabs of oak. Suddenly she scooped up the grimoire and hurled it at him. With a grunt, he caught it to his chest.

"You bastard! Is there anything you haven't lied to me about?"

Carefully, he smoothed the rumpled pages.

"If you're going to have an affair, you could at least go through the motions of deceit. I told you I would call, and the phone rang and rang until I was sure something must have happened to you. So back I came, leaving Mona, scared to death, speeding the whole way, and then I find you and your little friend. By the way, how long has this been going on?"

"Just today," he said. His voice sounded thick and hoarse. "It was—an accident."

"I see," she said icily. "The two of you accidentally fell upstairs, out of your clothes, and into bed. Conveniently, when I just happened to be gone."

He shook his head. There was no use trying to explain.

She lit another cigarette. When she spoke, she was calmer.

"Listen to me. I don't know what it is about this place, and I don't know what this"—her hand scattered the papers—"has to do with it, but Bertie was right, something is very wrong here. I never told you this, but I almost drowned in the pool the other afternoon. It was like something was holding me under. I tried to ignore it then, but I can't ignore it now. I want us out of here tonight. We don't even have to pack–just take what we need to travel. We'll have the rest sent on. We can go to Paris, or London, or home if you want. As long as it's far away."

McTell pressed a hand to his head. His left eye was throbbing, a drumbeat of blood.

"How old is she, John? Sixteen? Seventeen? There are laws against that sort of thing in this country too, you know. Christ, how long do you think you could keep that secret in a place like this?"

He stepped forward, reaching for the papers on the table. She caught his hand, stared at the mark.

"What," she breathed, "is that?"

He raised his palm before his face. It was unmistakable now, like a faint but clear brand: the outline of the symbol on the grimoire's cover.

"When I was climbing," he said in the same thick tone. "I scraped it." He turned and walked toward the stairs.

"You'll start packing?" she called anxiously.

He did not answer. Feeling her gaze on his back, he moved on heavily, with the tingling in his palm flaring into a ferocious surge of power through his body.

McTell placed the grimoire on the desk, opened it to the Book of the Pilgrim, and looked at the newest line of writing:

Solitudo tiliae viatori intellectum tribuit.

The linden's solitude brings understanding to the pilgrim.

248

Distantly, he realized that he had read the Latin as effortlessly as if he had been speaking it all his life.

The moon had slipped out from behind the restless clouds: pale, swollen full, too heavy for its own weight. McTell placed his hands on the windowsill and gazed at it with his eyes, but his mind looked inward.

To never see the girl again.

Or to subject his wife—his *wife*—to whatever shock had undone Mona.

If only he had time.

A tap came at the study door. He flipped the book closed and stood with his back to the desk. Linden's jaw was set, but her fingers twisted a handkerchief: and the defiance in her voice did not hide its tremor.

"I came to say that if you're not ready in twenty minutes, I'm going straight to that priest and tell him what happened."

McTell stared at her. She swallowed.

"I love you," she said, "I love the man I married. But something's been changing you. You even look different. It's for your own good, John. Start packing."

"All right," he said.

She waited, eyes wary.

"All right," he said again. "Twenty minutes."

Her shoulders drooped with relief.

He waited until her footsteps had gone down the hall to the bedroom. Then, palming the keys to the car, he walked noiselessly downstairs and out into the drive.

THIRTEEN

Étien Boudrie had once seen a photograph of several young Masai warriors who had just completed their initiation into manhood. They sat in a row, most with drooping heads, faint with exhaustion from the arduous tests they had undergone.

But one was looking straight into the camera. Boudrie remembered clearly how, in glancing at the photo, he had stopped short with a most unpleasant shock. The being that looked out from the young man's eyes, he understood instantly and instinctively, was something more—or less—than human. The gaze held the embodiment of calm, gloating evil; the lips were curved in a sly smile; and Boudrie could almost hear the whispered thought, "Now my time has come."

Whether this was the young man's true nature or an aberration brought on by his initiation trials, Boudrie could not know; nor whether there really were such beings as fallen angels dedicated to the destruction of mankind. But that evil existed, that it sometimes walked the earth in human form, he had no doubt. What else could Gilles de Rais, Torquemada, Vlad the Impaler, the more recent devil's children of the Third Reich, have been?

Or a man like Guilhem de Courdeval.

So. There it was at last, out in the open. And mad though the thought was, there was no denying that the story Philippe Taillou had told him matched in every particular the legend that had come down through the centuries. The tomb had been opened—and its seal of holy water broken.

Was it even thinkable that a man could, through some process beyond the grasp of the intellect, have survived physical death? That his spirit could have existed through centuries of imprisonment like a genie in a lamp, biding its time, plotting, waiting for the moment of its release, when it could resume its career of destruction? That it could send ominous visions to one woman, throw another into a coma, frighten a third nearly to death; shock a grown man into a stroke and haunt his son; even eviscerate a dog?

Almost as if that spirit, that will, were destroying all obstacles in its path? But to what?

Sins of the fathers.

Blood of a flower.

The drowned man.

The first two may have meant nothing, at least nothing apparent. But the third—

It has to do with water. Tainted somehow. Evil.

She was psychic, he reminded himself. She could have been unconsciously reading a mind, perhaps even his own. It was true that Courdeval had been present in

251

his thoughts since his talk with the Americans. Again he remembered the man McTell's too eager curiosity.

And then, with a jolt, came the obvious: If the legend was true, the water that had flowed over Guilhem de Courdeval's bones was going directly to the villa.

Angrily, he glared around the room, gulped from his glass, began to stalk. And what if it *was* true? To what did it add up? A series of events, unpleasant to be sure, but events that could be connected only by a madman or a child. You are old, Étien, he told himself cynically; the liquor that has been your life's blood is at last taking its toll.

But the ugly fear lying just beneath the surface of his consciousness—like a corpse in a shallow grave haunting a murderer's memory—rose up.

Was not the real heart of the matter that some deep part of him longed for the final, actual encounter: to look up and see it standing before him in all its hooved and horned menace, just so he would at last be certain beyond all doubt? Uneasily, he tried to push the thought away; to court it was the first step toward making it come true. A priest who failed in an exorcism, so legend had it, would himself be tormented by that spirit until his death—and after that, who knew?

He downed the last of the brandy and started off to bed. Weary though he was, he feared that sleep was yet a long way off. He mumbled a prayer that he might not pass another night tossing until dawn, his imagination fueled by this business—or grappling hopelessly with another dream of fire.

In the hallway he reached to turn out the light, but his hand hesitated. A little ashamedly, he left it on and went to his bedroom to put on the light there first. He had begun to undress when he heard the pounding at the door. Clumping back down the hall, he threw it open.

Mme. Durtal stood before him, holding her coat together as if it had no buttons. Her hands were thin and white, and there was fright in her eyes.

"It's Amalie, monsieur," she said in agitation. "She is tossing as if her soul struggles to leave her body."

He started for his visiting bag, with the thought fitting through his mind that he would have to go to the cathedral to get the oils for the administration of the Last Rites. Not until later did he wonder at his immediate certainty that the time for that had come.

". . . trying to speak," the woman was saying, "words that make no sense, but seem torn from her. Alysse, too, is unwell–"

"You've called Devarre?"

Her face took on a stubborn, miserly, peasant look.

"We have no telephone."

So you chose instead to get the priest, whom you will not have to pay, he thought.

"Wait in the car," he snapped. She turned back into the night. Numb with apprehension, Boudrie gripped the phone. He closed his eyes while it rang, hoping they had not gone out.

"It's me, Étien!" he yelled when the receiver was lifted. "*La Perrin* is dying."

"Five minutes," Devarre said, and hung up.

253

Boudrie slammed the door and set off at a clumsy run for the cathedral. Of all the times to worry about money! And what was it she had said? *Alysse, too, is unwell*–what did that mean?

"*Je vous salus, Marie, pleine de grâce, le Seigneur est avec vous,*" he mumbled as he flipped through his key ring. Dimly, he realized he had associated the action of his fingers with the rosary. At last he got the door open. The oils rested in an oak chest hundreds of years old. Forcing himself to overcome his impatience, he crossed himself, knelt, prayed briefly. When he rose, he lunged for the chest.

Outside again, he broke into an all-out run for the car.

Linden strode around the bedroom, emptying drawers and tossing their contents into suitcases, trying to keep her mind numb. Superimposed upon everything she had seen all evening was a single picture: her husband in bed, slumbering deeply, with a pretty teenaged girl nestled beside him. Beneath the surge of shock and disbelief, and yes, rage, there had been a fear that made her weak–too weak to scream, to leap upon them as she knew she should have done–and that left her capable only of turning and walking back downstairs to wait, as if she were in calm control

But the infidelity itself was not what had frightened her most. It was the contentment on his sleeping face, the passion she had sensed even in the relaxed muscles of the arm that cradled his bedmate. Somehow, she knew he did not look like that when he slept with her. She yanked open the closet and began emptying its contents by the armload.

Then there was this insanity about magic. A grown man. A distinguished professor. She had been running her mind back along the list of his relatives, trying to remember if there was any hint of mental instability that might be hereditary.

Where had he gotten that book? It was obviously very ancient. Even before she had read any of it, she had been strangely reluctant to touch it, quick to put it down. The *feel* of it was somehow bad.

Nerves. Whatever had gotten into him was working on her too. Doubtless, he'd found the book in the course of his work; he was always coming across such things.

But that did not explain why he was translating it, and why he had kept it a secret. Nor did it explain what Mona had told her. Was that nerves too? She remembered the terror in her sister's eyes, the choked, faint voice that had whispered the story. More insanity. A demon, of all things.

But what *had* it been?

The sound of a car engine starting brought her to herself. She gazed blankly at the doorway, torn from her vision of Mona's face.

Then she realized that the car was their BMW.

Dropping a pile of clothes, she hurried down-stairs—stunned at first, then breaking into a run—and threw open the main door just in time to see the disappearing taillights.

"You miserable son of a bitch," she breathed. But standing there in the windy night, her anger gave way to uncertainty. She stepped back inside, closed the door, and locked it.

Now what? Call the police? And complain about what: that she and her husband had had a fight, and he had driven off in his own car? There was no one else to call—certainly not Mona and Skip. She was stuck.

Wait for him to come back, then—if he did. And if not?

She folded her arms and walked back to the living room. There she paused, and suddenly she was hovering on the edge of tears, for loving a man who too often seemed not to need her, and now, even to want her.

But beneath her grief and rage remained the cold, creeping fear that he had truly gone mad. Perhaps it had been foolish to speak so sternly to him; she had not realized the extent of the problem. She would take care not to do it again; she would coax him if necessary, play along—whatever it took to get him to professional help.

In the meantime, there was nothing to do but wait. She touched her eyes with her handkerchief and went to pour herself a little brandy.

Suddenly, from deep in the forest came a strange whistle. It sounded very far away and close at the same time; quiet and yet piercing, with a mysterious, haunting quality. She waited, listening; it did not come again. Some night bird, no doubt, though she had never heard anything like it. For no reason, it increased her uneasiness. Realizing that the glass door to the patio was partly open and only screened, she went to lock it. Her gaze flicked over the moonlit pool outside.

She inhaled sharply.

Something in it was moving.

For long seconds she stared, telling herself it was the wind rippling the water, the reflected clouds passing before the moon.

But there it was again, a slow, steady, rhythmic movement.

Timidly, hardly breathing, she stepped closer.

"Who's there?" she called, and heard the quaver in her voice. "*Qui est là?*"

The movement continued, but only the wind answered back, with a sudden gust that sent leaves skittering across the patio. Slowly, she slid open the screen, leaning out into the night, waiting for her eyes to adjust.

As if the pool's dark glassy surface were a screen and the moonlight a beam projected onto it, two silhouetted figures seemed to be moving toward her. One was a man, very tall, with an enormous sword in one hand. The second came not quite to his waist, and was muffled in some sort of garment with a hood. It was the man's legs that were moving, in a steady menacing stride. The other creature seemed rather to glide. Wildly, her gaze flicked around the patio, to the forest, to the moon, to wherever the figures really were–to the source of this trick her eyes were playing on her.

But the figures were nowhere else. They were in the moonlight on the water, and they were getting bigger.

She whirled, fingers fumbling at the door latch. It refused to close.

The lights in the house flickered and died.

Fighting back the terror that leaped in her throat, she began to move, edging along the wall toward the phone, holding her breath, straining to hear. Something was rasping at the screen with what might have been claws. She moved faster, holding the wall for support.

The sound of the door slowly sliding open nearly made her scream. Moonlight cast a creeping, rising shadow that followed her own. It rustled, like something heavy being dragged. She reached the hallway. Her fingers groped around the corner for the phone.

Instead, they touched something that felt soft, rubbery, loathsome. She crouched, unable to pull her hand away, while her disbelieving mind struggled to identify it. Then it moved.

The scream, she had been holding burst from her lungs, and she fled blindly through the darkness, crashing into furniture and walls. A doorway loomed before her, a gaping patch of black. She plunged through, barely saving herself from falling headlong down the cellar stairs, and slammed the door behind. Her heels caught on the steps; she kicked off her shoes and stumbled on down, trying to silence her gasping breath. The stone walls were cold and rough against her hands, until she reached a corner and could go no father. Distantly, as if it were happening to someone else, she realized what she had done. There was no way out. She sank into a crouch and, with her ears straining, waited.

From the top of the stairs came the creak of hinges, a wedge of dim light. A thick dark shadow appeared, casting its head this way and that.

Then, with the same rustling sound, it began to descend. From behind came another sound, and though

Linden had never heard it before, she recognized the clanking of a man in armor.

Still breathing hard, Boudrie pulled up in front of the Perrin house. There was no sign yet of Devarre. As Mme. Durtal opened the door, Alysse walked past. She showed no indication of haste or upset, no recognition. Without speaking, she simply continued on into the kitchen. Stunned, Boudrie watched her disappear before he remembered to shut the door, and abruptly he realized that the house reeked of cooking cabbage. *Alysse, too, is unwell.* Mother of God, what was going on? Torn, he decided to ignore the girl for the moment—at least she was walking.

"Wait for Devarre," he told Mme. Durtal gruffly, and strode to the stairs.

Though the room was not warm, Amalie Perrin was perspiring heavily. The bedcovers were a twisted knot at her knees. The outline of her body through the linen nightgown was thin to the point of fragility; her hollow cheeks and shrunken limbs gave her the appearance of a bird. With clumsy gentleness, he untangled the covers and pulled them up to her shoulders.

"The girl," she rasped suddenly. So startled that he flinched, Boudrie held his breath to listen. She twisted, moving her head from side to side. Her hands clenched the sheets. "Not the little one. Save her, save her." The sound of her voice iced the blood in his veins. Swallowing, he leaned forward and took her hand.

"What girl, Amalie? What do you see?"

259

Her eyes opened so abruptly he dropped her hand and stepped back. She stared at him, pupils contracting like a cat's.

"The black robe," she said distinctly. Hope leaped in him—he was wearing a black robe. But as quickly, he understood that his was not the garment she meant—that whatever she was seeing was not in this world. He remembered the dreams Mélusine Devarre had described earlier. Brain whirling, he hurried to an open window to escape both his thoughts and the stifling, overwhelming reek of cabbage. He could have wept for gratitude when he heard a car door slam in the street.

Seconds later, Devarre walked into the room, with Mme. Durtal right behind. He nodded to Boudrie without pausing, opening his bag on the way to the bed. Once again, Boudrie watched him go briskly through the mechanics of pulse and temperature. Amalie Perrin moaned in protest at the thermometer.

Devarre straightened. His finger moved to encircle her wrist; he lifted it, displaying its matchstick thinness.

"I think this struggle is rapidly taking what remains of her strength," he said. "She should go to the hospital immediately."

Boudrie saw Mme. Durtal's head give a small shake, and in his heart he agreed. If she was going to die, better for her to die here in her own home than to waste away, plugged into a mysterious array of machines and bottles, among uncaring strangers. Suddenly he remembered the way he had been greeted.

"What about Alysse?" he said to the woman.

She shrugged hopelessly. "She seems to be in a dream, to have no real idea of what is taking place around her. She came home late, so I was forced to do the shopping. When I get back, the house smells like a gypsy camp, and poor Amalie is half-choked. Alysse has not spoken a word, not so much as walked upstairs to peek into her aunt's room. I shouted at her for filling this house with such a smell, and again to go fetch you, monsieur. She ignored me as if I did not exist." She spread her hands, her face expressing misery and worry.

But Boudrie was too numb for pity. Another steely probe had entered his mind: *Do you ever dream while you're awake?* How was it possible the girl had not realized what the cooking smell might do to her aunt? The implication was chilling, and the cold fear was rising in him that there were a good many questions he should have asked some time ago. He caught Devarre's eye and said to Mme. Durtal:

"Perhaps you'd better fetch Alysse." She looked doubtful, but left the room. To Devarre he said quietly, "We'll talk later, but for now, one question. I came prepared to administer the Last Sacrament."

The doctor's gaze seemed to turn inward.

"It is a thing not lightly done," Boudrie said.

"I can make no predictions. She's very weak."

"Her chances of regaining consciousness?"

Devarre hesitated, then shook his head. "If we rushed her to Grasse—"

"Would it help? Truly?"

He exhaled. "It's my duty as a physician to say yes, it's her only chance. The truth is, I don't believe there is any."

The door of the room opened. Mme. Durtal looked pale and haggard.

"Alysse is gone," she said.

It had to be black, that was the only thing Alysse was sure of. He wanted her in black. She had gone through her closet, vaguely aware that she did not own a single all-black dress–a sorry state of affairs. At last she remembered the slip she had bought a year before on a whim because it was so pretty, even though she really had nothing to wear it with. It came to just above her knees, and would do, although now she felt a little cold walking through the misty night. The stones on the roadside bruised her feet, and there was a dull ache somewhere near her middle. But that was not important. The whispering had been tugging at her for days now, confusing her, but at last it had all come clear. She had had to pick flowers, and then cook. Then she had to wait, confused again, until the whispering told her what to wear and do.

Now she was almost there. The only important things were that she hurry, and be wearing black. His face hung before her like a lamp, calling, guiding–the strong, hard face with its single eye that had been coming clearer in her mind for days now, though it kept blurring into a kind, handsome, familiar face she really preferred. Somehow, the two were one and the same, she was not sure how.

She knew she would understand, though, very soon.

The heat was stiffing, the darkness absolute. Chains bound Mélusine's wrists to a stone wall. From above came the harsh, guttural chanting of a single voice in a language she had never heard. The sound was atonal, discordant, making sudden bizarre shifts: an insidious beckoning like the tightening coils of a snake. The voice rose, fell, rose higher, like the fear in her chest. Abruptly it ceased.

From outside came the sound of footsteps on stone. Metal grated harshly as the door opened. The man was silhouetted by the torch he carried: a huge, broad man in a hooded black robe. His other hand gripped a dagger. He set the torch in a sconce and unlocked her chains. The dagger's point pierced her side, seared into her flesh. Gasping, she stumbled forward up a narrow flight of steps. Through blurred eyes she saw a fire—and an immense stone altar stained dark, emblazoned with a strange looping design. The firelight caught her captor's grim one-eyed face.

She had seen it before.

But now there was another face, a man's, as frightened as her own. The bigger man shoved her forward, held the dagger out hilt-first. Shaking his head in protest, agonized with fear, the other man nonetheless stepped closer and took the knife. With trembling hands, he raised it. And as his eyes met hers, she understood that this man who was about to take her life was not an enemy, but someone who loved her desperately. Her own desperation seized on his struggle; she threw her will against his.

Abruptly, she was lying on her own couch, eyes wide, powerless to move, with the dreadful sense of being pinned in a coffin. The image of the man with the knife flickered in and out of the bright familiar reality of her parlor. She fought, and as the knife trembled, about to fall, she cried out.

The image blurred. She leaped to her feet and rushed to the door.

This time there could be no waiting for what was sure to begin again. It was several blocks through the misty night to her husband, and safety. He had taken their car; her weak leg held her back. She moved as swiftly as it would allow, concentrating on the image of her great-aunt's face, struggling to hold off the creeping angry darkness that pressed around.

Not until she turned the corner to the Perrin house and saw the Citroën did she allow herself a sob of relief. It was then she discovered that the ache in her side was not a stitch from hurrying, but a wound seeping blood.

Gravel sprayed as McTell wheeled the BMW back into the driveway and gunned it toward the villa. He slammed on the brakes, threw open the door, pulled himself out.

The house was dark and silent.

He swallowed, the lump in his throat like a thick greasy ball. His left eye was throbbing steadily; when he covered the other with his hand, the vision was dark and blurred. He had been on his second brandy in the bistro

264

in Saint-Bertrand, trying to disguise the shaking of his hand as he raised the glass, when the image of the gutted hanging dog flared in his mind. For the second time in that same tavern, he had slammed down his drink half-finished and lunged for the door.

But as he stood in the misty night, staring at the darkened house, an awful gloating insistence gained steadily: *too late.*

Swallowing again, he began to walk.

He reached inside the hallway, touched the light switch. It was already on. He closed his eyes, remembering Mona, and flicked it back and forth. Nothing. It took him three attempts to clear his throat.

"Lin?" he called. The sound came out a hoarse, mocking croak. "Linden?"

The hallway loomed crypt-black and endless. He cursed himself for not having a flashlight in the car; his only one was still in his rucksack, and he was not even sure where that was. The only thing left was candles, in the kitchen. With them he could find the fuse box. He took several slow, steady breaths, lit a match, and began the step-by-step journey down the creaking hallway. His fingers whispered against the cold plaster of the wall.

The dining room was pale with faint moonlight. He crossed it quickly. In the kitchen he pulled open drawers, groping until his fingers found the candles. Shadows jumped with the flickering flame. He raised it–and saw that the cellar door was open.

It was always kept closed.

Feeling like an iron band was tightening around his chest, he edged toward it and peered down into the inky stairwell. Two white objects lay blurred by the candle's glow. He held the flame closer.

Shoes. Linden's.

The lights, he thought weakly. He had to fix the lights.

Instead, with terrible slowness, he began to descend. When he was halfway down, the candle flared, sputtered, died. He stood there in the sudden dark, shaking, barely able to hold off utter panic—and the urge to race back upstairs and out into the night, to charge blindly into the brush and run until he could run no more, then to bury himself with leaves and duff and crouch like a hunted animal until the morning sun.

He struck a match, relit the candle.

"Linden?" he whispered.

The walls were lined with shelves holding cans and jars that seemed to contain eerie floating shapes—fetuses, organs. Something brushed his ear. With a gasp he flailed at it, putting out the candle. He was barely able to make his hands light it again. The thing was a cobweb; a truculent black spider crouched near its edge, looking ready to pounce.

Then he saw her.

She was sitting up against the far wall, mouth open, staring sightlessly—exactly as Mona had been. McTell's blood surged in his veins. She was alive! He ran to her, dropping to one knee. The flame died again. Pale, ghostly moonlight filtering through a dirt-encrusted window allowed him to make out her face and dark eyes. Trembling with excitement, he touched her.

"Baby?" he whispered. "Are you all right?"

She made no move. Her flesh was cool. Gently, he touched the artery of her throat. Nothing. Panic rose again swiftly. He tugged at her blouse to feel her heart-beat. The cloth fell open, as if it had been slit. His fingers found a strange vertical ridge on her flesh. He lit the candle once more, pulled the blouse open, and leaned close.

Then he spun away, vomit burning his throat, and crashed blindly toward the stairs—holding before him the hand he had wet with blood as he had parted the flesh and peered in to see her spine.

FOURTEEN

Boudrie's hand made the so-familiar motions in the air: the names of the three persons of God, the sign that was tonight sending to her final rest the woman who had been his lover's sister, aunt to the girl who might well be his daughter. He stepped back from the bedside and took off his surplice, shedding with it his role as emissary of the faith that had dominated the Western world for twenty centuries, becoming again a simple man prey to every form of human weakness. The strange behavior and disappearance of Alysse had not left his mind for a second. Hurriedly, he folded the surplice and began to put away the oils.

Mme. Durtal rose from her knees, crossing herself.

"Some tea?" she said timidly.

"Tea," Boudrie growled. "My God, woman, haven't you got anything to drink in this house?"

Her eyes widened. "I'll look," she said, backing away.

Devarre was standing against the wall, hands folded before him, missing nothing. He cleared his throat.

"A word with you, Étien. Perhaps in the hall." The priest nodded, and paused to offer a final silent prayer. Though breath remained, she was almost there. He had seen it many times.

"I hate to pile on more bad news," Devarre said, "but you may as well know now. Not long before you phoned. I got a call from the hospital in Grasse. I seem to be doing a good deal of business with them these days."

An unpleasant premonition rose in Boudrie. "And?"

Devarre looked away. "The Taillou boy. It seems he was working by himself off in some field, hidden from view. He was operating his father's backhoe–whether he was qualified, I don't know–but apparently he had gotten off to poke around in the hole he was digging and the machine somehow broke loose and pinned him. He lay there for hours, until his mother missed him at dinner. Well, they found him at last and got an ambulance. It was one of those awful situations where as soon as they moved the machine, his death was virtually certain. The hospital wanted to know if I had his blood type, to be ready just in case."

There is no mercy, Boudrie thought, no relief. Heaven is a fantasy made up by cynics and believed by fools.

"He's dead?"

Devarre nodded. "Apparently he was conscious to the end, but he couldn't speak because of the weight on him."

A sharp knock came at the outside door. Alysse, Boudrie thought with relief. He heard it open, heard Mme. Durtal say:

"But come in, madame," sounding flustered as usual.

269

But it was not Alysse's voice that murmured thanks. Devarre was already striding down the stairs.

"I can't stand it any longer," Mélusine said into his chest. "It's going to drive me mad."

"Another—visitation?"

"'The worst yet. Some sort of ritual sacrifice. I couldn't make it stop. I think—this happened while it was going on." She took her husband's hand and touched it to her wound. His face went bloodless with rage. He glared around the room, but there was nothing to fight.

"We'll start by dressing that," he muttered, and turned to his bag.

Her gaze met Boudrie's. "A dreadful one-eyed man," she said quietly. "I had seen him once before."

He nodded, too numb to feign surprise.

Mme. Durtal was staring from one to the other, openmouthed, looking vaguely like a fish in an aquarium.

"Brandy," Boudrie told her gently, and her mouth snapped shut. She hurried out of the room.

Devarre was holding bandages and bottles.

"Come along, my dear," he said. "Unless you want to be undressed in public."

"It's nothing," she said. "A scratch."

"I'll use force if necessary." Reluctantly, she followed him to the bathroom.

Mme. Durtal returned with a dusty bottle and tray of glasses. Boudrie poured a drink distractedly, tossed it off, poured another. She watched with an astonishment that was beginning to annoy him. He took his glass to the window and stared down the street at the faint rainbow-hued haloes of mist around the lamps.

It was impossible, of course. But if the impossible had in some unfathomable way come true, was it simply random? Or was there a pattern, an object? For no reason he was again aware of the fading smell of cabbage.

Devarre walked back in with his arm around his wife; she was buttoning her blouse. Boudrie turned to Mme. Durtal.

"Alysse said nothing about where she might be?"

"I didn't even see her," she said despairingly. "One minute she's cooking cabbage, the next she's gone. She left her coat, even her purse."

Mélusine looked at them questioningly.

"She's disappeared," Devarre told her. "Apparently she's in some sort of daze."

"But where could she have gone? A friend's? A bistro?"

"With her aunt nearly dead upstairs?"

"My God," she breathed. "I'd forgotten all about it." She turned to Boudrie, eyes gone anxious. "Perhaps two weeks ago I sensed that something was bothering her, and made her tell me what. She'd been bathing, and thought she saw a man watching her—a big, ugly man with only one eye. Of course, it was impossible; the bathroom is secluded . . ."

"I think," Boudrie said slowly, "that we had better find her."

It was Mélusine who put words to his suspicion.

"Could she have gone back to the Americans?"

271

"For what?" said Mme. Durtal. "She was done for the day."

Boudrie ignored her, gazing at Mélusine.

"That tainted water you spoke of. I know now what it is." For a second he hung in indecision–to desert the dying was no small thing. But the living came first. He wheeled, looking for his bag., "You all must excuse me. I have a visit to pay."

"You'll want company," Mélusine said firmly.

"But it would look odd–"

"*Pah.*" She tossed her head impatiently. "Let's be truthful. There's something. We both know it. And it's very strong."

Mme. Durtal stared, bewildered.

"What is very strong? What do you keep talking about?"

"Pray, madame," Boudrie said, starting for the door. "Pray for your cousin, pray for yourself, pray for all of us. You'll be safe."

The three of them walked out into the misty night and climbed without speaking into Devarre's Citroën. There they paused and looked at each other.

"I hope," Mélusine said, "we go home feeling very foolish."

McTell threw himself up the cellar stairs, fell, lurched to his feet, and slammed the door against the horror behind him. He ran through the awful dark silence of the house and at last burst out into the night. There he raised his hands to the silhouetted, mist-shrouded ruin, clutching the empty dank air. The cry that

272

came from him was wordless: a long howl echoed by mocking laughter inside.

The linden's solitude brings understanding to the pilgrim.

Slowly, he let his hands fall. There was only the creak of branches, the faraway moaning of wind through the canyons, the dancing of the moon behind the heavy, swift clouds.

"All right," he whispered hoarsely. "All right, then."

He jerked open the door and strode back down the hall. In the kitchen he gripped a fistful of candles, lit them together, and held them before him like a torch as he climbed to his study. The grimoire lay where he had left it on his desk, inert, evil. Without pausing, he picked, it up and shook it open.

"This is the end of you," he said through clenched teeth, and thrust the flaming candles to the pages.

A flash of agony wrung a cry from him. He staggered back, flapping his arm. It felt as if his flesh were being ripped away with red-hot pincers. The vision in his left eye went black. A knife blade seemed to be scraping the depths of the socket. The pain surged until he thought his heart would explode. Frantically, knees giving out, he dropped the book and slapped at it, smothering the flames with his bare hands.

The pain began to subside. Trembling, he gathered the scattered candles and limped to the bookshelf. He stuffed them into a highball glass, then got hold of the Scotch decanter. The warm liquor made him gag. Vision began to filter back into his eye. The book lay on the floor, with the bottom corners of a dozen pages charred. An evil-emelling dark smoke bung in the air.

The burning sensation was mounting again in his hand—from putting out the fire, he thought at first. But it continued, harsh and stinging, and he suddenly realized what it was. Shaking his head and muttering, "No, no," he backed away. A burning flash shot up his arm, making him gasp.

Slowly, with tears in his eyes and dread in his heart, he knelt, picked up the book, turned to the page. In the flickering candlelight he could just make out the words:

Sanguis lilii viam terminat.

The blood of the lily brings the pilgrimage to its end.

From inside his mind, and yet somehow not from him at all, comprehension began to dawn. He watched with horrified fascination as his hands moved almost of their own will, paging through the translation until he came to the ritual, the murder of the peasant girl by her father, that had so puzzled him.

It puzzled him no longer.

He raised his face, understanding that he had no need of the translation after all—that in spite of passage of centuries, he remembered the ceremony in all its details with perfect clarity. He had rehearsed it against just this contingency.

Most important, the words of that secret incantation, which had been wrested from that unmapped city by only a few, were beginning to whisper themselves in his brain in a language men had never spoken.

A sound at the doorway made him, turn. Alysse was standing in it, wearing a lacy black slip, looking as calm as if she had just arrived for a day's work.

He turned back to the window. The clouds had parted. On a knoll beneath the ruin, two figures stood clearly silhouetted, one tall, one short.

John McTell picked up the grimoire and walked with it to the candles. He held it poised over the flame, inches away, already feeling the pain creeping through his limbs. An instant of courage, a few minutes of agony, and the pilgrimage would be truly at an end.

His hand faltered, and then, still holding the book, dropped to his side. He would need fire and one more thing, which he would find in the kitchen.

In his arms, Alysse was soft and warm as a kitten, seeming to weigh nothing. He carried her out the door and down the dark stairway. His strength was boundless.

But as he walked, a vast empty sadness touched his fading heart at the taunting inner whisper of that other voice, driving home the final nail. She had never really been his, had not given herself to him of her own free will.

He had allowed himself to be cheated even out of the one thing he had truly desired.

"Perhaps we should wait in the car," Mélusine said as they turned into the drive. "That way it won't seem quite so much like a storm-trooper attack."

Boudrie was about to agree when the Citroën's headlights flashed on the McTells' BMW. The driver's door hung open like a broken wing. Behind it, the house was dark. Devarre cut the engine.

"Someone was in a terrible hurry," the priest muttered.

"Drunk, maybe," said Devarre. He flicked on a flashlight. The BMW's keys were still in the ignition.

They exchanged glances and walked on to the house.

The heavy wooden door was wide open. Boudrie knocked loudly, the sound echoing through the emptiness inside.

Mélusine was shaking her head. "There's no one."

Boudrie turned to them, about to say, "Is this where we turn from mere rudeness to breaking and entering?" But Mélusine was already pushing past him, limping inside.

"Can you feel it?" she whispered. Her voice was chilled, and Boudrie's scalp prickled as he stepped inside the door. His groping hand found the light switch and flicked it without result.

"Odd," Devarre said, holding the flashlight beam on it. "The same thing happened the night I was called."

Mélusine was ahead of them. Her voice rang through the stillness:

"Madame? Monsieur?" The flashlight played around the kitchen, then came to rest on a box of candles that had been roughly torn open. Boudrie picked up two, lit them, and, with one in each hand, walked back to the living room. Mélusine was standing in its center. Nothing they could see in the dim light seemed out of order. In unspoken agreement, they started up the stairs. Devarre, walking and turning like a guard, brought up the, rear.

Something glinted in his other hand; Boudrie realized with distracted astonishment that it was a pistol.

They worked their way down the hall opening doors; paused at the sight of the half-packed suitcases in the master suite; then came to the study. A cluster of candles in a drinking glass guttered on a shelf. Boudrie stepped to the scattered papers on the desk, in the slender hope that a note or letter might provide a clue. While Devarre held the flashlight, he bent close and began to read the ufamiliar English. It was quickly apparent that the type-written pages were a translation of another text, and a very strange, sinister one: an account of some sort of ritualistic blood sacrifice. Madness, yes, but there was a tonc to the writing that was deliberate, authoritative, frightening.

What in the name of God had McTell been doing with something like this?

Boudrie forced himself to read faster, hands tightening on the edge of tile desk.

Mélusine spoke so abruptly he jumped: "But that's him!"

She was pointing in disbelief at a photograph on a shelf, dimly visible in the candle flame. She pulled the flashlight from her husband's hand and shone the beam on it. Boudrie recognized the couple immediately: Mc-Tell and his wife, posed in front of what looked like a château of the Loire. He looked austere, dignified–the eminent man of letters. His wife was smiling confidently.

"The other man in my dream tonight," Mélusine whispered. "The one who was holding the knife."

It came to him with a jolt that dropped his jaw:

277

Item, that he ascribed to the pagan belief of Hermes Trismegistus, that the spirit of the mage need not die, but could move from shape to shape at will; and that furthermore, if the accident of death should overcome his body, his spirit could gain another by means of a secret ritual. Such was the wickedness of this man, he was heard to declare that by causing some mortal to slay that which he loved most, the mage could then have that mortal in his power forever.

Sins of the fathers.

Blood of a flower.

"Alysse," he hissed.

Was that the form McTell's strange longing had taken: an obsession with a teenaged girl?

Never dreaming that he himself was being seduced in a far more profound and sinister way.

Boudrie turned to Mélusine.

"Madame." he said, forcing his voice to stay soft, "if an evil spirit were bent upon something besides causing mischief, what would it be?"

"A body," she said without hesitation. "It was my great-aunt who taught me that. Bad spirits suffer unendingly in their realm. They freeze, they burn, they are tormented by other spirits. This is the reason for possession. They wish to flee their torments, to enjoy again the warm things of life. But only the very strongest can effect it."

Boudrie strode to the window and stared out at the wind-tossed clouds. The moon danced behind them like a wanton harlot. The bleak silhouette of the ruin stared back as if in defiance. *I have stood for twelve centuries, it* seemed to say, my stones have been soaked a thousand times in blood. Do you come to challenge me?

"Unthinkable," Boudrie whispered.

He spun away and met Mélusine's eyes, dark with anxiety.

"You must tell us what you know, monsieur," she said. "You must have help."

"There is no time," he said, already moving toward the door.

Her hand caught his arm. He paused and met her eyes. The fear he saw in them touched his own heart, cold as twisting steel. But badly though I have lived, that life is past, he thought. This remains.

"I grow old, madame. I will never be stronger."

"But if you fail . . ."

Étien Boudrie smiled grimly and spoke words that would echo in her memory many times:

"Perhaps the early casualties in any battle are really the lucky ones."

"I'm sorry to always be the slow pupil." Devarre said in exasperation, "but fail at what?"

"No time," Boudrie said. He pushed past, gathering speed like a train.

"But where are you going?"

"No time!"

He took the stairs in jolting, jarring leaps, landed breathless at the bottom, lunged for the door. Behind him he heard Devarre yell:

"Damn it, Étien, wait!"

Then Boudrie was outside running into the night. May you be forgiven, Monsieur McTell, for what you have done, he thought. He plunged on, straining to pierce the darkness, vaguely aware of Devarre shouting again

When he crashed through the brush onto the old road to the ruin, he paused, panting. The heavy sky distorted the moon's shape. Windy whispers of night closed around him—like voices, he realized with dread, that he could almost understand.

He forced his heavy body into motion again, and as he lurched up the hill, he realized fleetingly that both Henri and Philippe Taillou were dead, and that he, Étien Boudrie, had told no one else about the secret of the hidden spring, whose breaching to fill a swimming pool had unleashed this wave of horror.

FIFTEEN

Roger Devarre stalked angrily back into the house.

"He disappeared before I could catch him," he said. "I wouldn't have believed he was so fast. He went charging into the brush like a mad bull."

She said nothing. She had limped downstairs after the running men, holding candles, silently watching.

"Do you know what he's doing?" Devarre said.

"Not the specifics, but in essence." The decision was a terrible one, the worst she had ever had to make; but there was no doubt. "You must go after him."

Devarre blinked.

"I don't like it either," she said.

"Let me get this straight," he said slowly. "You think there is some sort of evil influence at work that has something to do with those papers we found, that has led McTell and Alysse to climb that mountain in the middle of the night—"

"*Christ,*" she said impatiently. "Can't you see what's right in front of you?" She saw hurt come into his face, went to him, touched him. "I'm sorry," she said. "I'm frightened."

"I can only judge from what I know."

"But can't you believe me when I tell you I know some things, too? Do you think Étien is mad, or playing some game? Do you think I did this to myself?" She pulled his hand to her bandaged flank.

He exhaled and shook his head. "Forgive me," he murmured.

"Now, you must hurry. Fighting spirits is a priest's work, but the man may be physically dangerous as well."

"One more question. Is Étien really going to perform some sort of–exorcism?" The word came awkwardly from his mouth.

"Whatever it was he realized, he didn't say. Something he saw in those papers. But I think, when he said, '*Alysse!*'–don't you remember that when I asked the spirit what it wanted, it said, 'Blood of a flower'?"

"Good God!"

"That was what I was seeing in my dream tonight, I'm sure of it. But hurry! Can you find your way ?"

"I'm not looking forward to it, but I'll manage. When I was in the army, I crawled through plenty of brush." In the doorway he turned. "I can't stand the thought of leaving you here alone."

"Whatever is going to happen will happen up there," she said, trying to believe her own words. "I'd go with you, but my leg–"

"At least let me find the fuse box and get you some lights."

She shook her head firmly. "Every second matters."

Eyes full of anxiety, he kissed her and stepped out into the night.

She watched until his figure blended with the thick tangle of shadows. Immediately she wanted more light. She walked to the kitchen, lit several candles, and set them in dishes. It was then that she noticed the purse sitting on the counter. She turned it up and emptied it. Keys, cigarettes, several hundred francs, and a pack of playing cards fell out. There was also a wallet containing a passport. The photo was of Linden Anne Sumner McTell, a little younger, but unmistakably the same woman as in the picture upstairs in the study.

Mélusine stood holding it, turning slowly, searching the dim smoky air with her eyes. Suitcases on the bed, half-packed with a woman's clothes, and now this. In the confusion, none of them had thought to wonder about the wife. The sense of aloneness, of *wrongness,* rose sharply, pressing in around her like the dark.

Her moving gaze settled on something else that seemed out of place. A wooden holder for a graded set of fine Solingen carving knives had been thrown down carelessly. Two or three of the knives were partly displaced, and one of the larger ones was missing.

The sight suddenly brought back the memory of the knife in her own hand that had seemed to turn into a snake; and she remembered, too, what had been in her mind at that instant: a vow to protect Alysse.

As if you were its enemy.

She shivered, folded her arms, began to pace. There was nothing to do but wait.

Boudrie panted along at his rolling, lumbering trot, his thoughts half in his head, half-mumbled under his gasping breath.

The riddle was answered.

His body cried for rest, but he fought off the urge to turn back, to sink into blissful oblivion and never be forced to touch this monstrousness.

And what drove him on was not just the certainty that if he failed, Courdeval would destroy Alysse, and Mélusine, and himself, and God only knew who else. It was not even that this wickedest of men would again walk the earth–unknown, and free to move from shape to shape as others changed suits of clothes. It was understanding that in a direct and terrible way, he, Étien Boudrie, was responsible: that the life of the innocent Alysse was in jeopardy because her father had been a weak and sinful man, a priest who had broken his sacred vow.

For I the Lord your God am a jealous God, visiting the iniquity of the fathers upon the children to the third and fourth generation. And as he panted along, it seemed to Boudrie that a single word loomed before his mind's eye as if it were carved in immense blocks of stone, set against a horizonless landscape of twilight: RETRIBUTION.

He tried to forget that any hope, if there was any, rested in the body of a fat old priest running up a mountain at night.

When at last he reached the lip of the ravine that guarded the fortress, his breath was coming so hard it was almost a shriek. His legs ached as if wedges had been

284

driven into the bones. Fifty meters beyond lay the ruin's outer wall. There was no sound, no movement, except the writhing sea of thick black brush below, like a wall of night sprung up to defy the elusive moon. Sweating, staring, he stood terrified that he was about to deliver himself into the hands, not of an enemy, but of The Enemy. I cannot, he thought. I am no longer a young man.

He plunged down into the brush

The crossing seemed to take hours. He stumbled, caught and released branches only to have them whip across his face; he fell to a hand and knee when a root clutched at his ankle. He clung to the pain and fear, drove himself with them, lashed out ferociously at the grasping branches. When he dragged himself over the top, he was cut, bruised, exhausted, half-mad.

"Alysse!" he called hoarsely. Wind tore the sound from his lips, whirled it away into the rushing, whispering darkness. Suddenly enraged, he flailed at the empty air. "Alysse!"

Then a light-colored blur was moving swiftly toward him. Hope leaped in his heart–she was unharmed! As she came closer, he could see the dark cloud of hair, the white flowing gown. He stumbled forward, hands stretched out to her, nearly weeping with relief. "Alysse, my child–"

He stopped, stupefied. It was not Alysse.

It was her *mother*–the Céleste he had known so many years before. A mist swirled in his brain as she drew near, long hair tossing, eyes imploring.

"Étien," she called, and the youth in her voice unleashed a thousand memories he had kept firmly bolted in an unused compartment of his heart. Images whirled before him in a kaleidoscope of sight, scent, sensation: soft skin, liquid warmth, whispers and sighs. This woman who had been so outwardly prim—God, what passion, what abandon in her bed! Her voice came to him as from a vast distance:

"Do you not remember how I could make you roar as if your heart would burst?" His hands dropped to his sides, strength flowed from him like blood in a warm bath, and tears spilled from his eyes as he gazed into the face that had been, for him, the essence of love. Her fingers opened her gown and let it fall. His hands touched her breasts; her lips drew near, her eyes were shy but hungry—

And then, for the briefest flicker of time, he saw what lay far back in their depths.

With a bellow like an angry bear's, he wrenched himself free from the suddenly clutching hands, threw her from him, staggered back. His jaw went slack with horror as she swiftly bloated, hair dissolving into a limp, dripping mass, eyes filming over to the flat lifeless orbs of the drowned. For the first time since the war, he felt the cold sickening tug of his testicles trying to retract into his belly.

"Murderer," she whispered in a voice that came from the ocean floor

Then she was gone.

For a measureless time he stood, jerking with violent shudders; imagining voices in the night, their laughter in his mind, invisible bodies in the wind whipping around him. His fingers burned cold from touching her. Weakly,

286

he struggled against the urge to abandon all and throw himself back into the ravine, to run wildly down the mountain to lights and the company of men.

He started walking toward the ruin.

As he approached the entrance archway the sense of menace thickened around him like fog; the voices in the air changed from mocking to threatening. Around the corner ahead he heard a faint hissing noise. There was no knowing what it might be.

"Help me," he whispered, and stepped around the corner.

A long hopeless moan arose out of the gloom, along with the clank of chains. The hissing came from a brazier full of coals. Iron rods and pincers rested in them, glowing bright-hot red. A single hooded figure bent over the brazier. In amazement, Boudrie stared at the men who were chained to the wall. Christ! There were Pelissier, Lestraux, Blancard, all his brothers-in-arms from that night at Vézey-le-Croux. The faces were horrible, contorted with pain and despair. Opening his mouth to call out to them, Boudrie moved forward to their aid.

Then the hooded figure straightened up and turned, a glowing iron rod clasped in a thick glove. As he held it up, it illuminated his face.

And Boudrie recognized Augustin Marichal, his old master at the Grand Séminaire, the man among men he had admired to the point of worship—had known to be a living saint. But the old man's eyes burned with the fire of the coals, and his smile was twisted and gloating. He gestured with the blazing iron to a place on the wall where an empty set of manacles hung, waiting.

Boudrie was whirling away when the place exploded in flame. Burning bodies plunged from the windows of a fiery barn, shrieking, writhing, clutching at him. Their fingers flamed, their agonized faces were desperate with hate, and Boudrie heard his own voice screaming, "Jesus, mercy!"

The flames vanished, leaving only the cool wind and the obscenely gibbering voices. He fell back against the stone wall and put his hand over his eyes.

"No more,' he whispered. "I can bear no more."

He heaved himself off the wall and lunged into the fortress.

A small fire burned at the altar, illuminating three shapes. McTell stood stiffly, chanting in a strange harsh tongue. Something glinted in his hand. Behind him stood a taller figure hidden in shadow. The crumpled form on the altar could only be Alysse.

Slowly, the tall figure raised a gauntleted hand and pointed at Boudrie. A whistle rose, a high thin mournful sound with a quality of infinite dark distance.

The fourth figure appeared suddenly, as if from nowhere. It was wrapped in a dark hooded robe, coming fast, its grotesquely short limbs reaching. The hair on Boudrie's neck stood straight up. For the longest, worst instant of his life, he hung on the edge of flight.

Then he threw open his arms and charged.

At the instant of impact, a terrific cold stopped Boudrie's breath. His hands closed on the coarse hairy robe, something horribly wet and sharp ripped at his chest—

And then the creature's head jerked up, throwing back the hood.

Boudrie cried out, a cry that echoed through his mind as he fell and fell and fell, until at last he reached a place where the face he had seen could come after him no longer, where he was safe from the heart of evil.

At the altar, the man who was John McTell raised the knife slowly. Reflected firelight danced along the blade from the shaking of his hand.

SIXTEEN

Most of an hour had passed, and Mélusine waited beside the glass door, her eyes ceaselessly scanning the dark slope of Montsévrain, the silhouette of the ruin that came and went with the passing of the clouds over the moon. She had seen nothing. An hour was perhaps time enough for them to be back, if Boudrie had been wrong, if it was a false alarm. But it could as easily be all night–or never. The candles were half-gone, and she realized with growing anxiety that if they burned much further, she would have to begin prowling the closets and cellar in search of the fuse box. The thought was un-bearable. For the hundredth time, she forced herself to calm.

Suddenly she gasped. Two figures were climbing the steps: a man with his arm around someone–a woman, a girl. Alysse! She was safe, but moving slowly, and pale even in the moonlight. Overjoyed, Mélusine threw open the door. The man's face lifted sharply at the sound. Though she could not see him well, it had to be McTell.

"*Bonsoir,* monsieur," she called. "Please don't be angry. I'll explain who I am and what I'm doing in your house."

He said nothing, but guided Alysse across the patio to the door. Mélusine stepped aside uneasily; his walk was heavy, forced. Then she saw that his face and shirt were soaked, a rich dark red in the candlelight.

"But you're hurt! Come, let me help." She took the girl's hand and almost dropped it; it was as cold as if it had been in a refrigerator. She was wearing nothing but a black slip and a heavy red scarf around her neck. Mélusine looked anxiously into her eyes. They were dark and blank. What in God's name was going on? With anger rising swiftly to temper her relief, she made the girl sit in a chair and turned to McTell.

"We must get you help, monsieur," she said. "My husband should be back soon. And then I think you have some explaining to do."

To her amazement, he laughed—a harsh deep croaking sound without a trace of real mirth.

"I shall explain to thee, woman, fear not."

The voice was cold and hard as iron, and though he spoke in French, it was French such as she had never heard, the French of centuries ago.

He stepped forward, the candlelight illuminating his face clearly for the first time. One eye held a glare of triumph. The other was bleared and dead. Blood streaked his mouth, chin, chest, and he raised his hands for her to see; they, too, were stained and glistening. One of them clasped a dark leather-bound book.

"Do you not recognize the drowned man?"

"Oh God," she whispered. She took a step back.

"Do not allow yourself the luxury of hope." His voice was soft and creeping now, velvet-covered steel. "The priest is gone, to the realm of lost souls. He chose to play with a pet of mine. Your stupid husband yet thrashes through the brush, led astray by my servants. I toyed with his death; but better to let him live with his grief. It is *you* I want, madame: you, who thought to command me; you, who wished to keep me from what is mine."

He made a sudden imperious gesture. Alysse rose and walked dreamlike to stand by his side. His hand rested possessively on her shoulder.

"I would have destroyed you long ago, had I not hungered for this moment. In my youth I was rash, but I have learned to wait. At last the sin of a priest and the weakness of a scholar put occasion in my way. How carefully I lured that fool!"

Her voice came out a faint whisper: "What have you done with him?"

For the briefest of instants, both eyes lit up, and an altogether different being looked out of them—terrified, agonized, lost. Then he was gone.

"Have you not heard of the wages of sin?" the voice said mockingly.

Then the face went hard, ferocious. "We must say farewell, madame. Would that I could stay and tend to you, but I must leave that to my servants. Not again will I risk freedom, even for the pleasure you would bring me. This world is new; until I know it well, I will remain in secrecy. Your husband will think this night's work was the doing of a madman, and none other will ever tell the tale."

"Leave the girl," Mélusine said hoarsely. "I have lived my life. But leave her."

His smile widened, dark and malevolent.

"Show her, my love," he whispered.

Slowly, dreamily, Alysse's fingers moved to untie the scarf around her neck. One end fell against her breast with a small wet sound; and Mélusine finally understood that it was not a red scarf at all, but once white; and that the blood soaking McTell was not his own. She swayed, gripping the table for support.

"*Adieu,* madame, we have far to travel tonight. Take comfort in the knowledge that you and I will never meet again." Arm around Alysse, he turned and walked with his heavy gait out into the night.

For moments, Mélusine stood, unable to move, fingernails digging into her palms. Then she heard from the kitchen the distinct sound of a door opening.

A shadow, dim in the flickering light, appeared through the archway into the hall. A woman's sweep of hair was clearly outlined. The shape came into view, turning the corner, Mélusine recognized her instantly from the photos: McTell's wife. But something was terribly wrong with her movements.

The woman raised her face. The eyes that looked out were luminous green, thirsty with the lust to destroy–the eyes of an intelligent reptile that had a mouse safely trapped. The lips twisted in a leering smile. Mélusine stared, a scream trapped in her chest, her mind racing to the brink of consciousness while the hands of what had once been Linden McTell—as if they were opening a blouse—rose to her breasts and parted the flesh.

As in a dream, Mélusine felt a part of her mind take flight, unable to bear the reality of her earthbound body running clumsily, hopelessly, from the inescapable.

Cursing steadily under his breath, Roger Devarre shoved his way through the tangled underbrush in the ravine. Scratched and bruised, half-frightened and half-angry, he broke over the top and ran for the fortress entrance. All that talk about the supernatural had been working on him, stripping raw his nerves. Several times he had imagined that he was not alone on his dark journey through the woods, that unseen hands were pushing and tripping him, that threatening not-quite-heard voices were warning him to go back. Worse, he had gotten lost; nearly fifty minutes had passed on a climb that should have taken twenty. Now the very air around the ruin seemed blacker than elsewhere, thick with an ugly tension. He thought of his wife alone, and cursed again. How had she gotten that cut? With the Beretta held close to his thigh, he sprinted through the entrance, and stopped short.

Perhaps ten meters ahead, face down on the ground, a big dark-clothed body lay illuminated by the moon. Twenty meters farther, the embers of a small fire cast flickering shadows. There was no one else visible.

He dropped to his knees beside the priest, fingers reaching for a wrist.

"Étien," he said. Boudrie made no movement, no sound, but the pulse was there, slow and steady. Devarre felt carefully along the flanks for injuries, ran his fingers over neck and head; then, with an effort, turned him over.

White showed all the way around the pupils of Boudrie's staring eyes, and his expression made Devarre turn sharply away. He took several gulps of air, forced himself to look back, and slapped the priest's cheeks.

Nothing. He cursed himself for not having his bag, with its amyl nitrite. Then he saw the rent in the cassock. Quickly, he felt it. The flesh was bloodied but the wound superficial.

There was nothing to be done. He stood and strode to the fire, then sucked in his breath as the flashlight beam touched the great stone slab. It was wet with blood. At its foot lay a knife, dripping crimson.

He squeezed his eyes shut, opened them again. The flashlight moved around the ruin's interior. With that much blood, someone, or something, had died. Where was the corpse?

More important, where was the killer? The thought of the girl made him shiver.

He hurried back to Boudrie and quickly checked his pulse again. Nothing had changed. He took off his jacket,. folded it into a pillow, put it under the priest's head. Then he raised his face to the dark, windy sky. To carry the priest down was an impossibility; Boudrie weighed as much as two men. What, then? Wait with him?

With Mélusine alone in the house, and a murderer on the loose?

He knelt once more to murmur, "I'm sorry, Étien, I'll be back as soon as I can." Then, with a new meaning of the word fear in his heart, he began to run.

It had nearly gotten her, had gripped her hair as she yanked at the door, had torn a lock loose when she clawed at its eyes and broke free. It was very quick and strong, that thing which had once been a woman; she could never outrun it, not with her limp. She could feel it behind her now as she fled across the dark downstairs, could feel that it was leisurely in pursuit because it wanted to wring the utmost from her. It had plenty of time.

The stairwell beckoned like a dark mouth. She gripped the banister and pulled herself up, aware of the steady shuffling steps behind. The dim memory of the heavy oak dresser in the bedroom led her there. Panting, gasping, she tried to drag it back to block the door. On the thick carpeting it would not budge. She got to the other side and began to push.

A flash of gossamer moonlight through the window showed her the bedclothes. Something near the foot, beneath the covers, was squirming.

It dropped to the floor with a soft thud, dark coils writhing eagerly toward her.

The creature's hand brushed her almost playfully as she fled out into the hall. She burst through the doors at the end and hurled them closed behind her. Panting, she got to the balcony railing, and looked down: a drop of perhaps four meters, to concrete. Enough.

The silhouette was growing through the panes of glass. The wind was fierce now, tossing the black treetops, racing the clouds like schooner ships across the moon. She turned her back to the railing and stood straight, hair whipping, as the doors opened. The shape moved slowly forward.

A sadness, a weariness vaster than anything she had ever imagined, touched the deepest part of her. She thought fleetingly of her husband, of how good her life had been. The muscles in her strong leg tensed, ready to spring her headfirst over the rail into the next world.

Abruptly, her peripheral vision was caught by a vertical streak of shimmering light, so faint it was almost nonexistent, as much in her mind as in the air. Her gaze moved sharply to follow it, but it was gone before she could focus—only to reappear instantly at the farthest edge of her sight. Another streak appeared, and then another and another, filling her mind, swelling blindingly in a great wave that washed away her senses

Then she was in a place that was not a place, but a state of absolute stillness and clarity. Incomprehensibly, and yet beyond question, it was the culmination of being itself: the fulfillment of all her soul's inmost yearnings, the affirmation of every doubt, the resolution of every paradox. *Time is,* came a voiceless understanding, *time was, but time shall be no more.*

She saw without seeing that the battle of the two great principles of light and darkness had never begun and had already ended, and yet would rage on forever. Its field of combat was the human soul, and the only weapon, the human will: the divine spark of true freedom.

The war itself was what men called history, fought by the intelligences dimly perceived as spirits; and she understood that those not-quite-seen pillars of fire had converged to usher her to this final glimpse of truth.

The light within her faded softly, until she stood again in the stormy darkness, watching the woman-creature's approach. The human face had altered like a living mask, revealing the demonic fury beneath. From somewhere close by, Mélusine heard her husband's panicked voice shouting her name, but she did not turn. Unseen presences seemed to hover, urging her to courage, while others menaced and mocked.

Footsteps were pounding down the hallway. Devarre lunged through the doors, dropping into a crouch with the pistol aimed.

"*Arrêtez-vous, madame!*" he shouted.

Mélusine's hand rose palm-first. Devarre hesitated, and in that instant she took two firm steps, bent quickly forward, and kissed the creature on the lips.

Roger Devarre felt the hairs on the back of his neck separate and stand straight, as with a long shuddering groan, what he had thought was a living woman sank slowly to its knees and then collapsed, moonlight illuminating the rent in its chest.

SEVENTEEN

The detective in charge was named Bergerac. He was a small man with a big nose, and perhaps that, Mélusine thought, explained his lack of humor.

"It appears already that we will never know precisely how Monsieur McTell disposed of his wife's"—he looked away—"entrails, without leaving any sign. We must suppose that he buried them someplace. As to why, and why he then carried her upstairs to the balcony, we can only conjecture that he did so for the same reason he did the other things. He was insane."

The windows of the villa's study were filling with the gray light of dawn. Police in and out of uniform wandered through the rooms. The buzz of conversations blended with the static crackling of radios. A convoy of vehicles with flashing lights still blocked the driveway. Hours before, a team of medics had loaded the wide-eyed but still comatose Boudrie onto a helicopter. Now there remained the aftermath: the sleepless night, the thousand questions, the ebbing of adrenaline and the bone-deep weariness that came with it.

Bergerac lit a cigarette, looking around the room with his hard bright eyes.

"But then, there are many things we probably will never understand about this tragedy. The priest, for instance. Once again, we can only conjecture. Perhaps he was so horrified at what he had witnessed that he, too, lost his mind."

A subordinate entered the room, bent close to Bergerac's ear, said something in a rapid undertone, then saluted and left. He nodded sadly.

"As we had feared. We cannot say for certain that the blood at the ruin was Mademoiselle Alysse's until we find her body, but it is her type."

The Devarres exchanged glances.

"A man of surprising physical strength, this McTell," Bergerac said.

"Suppose," Mélusine said, "it could be shown that there was an influence on him that caused his actions."

"What sort of influence, madame?" Bergerac's eyes were cynical rather than interested.

"A possessing spirit."

Bergerac dragged on the cigarette, flicked the ash on the floor, gazed around the room.

"I presume you are suggesting something of a supernatural nature. I myself have never seen evidence of any such thing. Do you have any?"

He paused. Neither spoke. Waiting for the police to arrive, they had scanned the papers on McTell's desk. At Mélusine's insistence, Devarre had hidden them in the Citroën's trunk.

"Only rumors," she finally murmured. "There was suspicion in the village that he was dabbling in the occult."

"*Eh bien,*" Bergerac said, sounding resigned. "The events do seem to have been of a ritualistic nature, particularly the presumed murder of the unfortunate young woman. If this man McTell was, in fact, a believer in the supernatural, it may well have nurtured his madness. I have no experience with such things, but I have many times seen situations when a crime might not have occurred if something–a weapon, an occasion–had not presented itself. A young man with no money passes an unlocked vehicle with an expensive camera on the seat. In a passionate argument, someone lays hands on a heavy lamp or a knife. Or perhaps something as simple as a chance remark plants a seed of blackmail or revenge. I do not discount circumstances lending themselves to crime. But to go beyond that point–to speculate that possession may drive a man to murder–is something I cannot do."

Mélusine shook her head, remembering the terrified gaze of John McTell during the instant his body's captor had allowed it to show through.

"Perhaps we will learn more about these occult dealings," Bergerac went on, "and it will help us understand why McTell acted as he did. In the meantime, we're less concerned with his motives than with finding him. This. I assure you, we will do. He is on foot; he cannot get far.

"Madame, monsieur, I see no reason to keep you any longer tonight. You have been most helpful. If you would be so kind as to make yourselves available to come to the station tomorrow and issue formal statements of everything you remember, including these rumors of which you spoke–?" He snapped his fingers. A young policeman appeared. "Escort these good people to their car, and clear the drive for them." Bergerac bowed as they were ushered out of the room.

They sat dully in the Citroën, watching the *flic* direct the flashing vehicles aside.

"You were right." Devarre said. "There was no point in even bringing it up. God, what a useless fool I feel."

"There was nothing more we could have done, not really. Even Étien didn't understand until the very last. Perhaps those papers will tell us what he did not." The unspoken tag hung in the air: *and probably never will.*

Devarre let the clutch out; the car crept forward.

"How did you know to do that? To kiss that–poor woman?"

The policeman saluted as they turned onto the road. They waved wearily.

"I had help," she murmured. "I'll explain someday."

"One thing I promise you," he said quietly. "Never again will I doubt your word about anything of this sort." She leaned against him, and with his arm around her, Devarre drove slowly home.

Behind them, the gathering mistral sent leaves skittering across the concrete patio, covering the murky swimming pool like a blanket of decay.

EIGHTEEN

It was fitting. Mélusine though, that the nursing hospital for the clergy–old priests' home, her husband cynically persisted in calling it–should be in slummy Marseille, in a great stone building of cheerless gray that could easily have been mistaken for a prison. It sat on a bluff overlooking the Mediterranean, but even that one redeeming feature was small comfort on a day like this, with the sky and sea the same gray as the building, with the wind whipping the waves to the height of a house and cutting like an icy blade through her coat. A white-coiffed nun at the desk checked the appointment calendar. Yes, they were expected. Monsieur Boudrie would be brought down in a few minutes, if they would care to take a seat . . .

They stood in the bleak lobby, empty except for an occasional Sister moving with mouselike silence across the floor. The tables held stacks of out-of-date religious publications. Devarre's footfalls echoed strangely as he paced the room.

The police had found no trace of either McTell or Alysse. The trail was long since cold.

A pair of swinging doors opened; the black habit of a nun appeared, backing through. She turned, wheeling the chair she pushed. Her face was red from exertion.

He had shrunk, Mélusine saw, and his face had relaxed a little from the terrible look it had carried. Now he only stared, unmoving and, by all appearances, unseeing.

"You may take him on the grounds if you wish," the Sister said. "He's dressed warmly. But be careful of the wind in his eyes; he can't seem to close them. We have to put liquid in them frequently."

Devarre pushed the chair while she held the doors. By tacit consent they walked toward the sea. On a little bluff they paused, turning Boudrie obliquely to the wind. Surf thundered against the rocks below, with froth whipping across them. In the harbor, the small white fishing boats vanished and reappeared, as if swallowed and spat out again by giant watery jaws.

Mélusine took one of the priest's hands in both her own and bent over him, searching his empty face.

"What did you see, Étien Boudrie?" she said softly. "Will you never come back to tell us?"

Her grip tightened suddenly. For moments longer she stared, until her husband touched her shoulder.

She said nothing as they made their way back to the stark gray hospital. But her heart had already begun fanning into flame a spark of hope: that for the briefest of instants, as she had spoken Boudrie's name, she had seen a faint, bewildered awareness far back in his eyes.

ACKNOWLEDGMENTS

Re-releasing these novels has only been possible with great support and expertise on many levels.

Next, After Lucifer owes a particular debt to three classic stories of the supernatural: "Canon Alberic's Scrap-Book" and "Count Magnus" by M. R. James, and "The Book" by Margaret Irwin.

On a more personal level, the major pillars of this undertaking consist of a Gang of Three:

As always, my wife, Kim, has been my mainstay, both for her technical skills and for keeping me relatively sane.

Jason Neal is the genius behind everything from the website and Facebook pages to cover design.

Prof. Lisa Simon has added indispensable advice on editing, content, and shaping the overall process.

We've managed to have a pretty good time together along the way.

My family–who never knew quite what to expect from me, but it definitely wasn't this–have been rock solid, with special thanks to my brother and his wife, Drs. Dan and Barbara McMahon.

Jennifer Rudolph Walsh, at William Morris Endeavor Entertainment, has been my guardian angel for more than a decade. Also at WME, Britton Schey launched the ebooks with swift competence; Claudia Ballard and Eric Zohn retrieved the rights for these new publications; and other colleagues have tirelessly promoted my work.

My terrific editors at HarperCollins, Carl Lennertz and Dan Conaway, along with their colleagues, gave me major support through critical years.

Going back in time to when the books first came out:

Prof. Ted Ahern, of Boston College, kindly provided all Latin translations.

Tom Dunne and Michael Carlisle were the editor and agent who made it happen.

Heartfelt thanks to all of you, and to the many other friends who helped along the way.

NEXT, AFTER LUCIFER

Ancient evil awakens in a rural French village, in the form of a Templar knight who was burned at the stake in the 14th century for practicing black magic. Now it's the 1980s, and his undead spirit, bent on possession of a human body, invades the lives of a wealthy American couple renting a nearby villa. A genuinely frightening story–not recommended for children.

"A well-turned tale of supernatural terror in which lurks one of the best–or worst–monstrous creations to come along in a month of Black Sabbaths." (Houston Chronicle, 1987)

ADVERSARY

A sequel to *Next, After Lucifer,* with the evil Templar, Guilhem de Courdeval, surfacing in San Francisco. He poses as a spiritual teacher and gathers disciples, using a seductive philosophy that quickly fulfills their desires and solves their problems. At first, it all seems innocent—until they realize that his true goal is to turn them into servants of evil, and they're in too deep to back out.

"A storyteller of exceptional depth . . . The story blends black magic and mystery within a tight plot. One of the real delights, though, is his talent for describing people and places in few words but rich detail." (Evening News, Norwich, England, 1989)

CAST ANGELS DOWN TO HELL

Baby Selena, conceived and born under sinister circumstances, grows up into a beauty–but she remains shadowed by eerie mystery. The only men she'll take as lovers are loathsome criminals and scum–and they all soon die, raving mad suicides. Still, no one suspects her hellish secret: she's part demon child, cursed to be followed by nightmarish "companions" that feast on the souls of the men she beds. Her human side hates what she's forced to do, and so far she's thwarted the companions by giving them only the rotten meat of corrupt souls. But now they're demanding a goodhearted young doctor who's smitten by her–and her strength to fight them off is exhausted.

"A stylish semisequel to *Next, After Lucifer* (1987) and *Adversary* (1988) . . . Supple, moody prose lends an aura of ancient mystery to the story . . . it's his best yet–a haunting work." (Publishers Weekly, 1990)